THE NIGHT IN LISBON

BOOKS BY ERICH MARIA REMARQUE

All Quiet on the Western Front (1929)
The Road Back (1931)
Three Comrades (1937)
Flotsam (1941)
Arch of Triumph (1946)
Spark of Life (1952)
A Time to Love and a Time to Die (1954)
The Black Obelisk (1957)
Heaven Has No Favorites (1961)
The Night in Lisbon (1964)

THE
NIGHT
IN LISBON

ERICH MARIA REMARQUE

Translated by Ralph Manheim

HARCOURT, BRACE & WORLD, INC.

NEW YORK

To Paulette Remarque

THE NIGHT IN LISBON

CHAPTER 1

I stared at the ship. Glaringly lighted, it lay at anchor in the Tagus. Though I had been in Lisbon for a week, I hadn't yet got used to its carefree illumination. In the countries I had come from, the cities at night were black as coal mines, and a lantern in the darkness was more to be feared than the plague in the Middle Ages. I had come from twentieth-century Europe.

The ship was a passenger vessel; it was being loaded. I knew it was going to sail the next afternoon. In the harsh glow of the naked light bulbs, crates of meat, fish, canned goods, bread, and vegetables were being lowered into the hold; stevedores were carrying baggage on board, lifting up crates and bales as silently as if they had been weightless. The ship was being made ready for a voyage—like the ark in the days of the flood. It *was* an ark. Every ship that left Europe in those months of the year 1942 was an ark. Mount Ararat was America, and the flood waters were rising higher by the day. Long ago they had engulfed Germany and Austria, now they stood deep in Poland and Prague; Amsterdam, Brussels, Copenhagen, Oslo, and Paris had gone under, the cities of Italy stank of seepage, and Spain, too, was no longer safe. The coast of Portugal had become the last hope of the fugitives to whom justice, freedom, and tolerance meant more than home and livelihood. This was the gate to America. If you couldn't reach it, you were lost, condemned to bleed away in a jungle of consulates, police stations, and government offices, where visas were refused and work and residence permits unobtainable, a jungle of internment camps, bureaucratic red tape, loneliness, homesickness, and withering universal indifference. As usual in times of war, fear, and affliction, the individual human being had ceased to exist; only one thing counted: a valid passport.

That afternoon I had gone to the Casino Estoril to gamble. I still owned a good suit, and they had let me in. It was a last, desperate effort to blackmail fate. Our Portuguese residence permit would expire in a few days, and Ruth and I had no other visas. We had made our plans in France and drawn up a list of possible sailings for New York. This ship anchored in the Tagus had been the last on our list. But it was sold out for months; we had no American visas, and we were more than three hundred dollars short of the fare. I had tried to raise the money at least, in the only way still possible for a foreigner in Lisbon—by gambling. An absurd idea, for even if I had won, it would have taken a miracle to get us aboard. But in danger and despair you acquire a faith in miracles; without it you would go under.

I had lost fifty-six of the sixty-two dollars we still had left.

It was late at night and the quayside was almost deserted. But after a while, I became aware of a man not far off. First he paced aimlessly about, then he stopped and he, too, began to stare at the ship. Another stranded refugee, I thought, and took no further notice of him, until I felt that he was watching me. A refugee never loses his fear of the police, not even when he is asleep or when there is nothing to be afraid of—so I turned away with an affectation of bored indifference and started to leave the pier, slowly, like a man who has no ground for fear.

A moment later I heard steps behind me. I kept on walking but without hastening my step, wondering how I could let Ruth know if I were arrested. The pastel-tinted houses at the end of the pier, asleep like butterflies in the night, were still too far away to make a run for it and disappear in the tangle of narrow streets.

Now the man was beside me. He was a little shorter than I. "Are you a German?" he asked in German.

I shook my head and kept on walking.

"Austrian?"

I did not answer. I looked at the pastel-tinted houses, which were approaching much too slowly. I knew there were Portuguese policemen who spoke German very well.

"I'm not a policeman," the man said.

I didn't believe him. He was wearing civilian clothes, but plain-clothes men had arrested me half a dozen times in Europe. I had papers, not a bad job, done in Paris by a mathematics teacher from Prague, but they wouldn't have stood close scrutiny.

"I saw you looking at the ship," the man said. "That made me wonder . . ."

I mustered him with indifference. He didn't really look like a policeman, but the last plain-clothes man, who had nabbed me in Bordeaux, had looked as pathetic as Lazarus after three days in his grave, and he had been the most heartless of the lot. He had pulled me in even though he knew the Germans would be in Bordeaux next day, and it would have been all up with me if a kindly warden hadn't let me out a few hours later.

"Do you want to go to New York?" the man asked.

I did not reply. Twenty yards more would do it; then, if necessary, I could knock him down and run for it.

"Here," said the man, reaching into his pocket, "are two tickets for that boat."

I saw the tickets. I couldn't read the writing in the feeble light. But we had covered enough ground. It was safe to stop now.

"What is all this?" I asked him in Portuguese. I had learned a few words of the language.

"You can have them," said the man. "I don't need them."

"You don't need them? What do you mean?"

"I don't need them any more."

I stared at the man. I couldn't understand. He really didn't seem to be a policeman. If he had wanted to arrest me, he could have done so without these fancy tricks. But if the tickets were good, why couldn't he use them? And why did he offer them to me? Something began to tremble inside me.

"I can't buy them," I said finally in German. "They're worth a fortune. There are wealthy refugees in Lisbon; they'll pay anything you ask. You've come to the wrong man. I haven't any money."

"I don't want to sell them," said the man.

I looked back at the tickets. "Are they real?"

He handed them to me without a word. They crackled between my fingers. They were genuine. Possession of them was the difference between ruin and salvation. Even if I couldn't use them without American visas, I could still try next morning to get visas on the strength of them—or at least I could sell them. That would mean six months' more survival.

"I don't understand," I said.

"You can have them," he replied. "For nothing. I'm leaving Lisbon tomorrow morning. There's only one condition."

My arms sagged. I knew it was too good to be true. "What is it?" I asked.

"I don't want to be alone tonight."

6

"You want me to stay with you?"

"Yes. Until morning."

"That's all?"

"That's all."

"Nothing else?"

"Nothing else."

I looked at him incredulously. I knew, of course, that people in our situation could go to pieces; that solitude was sometimes unbearable. I knew this dread of the void that attacks people whose world has become a void, and I knew that the company even of a total stranger could save a man from suicide. But in such cases people helped each other as a matter of course; there was no need to offer a reward. And not such a reward! "Where do you live?" I asked.

He made a negative gesture. "I don't want to go there. Isn't there a bar that's still open?"

"There must be."

"Isn't there a place that caters to refugees? Like the Café de la Rose in Paris?"

I knew the Café de la Rose. Ruth and I had slept there for two weeks. The patron would let you stay as long as you pleased for the price of a cup of coffee. You spread out some newspapers and lay down on the floor. I had never slept on tables; you can't fall off the floor.

"I don't know of any," I replied. This was not true, but you don't take a man with two boat tickets to give away to a place frequented by people who would have sold their souls to get hold of them.

"I only know one place," said the man. "We can try it. Maybe it's still open."

He motioned to a solitary cab and looked at me.

"All right," I said.

We got in, and he gave the driver an address. I'd have liked to let Ruth know that I wouldn't be home that night; but as I entered the dark, foul-smelling cab I was assailed by so furious, so terrible a hope that my head almost reeled. Maybe all this was really true; maybe our lives were not at an end and the impossible was happening; maybe we were going to be saved. Once this thought had entered my head, I was afraid to leave this stranger out of sight for so much as a second.

We circled round the theatrical-looking Praça do Comércio and after a time came to a tangle of sloping alleys and stairways. I did not know this part of Lisbon; as usual, I was chiefly acquainted with the churches and museums—not that I was so much in love with God or art, but simply because in churches and museums no one asks for your papers. In the presence of Christ crucified and the great masters, you were still a human being—not an individual with dubious papers.

We left the cab and continued up the stairways and crooked streets. There was a smell of fish, garlic, night flowers, dead sunshine, and sleep. Under the rising moon, the St. George Castle rose up out of the night to one side, and the moonlight cascaded down the stairways. I turned around and looked down at the harbor. Down there lay the river, and the river was freedom and life; it flowed into the ocean, and the ocean was America.

I stopped still. "I hope you aren't playing tricks on me," I said.

"No," said the man.

"With the tickets, I mean." He had put them back into his pocket on the pier.

"No," said the man. "I'm not playing tricks." He pointed to a little square framed in trees. "That's the place I mean. It's still open. We won't attract attention. Almost all the customers are foreigners. They'll think we're leaving tomorrow and that we're celebrating our last night in Portugal before taking the boat."

The place was a kind of late restaurant with a small dance floor and a terrace, made to order for the tourist trade. Someone was playing a guitar, and in the background a girl was singing a *fado*. On the terrace several of the tables were occupied by foreigners. There was a woman in evening dress and a man in a white dinner jacket. We found a table at the end of the terrace. You could look down at Lisbon, at the churches in the pale light, the streets, the harbor, the piers, and the ship that was an ark.

"Do you believe in survival after death?" asked the man with the tickets.

I looked up. I had expected anything but that. "I don't know," I said finally. "In the last few years I've been too busy worrying about survival before death. I'll think about it when I'm in America," I added, to remind him of the steamer tickets he had promised me.

"I don't," he said.

I sighed with relief. I was prepared to listen to anything, but I couldn't have stood a discussion. I was too restless. Down there lay the ship.

The man sat there for a time as though sleeping with his eyes open. Then when the guitar player came out on the terrace, he woke up. "My name is Schwarz," he said. "That's not my real name; it's the name on my passport. But I've got used to it. It will do for tonight. Were you in France long?"

"As long as they let me stay."

"Interned?"

"When the war broke out. Like everyone else."

The man nodded. "So were we. I was happy," he said quickly and softly, with bowed head and eyes averted. "I was very happy. Happier than I had ever thought I could be."

I turned around in surprise. He really didn't look like a man who would talk like that. He seemed rather nondescript and retiring.

"When?" I asked. "In the camp?"

"No. Before."

9

"In 1939? In France?"

"Yes. The summer before the war. I still don't understand how it all came about. That's why I have to talk to somebody now. I don't know anyone here. But if I tell somebody about it, it will come back to me. It will become clear in my mind. And it will stay. I simply have to. . . ." He broke off. "Do you understand?" he asked after a while.

"Yes," I said. "It's not hard to understand, Mr. Schwarz."

"It's impossible to understand!" he replied with sudden violence. "She's lying down there in a room with closed windows, in a hideous wooden coffin; she's dead, she doesn't exist any more! Who can understand that? No one! Not you and not I, no one, and anyone who says he understands is a liar!"

I said nothing and waited. I had often sat with a man in a similar situation. Losses were harder to bear when you had no country of your own. There was nothing to sustain you, and the strange country became so terribly strange. I had been through it myself in Switzerland when I received the news that my parents had been killed and cremated in a concentration camp. The thought of my mother's eyes in the fire of the crematorium had haunted me. "I assume," said Schwarz more calmly, "that you know what refugee jitters are."

I nodded. A waiter brought us a bowl full of shrimp. I suddenly realized that I was very hungry and remembered that I hadn't eaten since lunchtime. I looked hesitantly across at Schwarz. "Go ahead and eat," he said. "I'll wait."

He ordered wine and cigarettes. I ate quickly. The shrimp were fresh and well seasoned. "Forgive me," I said, "but I'm very hungry."

I watched Schwarz while I ate. He sat there calmly, looking down at the great stage-set called Lisbon, and showing no sign of impatience or irritation. It gave me a kind of affection for him. He seemed to realize that whatever the book

10

of etiquette might say on the subject, a man could be hungry even in the presence of unhappiness without being unfeeling. If there's nothing you can do to help, you might just as well eat your food before it's taken away from you. Because that can happen any time.

I pushed the dish aside and took a cigarette. It was a long time since I had smoked. I had gone without in order to have a little more to gamble with.

"The jitters got into me in the spring of '39," said Schwarz. "I'd been a refugee for more than five years. Where were you in the fall of '38?"

"In Paris."

"So was I. I had given up. It was just before the Munich Pact. My fear had exhausted itself. I still hid and took precautions out of habit, but I had given up. There would be war and the Germans would come and get me. That was my fate. I was resigned to it."

I nodded. "That was the time of the suicide wave. It was a curious thing: when the Germans really came a year and a half later, there were fewer suicides."

"Then came the Munich Pact," said Schwarz. "That fall we won a new lease on life. Life was so sweet, so light, that we got careless. The chestnut trees actually blossomed a second time that year in Paris, do you remember? It went to my head; I began to feel human again, and, what was worse, to act human. So the police caught me and locked me up for four weeks for repeated unauthorized entry. It was the old game all over again: they pushed me across the border at Basel, the Swiss sent me back, the French sent me across at another place, I was locked up again—you know the routine, this game of chess with human . . ."

"I know. It was no joke in the wintertime. The Swiss prisons were the best. Heated like hotels."

I began to eat again. There's something good about un-

11

pleasant memories: they make you think you're happy when a moment before you were convinced of the contrary. Happiness is a question of degree. When you know that, you're seldom completely unhappy. I had been happy in Swiss prisons because they were not German prisons. But here in front of me sat a man who spoke as if he had a lease on happiness although somewhere in Lisbon a wooden coffin was standing in an airless room.

"The last time they released me they said they'd have to send me back to Germany if they caught me again without papers," said Schwarz. "It was only a threat, but it scared me. I began to wonder what I'd do if it really happened. I began to dream at night that I was in Germany with the SS on my tracks. I had that dream so often that I began to be afraid of falling asleep. Has that ever happened to you?"

"I could write a thesis about it," I replied.

"One night I dreamed I was in Osnabrück, the city where I had lived and where my wife was still living. I stood in her room and saw that she was sick. She was thin as a reed. And she was in tears. I woke up in a cold sweat. I hadn't seen her or heard from her in five years. I hadn't written either, because I didn't know whether her mail was being opened. Before I left, she had promised to get a divorce. I thought that would make it easier for her. And for a few years I thought she had done so."

Schwarz was silent for a time. I didn't ask him why he had left Germany. There were plenty of reasons, none of them interesting, because all were unjust. It's not interesting to be a victim. Either he was a Jew, or he had belonged to a political party hostile to the regime, or he had enemies who had risen to positions of influence—in Germany there were dozens of reasons for being thrown into a concentration camp or executed.

"I managed to get back to Paris," said Schwarz. "But that dream left me no peace. It kept coming back. At the same time the illusion of the Munich Pact was shattered. By spring everyone knew there was going to be war. You could smell it, as you smell a fire long before you see it. Only the diplomats shut their eyes and dreamed wishful dreams—of a second or third Munich, or anything but war. Never have so many people believed in miracles as in our times, when there aren't any."

"Oh yes there are," I said, "or we wouldn't any of us be alive today."

Schwarz nodded. "That's true. Private miracles. I had one myself. It began in Paris. I suddenly inherited a valid passport. That's the one in the name of Schwarz. It belonged to an Austrian I had met at the Café de la Rose. He died, leaving me his passport and his money. He had arrived only three months before. I had met him in the Louvre—looking at the Impressionists. I often went there in the afternoon to quiet my nerves. When you looked at those peaceful, sun-drenched landscapes, you just couldn't believe that a species capable of creating such paintings was going to unleash a murderous war—a soothing illusion that sent your blood pressure down for an hour or two.

"The man with the passport in the name of Schwarz often stood looking at Monet's nenuphars and cathedrals. We started to talk and he told me that after the *Anschluss* he had managed to get out of Austria by giving up his fortune, consisting of a collection of Impressionists. It had been seized by the state. He had no regrets. As long as paintings were shown in museums, he could regard them as his own, without having to worry about fire and theft. Besides, there were better pictures in the French museums than he had ever owned. Instead of being wedded to his own mediocre collection as a father is wedded to his family, under obligation to prefer his own, he now possessed all the pictures in the public museums without effort or responsibility. He was a strange man, quiet, gentle, and cheerful in spite of all he

13

had been through. He had been able to take very little money with him; but he had saved a number of old stamps. Stamps are the smallest things to hide, easier than diamonds. It's hard to walk on diamonds if you've hidden them in your shoes and you are called out of the train for questioning. You can't sell them except at a great loss, and a good many questions are always asked. Stamps are for collectors. Collectors aren't so curious."

"How did he get them out?" I asked, with the professional interest common to all refugees.

"He took some old, harmless-looking letters with him and hid the stamps under the lining of the envelopes. The customs officers checked the letters but not the envelopes."

"Not bad," I said.

"He also took two little Ingres portraits. Pencil drawings. He put them in hideous gilt frames and said they were portraits of his parents. He slipped two Degas drawings in between the portraits and the backing."

"Not bad," I said again.

"In April he had a heart attack. He gave me his passport, what stamps he had left, and the drawings. He also gave me the addresses of some people who would buy the stamps. When I dropped in to see him next morning, he lay dead in his bed, so changed by the silence that I could hardly recognize him. I took what money he had left and a suit and some underwear. He had told me to do so the day before; he preferred leaving his belongings to a companion in fate than to the landlord."

"Did you alter the passport?" I asked.

"Only the photo and the year of birth. Schwarz was twenty years older than I. Our first names were the same."

"Who did it? Brünner?"

"Somebody from Munich."

"That was Brünner, the passport doctor. He is an artist."

Brünner was well known for his skillful doctoring of identification papers. He had helped no end of people, but he himself had no papers when he was arrested. He was superstitious. He believed himself to be an honorable man and a public benefactor, and was convinced that nothing would happen to him as long as he did not practice his art for his own benefit. He had been the owner of a small print shop in Munich.

"Where is he now?" I asked.

"Isn't he in Lisbon?"

I didn't know, but it was possible, if he was still alive.

"Funny thing," said Schwarz II. "When I had the passport, I didn't dare to use it. Besides, it took me a few days to get used to my new name. I kept repeating it to myself. Crossing the Champs-Elysées, I mumbled my name and my new place and date of birth. I sat in the museum gazing at the Renoirs, and if I was alone, I'd rehearse an imaginary dialogue. Stern voice: 'Schwarz!' And I'd jump to my feet and answer: 'Here!' Or I'd snarl: 'Name!' and reply automatically: 'Josef Schwarz, born in Wiener Neustadt on June 22, 1898.' I'd even practice before I went to sleep. I didn't want to be awakened by a policeman and say the wrong name before I'd collected my wits. I had to forget my old name completely. There is a difference between having no passport and having a false one. The false one is more dangerous.

"I sold the two Ingres drawings. I received less for them than I had expected, but now I had money, more money than I had seen in a long time.

"Then one night I had an idea that stayed with me from then on. Wouldn't it be possible for me to go to Germany with this passport? It was almost genuine, and why should anyone get suspicious at the border? I could see my wife again. I could appease my fears about her. I could . . ."

Schwarz looked at me. "You must know that feeling. Refugee jitters in their purest form. That tightening in the stomach, in the throat, and in the back of the eyes. Everything you've been trying to bury for years, all the things you've done your best to forget, that you've avoided like the plague, come to life again. Memory is a deadly disease for a refugee; it's his cancer of the soul.

"I tried to down it. I kept going to see those paintings of peace and quietness, the Sisleys and Pissarros and Renoirs; I spent hours in the museum—but now it had the opposite effect on me. The pictures no longer pacified me—they began to cry out, to challenge, to remind me . . . of a country that hadn't yet been ravaged by the brown leprosy, of evenings in streets bordered by walls overgrown with lilac, of the golden sunsets in the old city, of green belfries with swallows flying round them—and of my wife.

"I'm a plain man without any special qualities. For four years I had lived with my wife as most men do: peacefully, pleasantly, but without great passion. After the first few months our relationship had become what is called a happy marriage—a relationship between two considerate people who don't expect too much. Our dreams belonged to the past, but we didn't miss them. We were reasonable people. And we were very fond of each other.

"Now I saw everything in a new light. I began to reproach myself; it was my fault that our marriage had been so commonplace. I had bungled everything. What had I lived for? What was I doing now? I had crawled into a hole, I was vegetating. How long would it go on? And how would it end? The war would come, and Germany was bound to win; no other country was fully prepared. And then what? Where could I crawl to, even assuming that I still had the time and strength? What camp would I starve in? Against what wall would I be shot—if I were lucky?

"The passport that should have given me peace drove me to despair. I wandered through the streets until I was dead tired. But I couldn't sleep, and when I did drop off, my dreams woke me up. I saw my wife in the cellars of the Gestapo; I heard her calling for help in the courtyard of my hotel; and one day, as I entered the Café de la Rose, I thought I saw her face in the mirror across from the door. For a moment she turned toward me—she was pale, her eyes were desolate—then she slipped away. I had seen her so clearly I was sure she was really there. I ran into the back room. As usual, it was full of people, but she was not among them.

"For a few days I was obsessed with the thought that she had come to Paris and was looking for me. Dozens of times I saw her turn the corner; I saw her sitting on a bench in the Luxembourg Gardens, and when I reached the spot, a strange face looked up at me in surprise; she crossed the Place de la Concorde just as the stream of traffic was about to start up again, and this time it was really she—her gait, the way she squared her shoulders; I even seemed to recognize her dress, but when the traffic policeman finally stopped the stream of cars and I was able to run after her, she had vanished, swallowed up by the black maw of the Métro. I raced down the stairs and was just in time to see the mocking taillights of the train receding in the darkness.

"I confided in a friend. His name was Löser; he sold stockings and had formerly been a doctor in Breslau. He advised me not to spend so much of my time alone. 'Find yourself a woman,' he said.

"It didn't help. You know these affairs born of misery, loneliness, fear. You hanker after human warmth, a voice, a body—and you wake up in a strange, awful room, feeling as though you'd fallen off the earth. In your desolation you're grateful for the sound of breathing beside you—but then your imagination starts working again, and after a while nothing is left but an ugly feeling of having abused yourself.

"When I talk about it now, it all sounds absurd and contradictory. It was different then. All my struggles added up to one thing: I had to go back. I had to see my wife again.

Possibly she had been living with someone else for heaven knew how long. That didn't matter. I had to see her. To me that seemed perfectly logical.

"Every day it became clearer that war was inevitable. Hitler had lost no time in breaking his promise to content himself with the Sudetenland and to spare the rest of Czechoslovakia. Obviously he was going to do the same with Poland. That meant war, because France and England both had alliances with Poland. And it was no longer a question of months, but of weeks or even days. For me, too. I'd have to decide quickly; my whole life depended on it. And I did decide. I decided to go back. What would happen afterward I didn't know. And I didn't care. If war came, I was lost in any case. I might as well do this insane thing.

"A strange peace came over me in the last few days. It was May, and the flower beds in the Rond-Point were bright with tulips. The evenings were bathed in the silvery light and blue shadows of the Impressionists. Behind the cold glare of the first street lamps rose the high, pale-green sky, and across the roofs of the newspaper buildings ran restless red ribbons of luminous writing, spelling out war for all who could read.

"First I went to Switzerland. I had to try out my passport in a safe place before I could really trust it. The French border guard handed it back to me with indifference; that I had expected. Only countries under dictatorship are hard to get out of. But when the Swiss guard came in, I felt something shrinking inside me. I sat there as nonchalantly as I could, but at the edges of my lungs I felt a fluttering, as of a leaf that begins to go wild on a windless day.

"The guard looked at my passport. He was a powerful, broad-shouldered man, who smelled of pipe smoke. As he stood in the doorway of the compartment, he blocked off the light, and for a moment I had the feeling that it was my freedom he was shutting out—that the compartment had become a prison cell. Then he handed me back the passport.

18

" 'You've forgotten to stamp it,' I said, so eased with relief that the words poured out much faster than I intended.

"The guard smiled. 'Don't worry. I'll stamp it. Does it make so much difference?'

" 'No. But to me it's a kind of souvenir.'

"The man stamped the passport and left. I bit my lips. How nervous I had become! Then it occurred to me that the passport looked a little more authentic with the stamp.

"In Switzerland I spent a day wondering whether I should take the train into Germany. In the end I was afraid to. I didn't know whether the passports of Germans, or even of former Austrians, returning home might not be examined with special care. Probably not; but still it seemed advisable to cross the border unofficially.

"In Zurich I went to the main post office, as I had on my first arrival years before. At the General Delivery window you were almost sure to meet acquaintances—homeless souls without residence permits, who could give you information. From there I went to the Café Greif—the Swiss version of the Café de la Rose. I met a number of people who had sneaked across the border, but no one who really knew how to cross safely back into Germany. That was understandable. Except for me, who would want to go to Germany? I noticed the way they looked at me. Then when they saw I was serious, they shrank away from me. Anyone who was planning to return must be a traitor; for who would go back unless he accepted the regime? And if a man could do that, what might he do next? Whom or what would he betray?

"I was alone. They avoided me as if I'd been a murderer. And I couldn't explain; when I thought about what I was going to do, I was so panic-stricken that I broke into a sweat; how could I possibly explain it to anyone else?

"At six o'clock the third morning the police came and pulled me out of bed. It was clear to me that one of my acquaintances had reported me. They looked at my passport suspiciously and took me along for questioning. It was lucky now that the passport had been stamped, because I was able to prove that I had entered the country legally and had only been there for three days. I shall never forget that early morning as I passed through the streets under guard. It was a clear day, and the towers and roofs of the city stood out sharply against the sky, as though cut out of metal. From a bakery came the smell of warm bread, and all the consolation in the world seemed to be in that smell. Do you know what I mean?"

I nodded. "The world never looks more beautiful than when you're being locked up. When you're about to leave it. If only we could always keep this feeling."

"I had that feeling."

"Were you able to hold it?" I asked.

"I don't know," Schwarz answered slowly. "That's what I want to find out. It slipped through my fingers—but even when I held it, did I have it completely? Can't I possibly win it back again, stronger than before, and hold on to it forever? Now that it can't change any more? Don't we always lose what we think we have hold of? Do we lose it because it moves? And does it stand still only when it's gone and can no longer change? Is it only then that it really belongs to us?"

His eyes were fixed on me in a rigid stare. It was the first time he had looked me full in the face. His pupils were dilated. A fanatic or a madman, I thought.

The woman in the evening dress at the next table stood up. She looked across the veranda down at the city and the harbor. "Darling, why do we have to go back?" she said to the man in the white dinner jacket. "If we could only stay here! I don't feel a bit like going back to America."

CHAPTER 2

"The police in Zurich," Schwarz went on, "held me for only one day. But it was a hard day for me. I was afraid they would check my passport. A phone call to Vienna would be enough. Or if they called in a specialist, he would discover the alterations.

"In the afternoon I calmed down. Whatever happened, it seemed to me, would be a kind of divine judgment. The decision was out of my hands. If they put me in prison, I'd have to abandon my idea of going to Germany. But late that afternoon they let me out, giving me to understand that I should leave Switzerland as quickly as possible.

"I decided to go by way of Austria. I had some familiarity with the Austrian border, and felt sure it would not be as closely guarded as that of Germany proper. Actually, why should either border be closely guarded? Who wanted to get in? But on the other hand, there were probably a good many wanting to get out.

"I took the train to Oberriet, planning to attempt the crossing somewhere in the vicinity. I'd have liked best to wait for a rainy day, but for two days the sky was clear. I left the third night, for fear that too long a stay would attract attention.

"The stars were all out that night, and it was so still that I seemed to hear the plants growing. In times of danger a different form of sight sets in. It's not a special focusing of the eyes, but something that spreads all over the body, as if you could see with your skin, especially at night. Your hearing moves into your skin, too, and you seem to *see* the slightest sound. You open your mouth and listen, and your mouth, too, seems to see and to hear.

"I shall never forget that night. I was alert in every fiber, all my senses were wide awake, I was prepared for anything, but utterly without fear. I felt as though I were crossing a high bridge from one side of my life to the other, and I knew that the bridge would fade away behind me like silvery smoke and that I'd never be able to return. I was passing from reason to feeling, from security to adventure, from rationality to dream. I was utterly alone, but this time my solitude was not a torment; there was something mystical about it.

"I came to the Rhine, which is young at this spot and not very wide. I undressed and made a bundle of my clothes, so as to hold them over my head. It was a weird feeling when I slipped naked into the water. It was black and very cool and strange. I felt I was plunging into the River Lethe to drink forgetfulness. It struck me as symbolic that I had to pass through it naked, as though leaving everything behind me.

"I dried myself, dressed, and continued on my way. Passing near a village, I heard a dog bark. I didn't know exactly how the border ran, so I kept to the edge of a road that skirted a forest. For a long while I met no one. I walked until dawn. A heavy dew was falling and there was a stag standing at the edge of a clearing. I went on until I heard peasants driving their wagons. Then I looked for a hiding place, not far from the road. I was afraid of arousing suspicion by being up so early and coming from the direction of the border. Later I saw two customs guards on bicycles. I recognized their uniforms. I was in Austria. Austria had belonged to Germany for just one year."

The woman in evening dress left the terrace with her escort. Her shoulders were very tan, and she was taller than the man who was with her. A few other tourists sauntered slowly down the steps. They all walked like people who had never been hunted—without looking around.

"I had some sandwiches," said Schwarz, "and there was a brook to drink from. At noon I went on. My goal was the town of Feldkirch, which I knew to be a resort, where a stranger would not attract attention. When I got there, I took the first train out of the dangerous border zone. I stepped into a compartment. Two uniformed SA men were sitting there.

"My experience with the police forces of Europe stood me in good stead, or I might have retreated. As it was, I went in and sat down in a corner next to a man in a loden suit, with a gun propped up beside him.

"It was my first encounter in five years with everything that to me was the essence of horror. In the preceding weeks I had often imagined this scene, but the reality was different. It was my body, not my head, that reacted; my stomach turned to stone, my mouth felt like a grater. The hunter and the SA men were talking about a widow Pfundner. She seemed to be the merry variety of widow, to judge by the love affairs they detailed. After a while they began to eat ham sandwiches. 'Where are you headed for, neighbor?' the hunter asked me.

" 'Back to Bregenz,' I said.

" 'You seem to be a stranger here?'

" 'Yes, I'm on my vacation.'

" 'And where have you come from?'

"I hesitated for a moment. If I had said Vienna, as indicated in my passport, they might have noticed that I didn't speak the soft Viennese dialect. 'From Hannover,' I said. 'I've been living there more than thirty years.'

" 'Hannover! Whew! That's a long way!'

" 'Yes, it's quite a way. But who wants to spend his vacation near home?'

"The hunter laughed. 'That's a fact. You've been lucky with the weather.'

"I felt my shirt sticking to my back. 'Yes, it's been marvelous, but it's as hot as midsummer.'

"The three of them started in again on the widow Pfundner. A few stations later they got out and I was left alone in the compartment. The train was passing through one of the most beautiful countrysides in Europe, but I saw very little of it. I was overcome by an almost intolerable feeling of regret, fear, and despair. Why on earth had I crossed the border? It was beyond me. I sat motionless in my corner, staring out the window. I was a prisoner, and I myself had allowed the lock to snap shut. I kept thinking I'd leave the train and try to get back to Switzerland during the night.

"But I didn't. My left hand clutched the late Schwarz's passport in my pocket, as though it might give me strength. I kept telling myself that by now it would do me no good to get out, and that the farther inland I went, the safer I'd be. I decided to travel through the night. In trains you're not so likely to be asked for your papers as in hotels.

"When you're in a panic, you always feel that a spotlight is on you, that no one has anything else to do but search for you.

"I closed my eyes. The temptation to give in to my panic was still greater because I was alone in the compartment. But I knew that every inch I gave now would become a yard

when I should really be in danger. I told myself that no one was looking for me; that I was of no more interest to the regime than a shovelful of sand in the desert, and that there was nothing visibly suspicious about me. This was true, of course. I looked hardly any different from the people around me. The blond Aryan is a German legend. Take a look at Hitler, Goebbels, Hess, and the rest of the leaders—all of them living disproof of their own delusions.

"In Munich I left the shelter of the railroad stations for the first time and forced myself to take an hour's walk. No knowing the city, I felt sure that no one would know me. stopped to eat at the Franziskanerbräu. The place was ful I sat down alone and listened. A few minutes later a stou perspiring man took a seat at my table. He ordered beer an boiled beef and unfolded a newspaper. So far it hadn't o curred to me to read the German papers. Now I bought tw of them. I hadn't read German for years, and it still seem strange to hear everyone talking it around me.

"The editorials were abominable, packed with bloodthirs arrogant lies. The whole outside world was represented as generate, treacherous, stupid, and good for nothing else bu be taken over by Germany. These were not small local pap they had formerly enjoyed a good reputation.

"I studied the man at my table. He ate, drank, and with pleasure. I looked around. Many of the diners reading papers, and in none of them did I detect any sig distaste. This had become their daily fare; it seemed ju natural to them as their beer.

"I continued to read until, among the short news i I found one about Osnabrück. A house on Lotterstrass burned down. I could see the street clearly. It began o the ramparts at Heger Gate and led away from the city. denly felt lonelier than I ever had in a foreign country.

"My state of mind fluctuated between shock and fa apathy, but soon I got used to it. I even began to fee

The danger would increase as I approached Osnabrück; that I knew. There would be people who remembered me from the old days.

"To avoid attracting attention at hotels, I bought a cheap suitcase and the usual articles required for a short trip. Then I took the train. I still didn't know how I was going to get in touch with my wife, and changed my plans every few minutes. I would have to trust to chance; I didn't even know whether she had given in to her family—staunch supporters of the regime—and married someone else. After reading the papers, I wasn't so sure that it would take an average mortal very long before believing what he read, especially when there was no possibility of comparison. Foreign papers were strictly censored in Germany.

"In Münster I went to an average hotel. I couldn't go on staying up at night and sleeping here and there in the day-time. I had to take the risk of staying in a hotel, where my arrival would be reported to the police. Do you know Münster?"

"A little," I said. "Isn't it an old city with a lot of churches, where the Treaty of Westphalia was signed?"

Schwarz nodded. "In Münster and Osnabrück in 1648. After thirty years of war. Who knows how long this one will last?"

"Not very long if it goes on like this. It took the Germans only four weeks to conquer France."

The waiter came and said the place was closing, that every-one else had left. "Isn't there some other place that's still open?" Schwarz asked.

There wasn't much night life in Lisbon, the waiter told us. But when Schwarz gave him a tip, he knew of a place, very secret, he said, a Russian night club. "Very chic."

"Will they let us in?" I asked.

"Of course they will, sir. I just meant that the ladies who go there are chic. All nationalities. Germans, too."

"How long does it stay open?"

"As long as there are customers. At this time of night there are always customers. Lots of Germans right now."

"What kind of Germans?"

"Germans."

"With money?"

"Of course." The waiter laughed. "The place isn't cheap. But very entertaining. Just say that Manuel sent you. Then you won't have to tell them anything else."

"Do you usually have to tell them something?"

"No. The doorman makes out a membership card for you with an imaginary name. Just a formality."

"Sounds all right."

Schwarz paid the check. We went slowly down the street with the stairs. As though leaning on each other's shoulders, the pale houses slept. Through the windows you could hear the moaning, snoring, and breathing of people without passport troubles. Our footfalls sounded louder than in the daytime.

"The lights," said Schwarz. "Do they startle you, too?"

"Yes. We're still used to blacked-out Europe. I keep thinking somebody has forgotten to turn them off and the planes will attack any minute."

Schwarz stopped. "Light was given to us as a gift from God," he said with emotion, "because there is something of God in us. And now we hide it because we are murdering the bit of God in us."

"As I remember the story," I said, "the gods didn't make man a gift of fire. Prometheus stole it. In return the gods gave him chronic cirrhosis of the liver."

Schwarz looked at me. "I stopped joking long ago. As long as people joke, they belittle the proportions of things."

"Perhaps," I said. "But isn't that better if it lets in a ray of hope?"

"You're right. I forgot that you are trying to get away.

How can a man who's trying to get away have time to think of proportions?"

"Aren't you trying to get away, too?"

Schwarz shook his head. "Not any more. I'm going back."

"Where?" I asked in amazement. I couldn't believe that he meant to go back to Germany a second time.

CHAPTER 3

The night club was typical of the places that White Russians have been operating all over Europe since the Revolution of 1917. They all have the same waiters, who all used to be aristocrats, the same choirs all made up of former officers of the guard, the same high prices, and the same melancholy atmosphere.

In addition, they all have the same dim lighting, and I was counting on that. Just as the waiter had said, there were Germans, and they were definitely not refugees. They were probably spies, members of the German legation, or employees of German firms.

"The Russians," said Schwarz, "have been more successful than we have in making a place for themselves. It's true they had a fifteen-year head start. Fifteen years of exile is a long time, a lifetime of experience."

"They were the first wave of refugees," I replied. "People were still sorry for them. They were given work permits and papers. Nansen passports. When we came, the world's supply of pity had long been used up. We were nuisances, termites; hardly anyone had a good word for us. We have no right to work, no right to exist, and we still have no papers."

I had been feeling nervous ever since we set foot in this place. It was probably a reaction to the closed-in, heavily curtained room, my awareness that there were Germans about, and the fact that I was sitting too far from the door for an easy getaway. I had long been in the habit of sitting near the exit wherever I went. It also made me nervous that from here I couldn't see the ship. Maybe some message had come and it would sail, ahead of time, that very night.

Schwarz seemed to read my thoughts. He reached into his pocket and put the tickets down in front of me. "Take them; I'm not a slave driver. Take them and go if you want to."

I was ashamed. "You've got me wrong," I said. "I have time. All the time in the world."

Schwarz did not reply. He waited. I took the two booklets and put them in my pocket.

"I arranged to take a train," he went on, as though nothing had happened, "that would reach Osnabrück early in the evening. I felt that I was crossing the border only now. Up until then, the people and things, even in my native land, had been strangers to me; but now every tree began to speak. I knew the villages we rode through; as a schoolboy I had gone there on excursions, or I had been there with Helen in the first weeks of our acquaintance. I had loved this country-side, as I had loved the city with its houses and gardens.

"Up until then, my horror had been abstract and all of a piece. What had happened had paralyzed me, turned me to stone. I had never felt the need to analyze it, to consider it in detail; actually, I had been afraid to do so. Now, suddenly, the little things began to speak, things that had nothing to do with the horror, and yet were part of it.

"The countryside hadn't changed. It was still the same.

The steeples still had the same soft green patina in the setting sun; the river still reflected the sky. It reminded me of the days when I had gone fishing and dreamed of adventures in strange lands—well, I had had plenty of those, but they weren't exactly what I had imagined. The meadows with their butterflies and dragonflies hadn't changed, nor had the hillsides with their trees and wild flowers; they were exactly as in the days of my youth, and in them lay my youth—buried, if I wanted to look at it that way, or ready to be rediscovered, if I tried to be more optimistic.

"And there was nothing to mar the scene. From the train I saw few people and no uniforms, only the countryside, gradually sinking into the dusk. There were roses and dahlias and lilies in the tiny gardens of the stationmasters. They were just as they had always been; the leprosy hadn't corroded them; they grew on wooden trellises, just as they did in France, and in the meadows stood cows just as in the meadows of Switzerland, brown and black and white—without swastikas—with the same old patient eyes. I saw a stork clattering on a farmhouse, and the swallows flew as they fly everywhere and always. Only the people had changed; I knew it, but that evening I couldn't see it, and I couldn't understand it either.

"Besides, they were not as uniformly different as I had foolishly imagined. The compartment filled up and emptied and filled up again. At that time of day there were few uniforms; nearly all the people were plain people, and their conversation was pretty much what I was accustomed to in France and Switzerland—about the weather, the harvest, the events of the day and the fear of war. They, too, were afraid of war; the only difference was that outside of Germany everyone knew that Germany had wanted it, whereas here I heard that other countries were forcing it on Germany. Almost everyone was for peace, as people always are just before a war breaks out.

"The train stopped. I squeezed through the gate with the

crowd. The inside of the station hadn't changed since I had last seen it; it only seemed smaller and dustier than I remembered.

"When I stepped out into the Bahnhofsplatz, everything I had been thinking fell away from me. Night was falling and the air was damp, as after a rain; I no longer saw my surroundings; everything trembled within me, and I knew that from then on I would be in great danger. At the same time I had the feeling that nothing could happen to me. It was as though I were standing under a glass bell that protected me but might shatter into bits at any moment.

"I went back in to the ticket window and bought a return ticket to Münster. I couldn't live in Osnabrück. It was too dangerous. 'When is the last train?' I asked the ticket seller, who sat in the yellow light behind his window, his bald head glistening, like a small-town Buddha utterly secure and immune to all vicissitudes.

" 'There's one at nine-twenty and another at eleven-twelve.'

"I went to a slot machine and bought a platform ticket. I wanted to have it handy in case I had to disappear in a hurry before train time. As a rule, station platforms are poor hiding places, but usually you have several to choose from—three in Osnabrück—you can jump into a train that's about to leave, explain to the conductor that you've made a mistake, pay the difference, and get out at the next stop.

"I had decided to call up a friend of former years, whom I knew to be no supporter of the regime. His tone on the telephone would tell me whether he could help me. I was afraid to call my wife directly, because I didn't know whether she lived alone.

"I stood in the little glass booth with the telephone book in front of me. My heart beat so hard as I turned the soiled and rumpled corners of the pages that I thought I could hear it; I even thought others could hear it, and bent low to avoid

32

being recognized. Unthinking, I had opened up to the letter with which my former name began. I found my wife's name, the phone number was the same, but the address had changed. Rissmüller-Platz was now called Hitler-Platz.

"The moment I saw the address it seemed to me that the dismal light bulb in the booth grew a hundred times stronger. I looked up, overcome by a feeling that it was black night outside and that I was standing in a brightly lighted glass box, or in the beam of a searchlight. Once again the madness of my undertaking struck me with full force.

"I left the phone booth and passed through the half-darkened station. The blue skies and happy faces of 'Strength through Joy' posters looked down at me menacingly. A train or two must have arrived; a swarm of travelers was coming up the stairs. An SS man stepped out of the throng and headed in my direction.

"I didn't run. Maybe he had someone else in mind. But he stopped right in front of me and looked me full in the face. 'Pardon me,' he said. 'Have you got a light?'

" 'A light?' I repeated. And then quickly: 'Yes, of course! A match!'

"I reached into my pocket and searched.

" 'Why a match?' said the SS man, surprised. 'Your cigarette's burning.'

"I hadn't even realized I was smoking. I held out my cigarette. He touched his to the incandescent tip and drew. 'What's that you're smoking?' he asked. 'Smells like a cigar.'

"It was a Gauloise. I had bought a few packs before crossing the border. 'A present from a friend,' I said. 'French. Black tobacco. He brought them back from France. They're too strong for me, too.'

"The SS man laughed. 'The best would be to stop smoking altogether. Like the Führer. But it's not easy, especially in times like this!' He saluted and left."

Schwarz smiled feebly. "When I was still a human being

with the right to go where I pleased, I used to have my doubts about the way writers describe terror—the victim's heart stands still, he can't move a limb, icy shivers run down his spine, his whole body breaks out in sweat; clichés and clumsy writing, I thought. Maybe so. But it's also the truth. It's exactly how I felt, though in my days of innocence such things had made me laugh."

A waiter approached. "Wouldn't you gentlemen like some company?"

"No."

He bent over me. "Before you say no, let me call your attention to the two ladies at the bar."

I looked at them. One of them seemed very well built. Both had on close-fitting evening dresses. I couldn't make out their faces. "No," I said again.

"They are ladies," said the waiter. "The one on the right is a German lady."

"Did she send you?"

"No, sir," the waiter replied with a disarmingly innocent smile. "It was my own idea."

"Good. Bury it. Bring us something to eat instead."

"What did he want?" Schwarz asked.

"To tie us up with Mata Hari's granddaughter. You must have given him too much tip."

"I haven't paid yet. You think they're spies?"

"Possibly. But for the one real International in the world: Mammon."

"Germans?"

"One of them, the waiter said."

"Do you think she's been sent to lure Germans back home?"

"I doubt it. That's more in the Russian line nowadays."

The waiter brought us a dish of canapés that I had ordered because the wine was going to my head. I was determined to keep my wits about me.

"Aren't you going to eat?" I asked Schwarz.

He shook his head absently. "It had never occurred to me

34

that those cigarettes might give me away," he said. "Now I checked through all my belongings. My matches were from France, too. I threw them away with the rest of my cigarettes and bought German. Then I remembered that my passport had a French entry stamp and visa; in case of questioning, I'd have had no difficulty in accounting for the French cigarettes. Bathed in sweat and furious with myself for my fears, I went back to the telephone booth.

"I had to wait. A woman with an enormous party badge called two numbers in succession and thundered commands. The third number didn't answer. The woman came out, self-important and furious.

"I called my friend's number. A woman's voice answered. 'May I speak to Dr. Martens, please?' I noticed that my voice was hoarse.

" 'Who is speaking?' the woman asked.

" 'A friend of Dr. Martens.' I couldn't give my name. The voice might be either his wife's or the maid's, but it would be a mistake to trust either of them.

" 'Your name please,' said the woman.

" 'I am a friend of Dr. Martens,' I answered. 'Please tell him that. On urgent business.'

" 'I'm sorry,' the woman's voice answered. 'If you won't tell me your name, I can't announce you.'

" 'You'll have to make an exception,' I said. 'Dr. Martens is expecting my call.'

" 'In that case, you can surely tell me your name. . . .'

"I racked my brains in desperation. Then I heard the receiver being hung up.

"I stood in the gray, windy station. My first move, which had seemed so simple, had gone wrong, and I had no idea what to do next. Maybe I'd have to call Helen directly and run the risk that a member of her family would recognize me by my voice. I could give a different name, but what name? Dr. Martens—I could think of no other at the moment. I hesitated. And then an idea dawned on me, so obvious that it would have come to me in a flash at the age of ten. Why not call Dr. Martens and give the name of my wife's brother? Martens knew him well and had taken an intense dislike to him ten years back.

"The same woman's voice answered. 'Georg Jürgens speaking,' I said briskly. 'Dr. Martens, please.'

" 'Are you the gentleman who called up before?'

" 'This is Sturmbannführer Jürgens. I wish to speak to Dr. Martens. Immediately.'

" 'Certainly,' said the woman. 'Just a moment.' "

Schwarz looked at me. "Do you know that terrible soft buzzing in the receiver when you're waiting for your life on the telephone?"

I nodded. "It doesn't even have to be life that you're waiting for. It can be the void that you're trying to exorcise."

Schwarz went on with his story. " 'Dr. Martens speaking,' I heard at last. Again I was in one of those states that would once have made me laugh. My throat was parched.

" 'Rudolf,' I whispered finally.

" 'I beg your pardon?'

" 'Rudolf,' I said. 'This is a relative of Helen Jürgens.'

" 'I don't understand. Aren't you Sturmbannführer Jürgens?'

" 'I'm calling for him, Rudolf. For Helen Jürgens. Don't you understand now?'

" 'I don't understand a thing,' said the voice in the phone with irritation. 'I'm in the middle of a consultation. . . .'

" 'Couldn't I come to your office, Rudolf? Are you very busy?'

" 'What are you driving at? I don't even know you, and you . . .'

" 'Old Shatterhand,' I said.

"Suddenly I had remembered the names we had called each other by as boys playing Indians, names from the novels of Karl May that we had devoured at the age of twelve. For a moment I heard nothing. Then Martens said softly: 'What's that?'

" 'Winnetou,' I answered. 'Have you forgotten the old names? Why, those are the Führer's favorite books.'

" 'That's true,' he said. It was generally known that the man who was starting the Second World War had by his bed-side the thirty or more volumes of Karl May's collected works and that these books about Indians, trappers, and hunters, which strike any normal boy of fifteen as at least slightly ridiculous, were his favorite reading matter.

" 'Winnetou?' Martens repeated in a tone of incredulity.

" 'Yes. I've got to see you.'

" 'I don't understand. Where are you?'

" 'Here. In Osnabrück. Where can we meet?'

" 'I'm having consultations,' said Martens mechanically.

" 'I'm sick. Can I come and consult with you?'

" 'What's the point in all this?' said Martens in a voice that showed he had decided what to do. 'If you're sick, just come and see me. Why bother to phone?'

" 'When?'

" 'The best time would be seven-thirty. Seven-thirty,' he repeated. 'Not before.'

" 'Good. I'll see you at seven-thirty.'

"I put down the phone. I was bathed in sweat. Slowly I made my way to the exit. A pale half-moon appeared for an instant between the clouds. In just a week, I thought, it will be the new moon. A good time to cross the border. I looked at the clock. I still had three-quarters of an hour's time. Better get away from the station. People who hang around stations always look suspicious. I took the street that was darkest and least frequented. It led to the old ramparts. One section had been leveled and topped with tall trees. An-other, along the river, remained as it had been. I followed the ramparts, crossed a square, and passed the Church of the Sacred Heart.

"From the upper ramparts you could look across the river

at the roofs and towers of the city. The baroque dome of the cathedral glistened in the wavering moonlight. I knew this view; it was reproduced on a thousand postcards. I also knew the smell of the water and the smell of the linden trees on the avenue that skirted the ramparts.

"I saw lovers sitting on the benches that had been set up between the trees, offering a view of the river and the city. I sat down on an empty bench to kill the half hour before I could go to see Martens.

"The bells of the cathedral began to ring. I was so agitated that the vibrations literally shook me. It was like observing an invisible game of tennis. One of the players was my old self I knew so well, who trembled and was afraid and didn't dare to reflect on his situation. The other was my new self, who was bold and risked his life as if there were no other possible course—a strange schizophrenic contest, observed by a passive, objective arbiter, who for all his objectivity hoped in his heart that the new self would win out.

"I remember that half hour in every detail. I even remember my amazement at taking such a clinical view of myself. It was as if I were standing in a room with facing mirrors; they cast my reflection back and forth in an infinity of empty space, and behind every reflection I discovered another, looking over the preceding one's shoulder. The mirrors seemed old and tarnished, and I couldn't make out whether the expression was questioning, sad, or hopeful. The images were blurred by the silvery darkness.

"A woman sat down beside me. I didn't know what she wanted, and I had no idea whether the barbarian regime had by now reduced even these things to military exercises. So I stood up and left. I heard the woman laughing behind me, and I've never forgotten the soft, rather contemptuous, commiserating laugh of that unknown woman on the Herrenteichswall in Osnabrück.

38

CHAPTER 4

"The waiting room was empty. Plants with long, leathery leaves stood on a shelf by the window. On the table lay magazines, the covers showing pictures of party bigwigs, soldiers, a detachment of Hitler Youth. I heard swift steps. Martens stood in the doorway. He stared at me, took off his glasses, and blinked. The light in the waiting room was dim. He did not recognize me at first, probably because of my mustache.

" 'It's I, Rudolf,' I said. 'It's Josef.'

"He motioned me to speak softly. 'Where have you come from?' he whispered.

"I shrugged. What did that matter? 'I'm here,' I said. 'You've got to help me.'

"He looked at me. His nearsighted eyes in the dim light seemed like the eyes of a fish in a bowl. 'Have you permission to be here?'

" 'Only from myself.'

" 'How did you cross the border?'

39

" 'That doesn't matter. I've come to see Helen.'

"He gaped at me. 'So that's what you've come for?'

" 'Yes,' I said.

"Suddenly I felt calm. I had been trembling as long as I was alone. Now all my agitation left me; my problem was to calm my perturbed friend.

" 'To see Helen?' he asked.

" 'Yes, to see Helen. And you've got to help me.'

" 'Good God!' he said.

" 'Is she dead?' I asked.

" 'No, she is not dead.'

" 'Is she in town?'

" 'Yes. At least she was a week ago.'

" 'Can we speak here?' I asked.

"Martens nodded. 'I've sent my receptionist away. If any patients turn up, I can send them away, too. I can't ask you to my home. I've married. Two years ago. You understand. . . .'

"I understood. Relatives were not to be trusted in the Thousand-Year Reich. Denunciation was looked upon as a national virtue by the saviors of Germany. Of that I had first-hand experience. It was my wife's brother who had denounced me.

" 'My wife isn't in the party,' said Martens quickly. 'But we've never'—he looked at me with confusion—'discussed a case like this one. I'm not exactly sure what she would think. Come in here.'

"He opened the door of his consultation room and locked it behind us. 'Leave it open,' I said. 'A locked room is more suspicious than if we were to be seen.'

"He turned the key back in the lock and looked at me. 'Josef, for God's sake, what are you doing here? Have you come secretly?'

" 'Yes. And you don't have to hide me. I'm staying at a hotel outside the city. I've come to you because you're the

40

only one who could let Helen know I am here. I haven't heard from her in five years. I don't know what's become of her. I don't know even whether she has remarried. If she has . . .'

" 'And that's why you've come?'

" 'Yes,' I replied in astonishment. 'Why else would I come?'

" 'We've got to hide you,' he said. 'You can spend the night here on the couch. I'll wake you before seven. At seven the maid comes in to clean up. After eight you can come back. There are no patients before eleven.'

" 'Is she married?' I asked.

" 'Helen?' He shook his head. 'I don't even think she's divorced from you.'

" 'Where is she living? In the old apartment?'

" 'I think so.'

" 'Is anyone living with her?'

" 'What do you mean?'

" 'Her mother. Her sister. Her brother. Or some other relative.'

" 'I'm not sure.'

" 'You've got to find out,' I said. 'And you've got to tell her I'm here.'

" 'Why don't you tell her yourself?' Martens asked. 'There's the phone.'

" 'And suppose she's not alone? What if her brother is there? He has already denounced me once.'

" 'That's true. She'd probably be just as flabbergasted as I was. That could give her away.'

" 'I don't even know how she feels about me, Rudolf. It's been five years, and we were only married for four. Five years are more than four—and separation cuts more ice than a life together.'

"He nodded. 'I don't understand you,' he said.

" 'I can see that. I don't understand myself either. We lead different lives.'

" 'Why didn't you write her?'

41

" 'I can't explain all that now, Rudolf. Go to see Helen. Talk to her. Find out how she feels. If it seems like the right thing to do, tell her I'm here and ask her how we can meet.'

" 'When do you want me to go?'

" 'Right away,' I said, startled. 'Why wait?'

"He looked around. 'Where will you go in the meantime? It's not safe here. My wife is likely to send the maid down for me. I usually go upstairs after my office hours; she's used to it. I could lock you in, but that would look suspicious.'

" 'I don't want to be locked in,' I said. 'Can't you tell your wife you have to visit a patient?'

" 'I'll tell her that when I come back. It's simpler.'

"I saw a twinkle in his eyes, and for a moment the left one seemed to wink ever so slightly. That reminded me of our childhood days. 'I'll wait in the cathedral. Nowadays churches are almost as safe as in the Middle Ages. When should I call you up?'

" 'In an hour. Say your name is Otto Sturm. How can I find you? Wouldn't you rather go some place where there's a phone?'

" 'Places with phones are dangerous.'

" 'Yes, maybe so.' For a moment he stood hesitant. 'Yes, maybe you're right. If I'm not back, call again, or leave a message saying where you are.'

" 'Good.'

"I took my hat.

" 'Josef,' he said.

"I turned around.

" 'How is it out there?' he asked. 'You know what I mean. Without . . . without everything . . .'

" 'Without everything?' I answered. 'Yes, that's about it. Without everything. But not entirely. And how is it here? With everything except the one thing that counts?'

" 'Not so good,' he said. 'Not so good, Josef. But shiny on the surface.'

* * *

42

"I took the emptiest streets to the cathedral. It was not far. In Krahnstrasse a company of marching soldiers passed me. They were singing a song I did not know. On the Domplatz there were more soldiers. A little farther off, by the three crosses of the Little Church, a crowd had gathered—two or three hundred people, most of them in party uniform. I heard a voice and looked for the speaker; there wasn't one. Finally my eyes lit on a black loud-speaker propped up on a platform. It stood there under a light, naked and alone, an automaton, screaming about the right to reconquer every inch of German soil, the Greater Germany, revenge. The peace of the world, it roared, could be safeguarded in only one way: the world must do what Germany wanted. That was right and just.

"The wind had risen again, and the swaying branches cast their restless shadows on the faces, the howling machine, and the silent stone sculptures on the church wall behind them: Christ on the cross between the two thieves. The faces of the listeners were concentrated and transfigured. They believed what the automaton was screaming at them; in a strange state of hypnosis, they applauded this disembodied voice as if it were a human being. The scene struck me as typical of the sinister, demonic mob spirit of our times, of all the frightened, hysterical crowds who follow slogans. It makes no difference whether the slogans come from the right or the left, as long as they relieve the masses of the hard work of thinking and of the need to take responsibility.

"I hadn't expected to find so many people in the cathedral. Then I remembered that services were held every evening in May. For a moment I wondered whether a Protestant church mightn't be better; but I didn't know whether they were open in the evening. I squeezed into an empty pew near the entrance. There was a blaze of candles at the altar, but the rest of the church was dimly lighted, and it would not have been easy to recognize me.

"The priest moved about the altar in a cloud of incense and candlelight, surrounded by altar boys in red cassocks and white surplices, one of them swinging the steaming censer. I heard the organ and the singing, and it seemed to me that I was looking upon the same transfigured faces as outside, the same ecstatic sleepwalkers' eyes, full of unquestioning faith and yearning for security without responsibility. The atmosphere in the church was gentler, milder; but this religion, which tells us to love God and our neighbor, had not always been so mild: in long centuries of darkness it, too, had shed a great deal of blood. The moment it had ceased to be persecuted, it had begun to persecute in turn, with fire and sword and rack. Helen's brother had made that point when he spoke to me in the concentration camp: 'We have taken over the methods of your Church. Your Inquisition with its tortures in God's name taught us how to deal with enemies of the faith. Actually, we are not so cruel: it's only in special cases that we burn people alive.' I was hanging on a cross when he said that to me—that was one of their gentler ways of getting information out of prisoners.

"The priest at the altar raised the golden monstrance and blessed the congregation. I sat very still, but I felt as if I were floating in a tepid bath of incense, consolation, and light. Then the last hymn struck up: 'Be thou in this night my shield and my guard.' I had sung that as a child; in those days the darkness of night had frightened me—now it was the light that I feared.

"The people began to leave. I had another fifteen minutes to wait. I slid into a corner beside a great pillar that supported the vaulting.

"At that moment I saw Helen. I didn't recognize her at first, because I hadn't expected her here. Then when she had gone a few steps past me and reached a spot where the crowd had thinned out, I recognized her by the way she moved her shoulders in working her way forward. She didn't seem to touch anyone, but to glide in between people. Suddenly she was standing almost disengaged in the wide center aisle, against the candles and the blue-and-red darkness of the tall Romanesque windows. She looked small and slender and lost.

"I stood up, trying to catch her eye. I didn't dare to beckon. There were still too many people; it would have attracted attention. She's alive, was my first thought. She's not dead and she's not sick. In our situation, that's always the first thought. You're so surprised that something is still the same as before—that someone is still there.

"She hurried on to the choir. I slipped out of my pew and followed her. At the communion rail she stopped and turned around. She carefully examined the people still kneeling in the pews, then returned slowly down the aisle. I stood still. She was so sure of finding me in one of the pews that she passed right beside me, so close that we almost touched. I followed her. When she stopped again, I stopped right behind her. 'Helen,' I said. 'Don't turn around. Go outside. I'll follow you. We mustn't be seen here.'

"She quivered as if she had been struck, but she went on. Why on earth had she come here? We were in great danger of being recognized. But I myself hadn't known there would be so many people.

"I saw her walking along ahead of me; but all I felt was impatience to be out of the church as quickly as possible. She had on a black suit and a very small hat, and she held her head very erect and a little to the side, as though listening to my footsteps. I lagged a few steps behind, remaining just near enough to keep her in sight; I had learned by experience that you are often recognized simply because you are too close to someone else.

"She passed by the stone holy-water fonts and through the great portal. Then she turned left. Alongside the cathedral there was a broad walk paved with stone flags, barred off from

45

the square by iron chains affixed to sandstone posts. She jumped over the chains, took a few steps into the darkness, stopped, and turned around. When I say that I felt in that moment that this was my life, my whole life walking ahead of me and apparently away from me, and then suddenly it turned back to me, that's another cliché, and it's both true and untrue. Just the same, I felt it, but that wasn't all I felt. I walked toward Helen, toward her dark figure, toward her pale face and her eyes and her mouth, and I left behind me everything that had been. The years during which we had not been together did not evaporate; they still existed, but they were something I had read about, not something I had experienced.

" 'Where have you come from?' Helen asked in a tone that was almost hostile, before I had reached her.

" 'From France.'

" 'And they let you in?'

" 'No, I crossed the border illegally.'

"Those were almost the same questions that Martens had asked. 'Why?' she asked.

" 'To see you.'

" 'You shouldn't have come.'

" 'I know. I said the same thing to myself day after day.'

" 'And why have you come?'

" 'If I knew that, I wouldn't be here.'

"I didn't dare to kiss her. She stood right in front of me, but so rigid I thought she might break if I touched her. I didn't know what she might be thinking, but I had seen her again, she was alive, and now I could go, or wait to see what would happen.

" 'You don't know?' she asked.

" 'I'll know tomorrow. Or next week. Or later.'

"I looked at her. What was there to know? Knowledge was a speck of foam dancing on top of a wave. Every gust of wind could blow it away; but the wave remained.

" 'You've come,' she said. Her face lost its rigidity and

46

grew gentle. She came a step closer. I held her by the arms, and her hands were pressed against my chest as though to hold me at a distance. I had the feeling that we had stood a long while face to face and alone on the dark windy square; the street sounds seemed muffled, as though cut off from us by a glass wall. At the end of the square to the left of me, about a hundred paces distant, lay the brightly lighted Stadttheater with its white steps, and for a moment, I remember, I was vaguely surprised that plays were still being shown and that the theater hadn't been turned into barracks or a prison.

"A group of people passed us. One of them laughed and some of them looked around at us. 'Come,' Helen whispered. 'We can't stay here.'

" 'Where can we go?'

" 'To your apartment.'

"I thought I must have heard wrong. 'Where?' I asked again.

" 'To your apartment. Where else?'

" 'Someone might recognize me on the stairs. Aren't the same people living in the house as before?'

" 'They won't see you.'

" 'And the maid?'

" 'I'll give her the night off.'

" 'And tomorrow morning?'

"Helen looked at me. 'Have you come so far just to ask such questions?'

" 'I haven't come to be caught and sent to a concentration camp, Helen.'

"At last she smiled. 'Josef,' she said, 'you haven't changed. How did you ever get here?'

" 'I don't know myself,' I answered, and had to smile, too. I remembered how sometimes in the past she had taken the same tone in exasperation at my pedantry. That memory effaced the danger. 'But I'm here,' I said.

"She shook her head, and I saw that her eyes were filled

47

with tears. 'Not yet,' she answered. 'Not yet. And now come along, or they really will arrest us; it looks as if I were making a scene.'

"We crossed the square. 'I can't come with you right away,' I said. 'You'll have to send the maid away first. I've taken a room in a hotel in Münster. No one knows me in Münster; my idea was to stay there.'

"She stopped still. 'For how long?'

" 'I don't know,' I answered. 'I've never been able to think ahead. All I knew was that I wanted to see you and that I'd have to go back some time.'

" 'Across the border?'

" 'Of course.'

"She bowed her head and went on. I reflected that I should now be very happy, but I didn't feel that way. It's only later that you really feel it. Now—now I know that I was happy.

" 'I've got to call Martens,' I said.

" 'You can call him from your apartment,' Helen replied. It gave me a jolt every time she said 'your apartment.' She was doing it on purpose. I didn't know why.

" 'I promised Martens to call him in an hour,' I said. 'That means now. If I don't call, he'll think something has gone wrong. He might do something foolish.'

" 'He knows I was going to meet you.'

"I looked at my watch. I ought to have called fifteen minutes before. 'I'll call him from the nearest café,' I said. 'It will only take a second.'

" 'Goodness, Josef,' said Helen angrily, 'you really haven't changed. You're even more pedantic than you used to be.'

" 'Maybe so,' I said. 'But I know from experience what calamities can come from inattention to details. And I also know what it feels like to wait when there's danger in the air.' I took her arm. 'If I weren't pedantic, Helen, I wouldn't be alive.'

"She pressed my arm. 'I know,' she murmured. 'But don't you understand that I'm afraid something will happen if I leave you alone for one minute?'

"I felt all the warmth in the world. 'Nothing will happen, Helen.'

"She smiled and raised her pale face. 'Go telephone. But not in a café. There's a booth over there. They put it up while you were away. It's safer than a café.'

"I went into the glass booth. Helen stayed outside. I called Martens. The line was busy. I waited a little while and called again. The coin was returned with a tinkle. The line was still busy. I grew anxious. Through the glass I could see Helen pacing attentively back and forth. I motioned to her, but she didn't see me. She was watching the street but trying not to show it, sentinel and guardian angel in one, in a very becoming suit, as I now noticed. I also saw, as I waited, that she had on lipstick. In the yellow light it seemed almost black. I remembered that rouge and lipstick were frowned on in the new Germany.

"At the third attempt Martens answered. 'My wife was on the phone,' he said. 'For almost half an hour. I couldn't interrupt her.'

" 'Where is she now?'

" 'In the kitchen. I had to let her talk. You understand?'

" 'Of course I do. Everything is all right. Thank you, Rudolf. Forget you saw me.'

" 'Where are you?'

" 'In the street. Thank you, Rudolf. I don't need anything now. I've found what I was looking for. We're together.'

"I looked at Helen through the glass wall and wanted to hang up. 'Do you know where you'll stay?' Martens asked.

" 'I think so. Don't worry. Forget this evening; pretend you dreamt it.'

" 'If there's anything else I can do,' he said hesitantly, 'let me know. I was too surprised at first. You understand. . . ?'

49

" 'Yes, Rudolf, I understand. If I need anything, I'll let you know.'

" 'If you want to spend the night here . . . we could talk. . . .'

"I smiled. 'We'll see. I've got to hang up now. . . .'

" 'Yes, of course,' he said quickly. 'Forgive me. I wish you the best of luck, Josef. I really do.'

" 'Thank you, Rudolf.'

"I stepped out of the airless telephone booth. A gust of wind nearly blew my hat off. Helen rushed over to me. 'Come home now! You've infected me with your caution. I feel as if a hundred eyes were staring at us out of the darkness.'

" 'Have you still the same maid?'

" 'Lena? No, she was spying for my brother. He wanted to know if you wrote me. Or if I wrote you.'

" 'And the present one?'

" 'She's dumb and she doesn't care what I do. If I give her the weekend off, she'll be delighted. She won't think anything.'

" 'You haven't sent her away yet?'

"She smiled and was very beautiful. 'I had to make sure you were really here.'

" 'You've got to get rid of her before I come in,' I said. 'She mustn't see us. Couldn't we go somewhere else?'

" 'Where?'

"Where indeed? Helen laughed. 'Here we stand like two teen-agers, wondering where they can meet in secret because their parents think they're too young. Where can we go? To the Castle Park? It's closed at eight o'clock. Sit on a bench in the municipal gardens? A pastry shop? That would be dangerous.'

"She was right. These were the details that I had not foreseen—you never do. 'Yes,' I said. 'Here we stand like teen-agers.'

"I looked at her. She was twenty-nine; but she hadn't changed. The five intervening years had slid off her like water

50

from a young seal. 'I came here like a teen-ager, too,' I said. 'All reason was against it. But I didn't think ahead. I didn't even know whether you were married to me or to somebody else.'

"She did not answer. Her brown hair shone in the light of the street lamp. 'I'll go ahead and send the girl away,' she said. 'But I hate leaving you alone in the street. You might disappear as suddenly as you came. Where will you go in the meantime?'

" 'Where you found me. In a church. I could go back to the cathedral. Churches are safe, Helen. I've become an expert on French, Swiss, and Italian churches and museums.'

" 'Come back in half an hour,' she whispered. 'Do you remember the windows of our apartment?'

" 'Yes,' I said.

" 'If the corner window is open, the coast is clear and you can come up. If it's closed, wait until I open it.'

"I was reminded of my childhood, when I had played Indians with Martens. In those days the signal had been a light in the window; Old Shatterhand or Winnetou would be waiting down below. Did life repeat itself? Could anything really be repeated?

" 'Good,' I said, and began to walk away.

" 'Where are you going?'

" 'I'll see if St. Mary's is still open. If my memory doesn't deceive me, it's a fine example of Gothic architecture. I've learned to appreciate those things.'

" 'Stop the nonsense,' she said. 'It's bad enough having to leave you alone.'

" 'Helen,' I answered, 'I've learned to take care of myself.'

"She shook her head. The bravery went out of her face. 'Not well enough,' she said. 'Not well enough. What will I do if you don't come back?'

" 'There's nothing you can do. Your telephone number's still the same, isn't it?'

" 'Yes.'

"I touched her shoulder. 'Helen,' I said. 'Everything will be all right.'

"She nodded. 'I'll take you to St. Mary's. I want to be sure you get there.'

"We walked in silence. It was not far. Helen left me without a word. I looked after her as she crossed the old market place. She walked quickly without looking back.

"I stopped in the darkness beneath the portal. To the right lay the city hall, in shadow except for the carved stone faces which caught a faint glow of moonlight. In 1648 the end of the Thirty Years' War had been proclaimed on the steps outside that city hall; so had the beginning of the Thousand-Year Reich in 1933. I wondered whether I would live to witness the announcement of its end. I had little hope.

"I did not try to go inside the church. I was suddenly repelled by the idea of hiding. I was still determined to be careful, but since I had seen Helen, I didn't want to act like a hunted animal any more, unless I had to.

"Still, it wouldn't be safe to stay here too long, so I began to stroll about. The city, which before had seemed dangerous, familiar and at the same time strange, now came to life. I sensed that this was so because I myself had begun to live. It came to me that my anonymous existence of the last few years, which had seemed so empty, a sheer fight for survival, had not been so useless. It had molded me, and now, like a flower that had opened during the night, a sense of life that I had not known before was within me. There was nothing romantic about it; but it was new and exciting, as if an enormous, bright-colored tropical bloom had appeared by magic on a common garden plant that might at best have been expected to produce a measly bud or two. I came to the river, stopped on the bridge, and looked down over the rail at the water. To the left of me stood a medieval watchtower, which now housed a laundry. The windows were lighted, and the girls were still at work. The light came blowing across the river in broad beams. The black wall with the linden trees stood out against the tall sky, and to the right lay gardens and the silhouette of the cathedral.

"I stood very still, completely relaxed. There was nothing to be heard but the splashing of the water and the muffled voices of the laundry girls behind the windows. I couldn't make out what they were saying. All I heard seemed to be human sounds that had not yet shaped themselves into words, signs of human presence, but not yet, as finished words would have been, signs of falsehood, betrayal, stupidity, and frantic loneliness, ugly overtones disfiguring what had been conceived as a pure melody.

"I breathed, and it seemed to me that I was breathing in the same rhythm as the water. For a timeless moment I even felt that I was a part of the bridge, that the water was flowing through me with my breath. This seemed perfectly natural, and I was not surprised. I didn't think; my thoughts had become as unconscious as my breathing and the water.

"A subdued light moved quickly through the line of lindens at my left. My eyes followed it, and then I heard the voices of the girls again. I realized that for a time I had not heard them. And again I noticed the smell of the lindens, carried across the water by the breeze.

"The moving light went out and at the same time the windows behind me darkened. For a minute the water lay black as pitch, then I saw the little spangles of moonlight that had been drowned out by the light of the laundry. Now that the moonlight was alone, its play was more delicate and varied than the coarse yellow light it had replaced. I thought of my life, in which years before a light had been extinguished, and I wondered whether a multitude of soft lights that I had never seen before might not reappear in it—like the sparkling moonlight on the river. Until then I had only been aware of my loss—it had never occurred to me that I might have gained something by it.

* * *

"I left the bridge and walked back and forth between the dark lines of trees on the ramparts until the half hour was up. The smell of the lindens grew stronger as the night advanced, and the moon sprinkled the roofs and towers with silver. It was as though the city were doing everything in its power to show me that I had built up a lie, that there was no danger lurking in wait for me anywhere, that I could go home with an easy heart after a long and aimless journey, to be myself again.

"There was no need to be on my guard against this feeling. Something within me watched of its own accord, peering out in all directions. Too many times I had been arrested in Paris, Rome, and other cities in exactly this state of mind— surrendering to beauty and lulled to security by delusions of love, understanding, and forgetfulness. The police never forgot. Moonlight and the scent of linden trees didn't make saints of stool pigeons.

"Cautiously, my senses alert like bats' wings, I made my way to Hitler-Platz. The house was on a corner, where a street entered the square. The street still had its old name.

"The window was open. I remembered the story of Hero and Leander and the fairy tale about the prince and princess in which the nun puts out the light and the prince drowns; I wasn't a prince, I thought; the Germans had lots of beautiful fairy tales, nevertheless, or perhaps for that very reason, the most revolting concentration camps in the world. Calmly I crossed the street, and it was not the Hellespont and not a northern sea.

"When I reached the entrance, I saw someone coming down the hallway. It was too late to turn back; I walked on toward the stairs with an air of knowing where I was going. It was an elderly woman I had never seen before. My heart stood still—" Schwarz smiled. "That's another cliché that you don't believe until you've felt it. I didn't look around. I heard the house door close, and ran quickly up the steps.

"The door was slightly ajar. I pushed it open and there was Helen. 'Did anyone see you?' she asked.

" 'Yes, an old woman.'

" 'Without a hat?'

" 'Yes, without a hat.'

" 'It must have been the maid. Her room is in the attic. I gave her off until Monday afternoon; she must have spent all that time primping. She thinks people have nothing else to do than to find fault with her dress.'

" 'Don't worry about her,' I said. 'Whether it was she or not, she didn't recognize me. I know when somebody recognizes me.'

"Helen took my raincoat and hat. She was going to hang them in the vestibule.

" 'Don't leave them here,' I said. 'Somebody might see them. Put them in a closet.'

" 'Nobody will be coming,' said Helen, and led the way to the living room.

"Before following her, I turned the key in the lock.

"In the first years of my exile I had often thought of my home; then I had tried to forget it. Now that I was in it, I didn't feel much. It affected me like a picture that had once belonged to me and that reminded me of a certain period of my life. I stood in the doorway. Hardly anything had changed. The couch and the chairs had been done over.

" 'Weren't they green before?' I asked.

" 'Blue,' said Helen."

Schwarz turned to me. "Things have a life of their own, and it's terrible when you compare them to yours."

"Why make comparisons?" I asked.

"Don't you?"

"Yes, but in a different way. I stick to myself. When I'm hungry on the water front, I compare myself with an imaginary me, who, in addition to being hungry, has cancer. That makes me happy for a minute, because I'm only hungry, without the cancer."

"Cancer," said Schwarz, and stared at me. "What makes you think of that?"

"I could have said syphilis. Or tuberculosis. Cancer seemed the most plausible."

"Plausible?" Schwarz was still looking fixedly at me. "There's nothing plausible about cancer. It's unthinkable."

"All right," I said in a conciliatory tone. "I just took it as an example."

"It's simply inconceivable."

"That's true of every fatal illness, Mr. Schwarz."

He nodded in silence. "Are you still hungry?" he asked after a while.

"No. Why?"

"You said something about hunger."

"I've eaten dinner twice since I've been with you."

He was silent. After a while he said more calmly: "The chairs were yellow. They had been done over; that was all that had happened there in five years, while I had been suffering all the ironies of fate. Sometimes things are incongruous, that's what I meant."

"Yes," I said. "A man dies, but his bed is still there. His house is still there. Objects remain as they were. If we could only destroy them, too!"

"Not if they don't mean anything to us."

"That's right," I said. "Besides, a human life isn't that important."

"No?" said Schwarz, and there was agony in the face he raised to me. "Not important? No, of course not. But tell me, if a life isn't important, what is?"

"Nothing," I said, knowing even as I spoke that it was true and yet untrue. "It's we ourselves who make things important."

Schwarz took a quick gulp of the dark wine. "And why

not?" he asked in a loud voice. "Can you tell me why we shouldn't make them important?"

"No, I can't tell you that. Anyway, it was just a silly manner of speaking. I myself take life seriously enough."

I looked at my watch. It was a little after two. The band was playing dance music, a tango. The short, muted notes of the horn reminded me of the far-off sirens of a departing ship. Only a few hours until dawn, I thought; then I'll be able to get out of here. I felt for the tickets in my pocket. They were still there. I had almost expected them not to be; the unaccustomed music, the wine, the curtained room, and Schwarz's voice created an atmosphere of drowsy unreality.

"I was still in the doorway of the living room," Schwarz went on. "Helen looked at me and asked: 'Has your home become so strange to you?'

"I shook my head and took a few steps forward. A curious embarrassment had come over me. The objects in the room seemed to be reaching out for me; but I no longer belonged to them. Perhaps I no longer belonged to Helen either. 'Everything is the same,' I said quickly, with a desperate fervor. 'Everything is the same, Helen.'

" 'No,' she answered. 'Nothing is the same. Why have you come back? For that? So everything would be the same?'

" 'No,' I said. 'I know that can't be. But didn't we live here? Where are those years?'

" 'Not here. And they aren't in the old clothes that we've thrown away. Or is that what you thought?'

" 'No. I'm not asking for myself. But you've been here the whole time. I'm asking for you.'

"Helen gave me a strange look. 'Why didn't you ever think of that before?' she said.

" 'Before?' I asked uncomprehending. 'What do you mean? I couldn't come back any sooner.'

" 'That's not what I mean. I mean before you went away.'

"I didn't understand. 'What should I have asked, Helen?'

"She did not reply at once. Then she said quickly: 'Why didn't you ask me to go with you?'

"I stared at her. 'With me? To leave your home? Your family? Everything you loved?'

" 'I hate my family.'

"I was utterly bewildered. 'You don't know what it's like out there,' I murmured finally.

" 'You didn't either, then.'

"That was true. 'I didn't want to take you away from here,' I said feebly.

" 'I hate it,' she answered. 'I hate everything here. Why have you come back?'

" 'You didn't hate it then.'

" 'Why have you come back?' she repeated. She was standing at the other end of the room, separated from me by the yellow chairs and more than five years. A wave of hostility and bitterness struck me full in the face. At the time of my flight my conduct had seemed perfectly natural. How could I involve Helen in the dangers and uncertainties of a life in exile? Now it came to me that perhaps I had offended her deeply by running off and leaving her alone.

" 'Why have you come back, Josef?' she asked.

"I should have liked to say that I had come back for her sake. But at the moment I couldn't. It was not so simple. I saw what I had never seen before: what had driven me back was a quiet, stark desperation. My reserves had been used up; my naked instinct of self-preservation had not been strong enough to endure the chill of loneliness any longer. I had not been able to build up a new life. In my heart I had never really wanted to, because I had never really put my old life behind me. I couldn't forget it, and I couldn't overcome it. Gangrene had set in, and I had to choose. I could let myself rot away, or I could go back and try to get well.

"I had never figured all this out, and even now it was only half clear to me; but it was an enormous relief to know even as much as I did. My feeling of oppression and embarrassment left me. Now I knew why I was here. From five years of exile I had brought nothing with me but my sharpened senses, an eagerness to live, and the caution and experience of a fugitive criminal. In all other respects, I was bankrupt. The nights in the no man's land between borders, the cruel boredom of a life spent fighting for a little food and a few hours of sleep, the underground existence of a mole—all this fell away from me as I stood here on the threshold of my home. I was bankrupt, but at least I had no debts. I was free. This was not a return. The self of those years had committed suicide when I crossed the border. It was dead. Another self was alive, and it was a gift, involving no responsibility." Schwarz turned to me. "Do you know what I mean? I repeat myself and talk in contradictions."

"I think I understand you," I answered. "The possibility of committing suicide is a blessing, though we seldom appreciate it. It gives you the illusion of free will. And probably we commit suicide more often than we suspect. We just don't know it."

"That's it!" said Schwarz eagerly. "If we only knew it for suicide! Then we'd also be able to rise from the dead. We'd have several lives instead of dragging the ulcers of experience from one crisis to the next and succumbing to them in the end.

"Of course I couldn't explain that to Helen," he continued. "And I didn't have to. All at once I felt so light that there was no need to explain. On the contrary, I felt that explanations would only make for confusion. She probably wanted me to say that I had come back on her account; but I knew with my new insight that that would have been my ruin. The past would have broken over us with all its reproaches, with all its guilt and lost opportunities and offended love, and we would never have found our way out. If this idea of spiritual suicide, which now seemed almost joyful, was to have any meaning, it had to be complete; it had to take in not only the years of exile, but also the years before it; otherwise a second gangrene, even older than the first, would set in. Helen stood there, an enemy, ready to strike out at me with love and an exact knowledge of my vulnerable points, and I wouldn't have had a chance. The suicide that had held out hope of liberation would become an excruciating moral agony —no longer death followed by resurrection, but complete annihilation. It is a mistake to explain too much to women. The thing to do is to act.

"I approached Helen. When I touched her shoulder, I felt her tremble. 'Why have you come?' she asked again.

" 'I've forgotten,' I said. 'I'm hungry, Helen. I haven't had anything to eat all day.'

"Beside her on a little painted Italian table was the silver-framed photograph of a man I did not know. 'Do we need that?' I asked.

" 'No,' she said in surprise. She took the picture and shoved it into the table drawer."

Schwarz looked at me and smiled. "She didn't throw it away," he said. "She didn't tear it up. She put it in the drawer. She'd be able to take it out and set it up again any time she pleased. I don't know why, but the discreet calculation of her gesture delighted me. Five years before, I would not have understood it. I would have made a scene. Now it put an end to a situation that was threatening to get stuffy. We can stomach big words in politics, but not in love. Unfortunately. It would be better the other way around. Helen's rationalistic gesture was not loveless; this was love seasoned with feminine perspicacity. I had disappointed her once; why should she be in any hurry to trust me? I, for my part, hadn't lived in France for nothing; I asked no questions. And what could I have asked? And by what right? I laughed. She was taken aback. Then her face brightened and she laughed, too. 'Tell me,' I asked, 'have you divorced me?'

"She shook her head. 'No. I refused. But not on your account. It was to annoy my family.'

CHAPTER 5

"I didn't sleep much that night," said Schwarz. "I was very tired, but I kept waking up. The night pressed into the little room where we lay. I thought I heard sounds. I would half drop off and dream that I was running and being pursued. I started in terror.

"Helen woke up only once. 'Can't you sleep?' she asked through the darkness.

" 'No. I didn't expect to.'

"She put on the light. The shadows leapt from the window. 'There's no use expecting too much,' I said. 'I have no control over my dreams. Is there any wine left?'

" 'Plenty. That's one thing I can count on from my family. When did you begin to drink wine?'

" 'Since I've been in France.'

" 'That's good,' she said. 'Do you know anything about wines?'

" 'Not much. What I know best is the cheap red stuff.'

"Helen went to the kitchen and came back with two bottles and a corkscrew. 'Our glorious Führer has changed the regulations about wine making,' she said. 'There used to be a law against adding sugar to natural wines. Now wine makers are even allowed to interrupt the fermentation.'

"She saw by the look on my face that I wasn't up on these things. 'They do that in bad years to make sour wine sweeter,' she explained with a laugh. 'It's a swindle that the master race thought up to help the export trade and take in hard currency.'

"She handed me the bottles and the corkscrew. I opened a bottle of Moselle. Helen brought in two thin glasses. 'How did you get so brown?' I asked.

" 'I was in the mountains in March. Skiing.'

" 'You ski in the nude?'

" 'No, but you don't need clothes for sun-bathing.'

" 'Since when have you known how to ski?'

" 'Someone taught me,' she said with a look of defiance.

" 'That's nice,' I said. 'It's supposed to be very good for you.'

"I filled a glass and held it out to her. The wine was tart and more aromatic than Burgundy. I hadn't had any like it since I had left Germany.

" 'Don't you want to know who taught me?' Helen asked.

" 'No.'

"She looked at me in surprise. In former days I would probably have questioned her all night. Now I didn't care in the least. The weightless unreality of the early evening was back again. 'You've changed,' she said.

" 'You've said the opposite at least twice,' I countered. 'It makes no difference either way.'

"She held her glass, but did not drink. 'Maybe I'd rather you hadn't changed.'

"I drank. 'Because that would make it easier to crush me?'

" 'Did I crush you before?'

62

" 'I don't know. I don't think so. It's been a long time. When I remember how I was then, I can't see why you shouldn't have tried.'

" 'One always tries; don't you know that?'

" 'No,' I said. 'But you've warned me at least. The wine is good. I guess the fermentation wasn't interrupted.'

" 'Like yours?'

" 'Helen,' I said, 'you're very exciting—and funny to boot. That's a most unusual and delightful combination.'

" 'Don't be so sure,' she said irritably, and sat down on the bed, still holding her glass.

" 'I'm not sure of anything,' I said, smiling. 'But uncertainty has its points. If it doesn't kill you, it can lead to an unshakable certainty. That's a lot of big words, but they only reflect the experience of a rolling stone.'

" 'Rolling stone?'

" 'Like me. A man who can't stop anywhere, who can never settle down. The existence of a refugee. Or a Buddhist mendicant monk. Or modern man. There are more refugees in the world than you think. A good many of them have never left home.'

" 'That doesn't sound so bad,' said Helen. 'Better than bourgeois stagnation.'

"I nodded. 'But it can be described in a different way; then it's not so attractive. Luckily we lack imagination. Otherwise so many people wouldn't volunteer to go to war.'

" 'Anything is better than stagnation,' said Helen, draining her glass.

"I watched her as she drank. How young she is, I thought, how young and inexperienced, how defiant and lovable, how dangerous and foolish. She doesn't know a thing. She doesn't even know that bourgeois stagnation is a moral, not a geographical, condition.

" 'Would you like to go back to it?' she asked.

" 'I don't think I could. My country has made me a cosmopolitan against my will. I can't change now. It's never possible to go back.'

" 'Not even to a person?'

" 'Not even to a person,' I said. 'Even the earth rolls. It's a refugee from the sun. You can never go back. It's no use trying; you come to grief.'

" 'Thank the Lord for that.' Helen held out her glass to me. 'Haven't you ever wanted to go back?'

" 'Always,' I said. 'I never follow my theories. That's what makes them so endearing.'

"Helen laughed. 'You've been talking a lot of nonsense.'

" 'Of course. It's pure flimflam to hide something else.'

" 'What?'

" 'Something that can't be put into words.'

" 'Something that happens only at night?'

"I did not answer. I sat quietly on the bed. The wind of time had been howling in my ears. Now it had stopped blowing. I felt as if I had moved from a plane to a balloon. I was still floating through the air; but there was no longer any sound of engines.

" 'What's your name now?' Helen asked.

" 'Josef Schwarz.'

"She pondered a moment. 'Then am I Mrs. Schwarz?'

"I had to smile. 'No, Helen. It's just a name. The man I got it from had inherited it himself. I'm the third generation. A long-dead Josef Schwarz is living on in me like the Wandering Jew. A total stranger, but my spiritual ancestor.'

" 'You didn't know him?'

" 'No.'

" 'Does it make you feel different to have another name?'

" 'Yes,' I said. 'Because a piece of paper goes with it. A passport.'

" 'Even if it's false?'

"I laughed. That was a question from another world. The authenticity of a passport depended on the policeman who checked it. 'You could write a philosophical parable about that,' I said. 'It would begin with the question of what a name is. Accident or identification.'

" 'A name is a name,' said Helen with obstinacy. 'I defended mine. It was yours. Now you come along and you've picked up another one somewhere.'

" 'It was a present,' I said. 'To me it was the most precious present in the world. I'm glad to bear it. To me it means kindness. Humanity. If I ever despair, it will remind me that kindness is not dead. What does your name remind you of? Of a family of Prussian soldiers and hunters with the mentality of foxes, wolves, and peacocks.'

" 'I didn't mean *my* family's name,' said Helen, balancing a slipper on her toes. 'I still bear yours. The old one, Mr. Schwarz.'

"I uncorked the second bottle of wine. 'I've been told that it's the custom in Indonesia to change names now and then. If you're sick of your personality, you change it, take a new name, and start a new life. A good idea!'

" 'Have you started a new life?'

" 'Today,' I said.

"She let the slipper fall to the floor. 'Don't people take something with them into a new existence?'

" 'An echo,' I said.

" 'No memory?'

" 'That's what an echo is. A memory that has stopped hurting and making you feel ashamed.'

" 'Like looking at a film?' Helen asked.

"She looked as if she were going to throw her glass in my face any minute. I took it from her hand and poured in some wine from the second bottle. 'What kind of wine is this?' I asked.

" 'Schloss Reinhartshausener. A great Rhine wine. Fully matured. Fully fermented. Not tampered with. Doesn't try to palm itself off as something else.'

" 'Not a refugee?' I said.

" 'Not a chameleon that changes color. Not somebody who side-steps his responsibilities.'

" 'Good Lord, Helen! Do I hear sounds of bourgeois respectability? Weren't you trying to get away from stagnation?'

" 'You make me say things I don't mean,' she answered angrily. 'What are we talking about? And what for? The first night! Why don't we kiss or hate each other?'

" 'That's just what we're doing.'

" 'Words. Where do you find so many words? Is it right that we should be sitting here talking?'

" 'I don't know what's right.'

" 'Where do you get all the words? Have you been talking so much? Have you had so much company?'

" 'No,' I said. 'So little. That's why words come tumbling out of me now like apples out of a basket. I'm just as surprised as you are.'

" 'Is that the truth?'

" 'Yes, Helen,' I said. 'It's the truth. Don't you see what it means?'

" 'Can't you say it more simply?'

"I shook my head.

" 'Why not?'

" 'Because I'm afraid of direct statements. And afraid of words that add up to a statement. You may not believe me, but it's so. And besides, there's my fear of the anonymous fear that is slinking through the streets somewhere, that I don't want to think or talk about, because of a stupid superstition which tells me that danger isn't there if I take no notice of it. That's why we talk in this way. When we talk like this, time seems suspended—as in a film that's torn. Everything stands still. Nothing can happen.'

" 'That's too deep for me.'

" 'For me, too. Isn't it enough that I'm here with you, that you're still alive, and that I haven't been caught yet?'

" 'Is that what you've come for?'

66

"I didn't answer. She sat there like a diminutive Amazon, naked, holding a glass of wine, demanding, giving no ground, crafty and bold, and I realized that in our former life I had known nothing about her. I couldn't see how she had endured life with me. It was as if I had had a pet, a sweet little lamb—or so I thought—and treated it like a lamb, and as though my pet had turned out to be a young puma, who had no interest whatever in blue ribbons and soft brushes, and was perfectly capable of biting the hand that reaches out to caress her.

"I was on dangerous ground. As you can imagine, I hadn't given a very good account of myself this first night. My failure had been classical, abject. I had expected as much, and maybe it happened because I expected it. The truth is that I was impotent, but luckily, because I had expected to be, I hadn't made the desperate efforts that are usual in such cases. It's all very well to be superior about it and say that only stable-boys are immune to that kind of thing. Women may even pretend to understand and respond with embarrassing motherly kindness, but any way you look at it, it's a miserable business, and the more seriously you take it, the more ridiculous it becomes.

"Since I had given none of the usual explanations, Helen was upset, and because she was upset, she attacked me. She couldn't understand why I hadn't made love to her, and she felt offended. I should simply have told her the truth, but I'd have had to be calmer than I was. There are two kinds of truth in such matters—one, in which you expose yourself, and a second, strategic truth, in which you don't risk anything. I had learned in the course of five years that if you stick your neck out, you shouldn't be surprised to be shot at.

" 'People in my situation get superstitious,' I said to Helen. 'They imagine that if they say or do something directly, the opposite will happen. That's what makes them so careful. With their words, too.'

" 'How senseless.'

67

"I laughed. 'I gave up trying to make sense out of things long ago. If I hadn't, I'd be as bitter as a wild lemon.'

" 'I hope you're not too superstitious.'

" 'I'll tell you how superstitious I am,' I said very calmly. 'I honestly believe that if I were to tell you I loved you beyond all measure, I'd hear the Gestapo pounding on the door a minute later.'

"For a moment she held as still as an animal that has heard an unaccustomed sound. Then she slowly turned her face toward me. It had changed completely. 'Is that really the reason?' she asked softly.

" 'That's only one reason,' I replied. 'How can you expect me to keep my thoughts in order when I've just been transported from a complete hell into a dangerous paradise?'

" 'I've often tried to imagine what it would be like if you came back,' she said after a while. 'The reality is entirely different.'

"I was careful not to ask in what way. People tend to ask too many questions in love, and once you begin really wanting to know the answers, love is on its way out. 'It's always different,' I said. 'Thank heaven.'

"She smiled. 'It's never different, Josef. It just seems so. Is there still any wine?'

"She circumnavigated the bed like a dancer, put her glass down on the floor beside her, and stretched out. She was tanned by a sun I had never seen and carefree in her nakedness—after the manner of a woman who knows she is desirable and has often been told so.

" 'When do I have to leave?' I asked.

" 'The maid won't be here tomorrow.'

" 'The day after?'

"Helen nodded. 'It was simple. This is Saturday. I told her to take the weekend off. She won't be back until Monday noon. She has a lover. A policeman with a wife and two children.'

"She peered at me from under half-closed eyelids. 'She was delighted.'

"From outside came singing and the sound of marching. 'What's that?' I asked.

" 'Soldiers or Hitler Youth. Here in Germany somebody is always marching.'

"I stood up and looked out between the curtains. It was a detachment of Hitler Youth. 'It's weird,' I said, 'the way you don't take after your family.'

" 'It must be my French grandmother,' said Helen. 'They keep her a secret, as if she had been Jewish.'

"She yawned and stretched. All at once she was perfectly relaxed, as though we had been living together for weeks and there was no danger to be feared from outside. So far we had both done our best not to speak of danger. And Helen had asked me nothing about my life in exile. I didn't realize that she had seen through me and already made a decision.

" 'Don't you want to sleep some more?' she asked.

"It was one o'clock. I lay down. 'Can't we leave a light on?' I asked. 'I sleep better that way. I'm not used to the German darkness yet.'

"She gave me a quick look. 'Leave them all on if you want to, dearest.'

"We lay close together. I could hardly remember that once upon a time we had slept in the same bed night after night. It was like a pale shadow, a colorless memory. Helen was with me, but in a different way, with a strange new intimacy. I recognized only the anonymous things about her, her breath, the smell of her hair, but most of all the scent of her skin, long lost and not yet fully returned, but there just the same, and already wiser than the brain. What comfort there is in the skin of someone you love! How much more intelligent it is than the mouth with its lies! I lay awake that night and held Helen in my arms and saw the light and the room that I knew and did not know, and in the end I stopped asking myself questions. Helen woke up once again. 'Did you have many women in France?' she murmured without opening her eyes.

" 'No more than necessary,' I replied. 'And none like you.'

"She sighed and tried to turn over, but sleep overpowered her first and she sank back. Slowly sleep overcame me, too, no dreams came, and toward morning I awoke and every barrier between us was gone. I reached out for her and she came to me willingly. We fell back into sleep as into a cloud gleaming with light, and there was no more darkness.

CHAPTER 6

"In the morning I phoned the hotel in Münster where I had left my suitcase and explained that I had been detained in Osnabrück but would be back that night; they should keep the room for me. That was a precaution; I didn't want to be reported on suspicion of trying to beat my hotel bill and find the police waiting for me. An indifferent voice said yes, of course, they would keep the room. I asked if there were any mail for me. No, there was no mail.

"I hung up. Helen was standing behind me. 'Mail?' she said. 'Whom are you expecting to hear from?'

" 'No one. I only said that to avert suspicion. Somehow people who are expecting mail aren't taken for swindlers.'

" 'Are you a swindler?'

" 'Against my will. But there can be a certain amount of fun in it.'

"She laughed. 'You're going back to Münster tonight?'

" 'I can't stay here any longer. Your maid will be back tomorrow. It would be too risky to take a hotel room in Osna-brück. In Münster no one is likely to recognize me on the street, and it's only an hour away.'

" 'How long are you planning to stay in Münster?'

" 'I won't know that until I'm there. In time you develop a kind of sixth sense—for danger.'

" 'Do you sense danger here?'

" 'Yes,' I said. 'Since this morning. I didn't yesterday.'

"She knit her brows. 'Of course you mustn't go out,' she said.

" 'Not before dark. And then only on my way to the sta-tion.'

"Helen did not comment. 'Everything will work out all right,' I said. 'Don't give it a thought. I've learned to live from hour to hour, but without quite forgetting the next day.'

" 'Have you?' Helen asked. 'That's convenient.' She had the same tone of slight annoyance as the evening before.

" 'It's not just convenient,' I said. 'It's necessary. But even so, I forget things now and then. I should have brought a razor from Münster. By evening I'll look like a tramp. Accord-ing to the refugee's handbook, that's the first thing to avoid.'

" 'There's a razor in the bathroom,' said Helen. 'The one you left five years ago. You'll find shirts and underwear, too, and your old suits are hanging in the closet.'

"She said that as if I had left her five years before with another woman and had come back alone to get my things and leave again. I made no attempt to set things right; it would have done no good. She would only have looked at me in amazement and said no such thought had entered her head but if that was how I felt about it . . . and I would have been drawn into a senseless argument. Strange how compli-cated we can make things just to avoid showing what we feel!

"I went into the bathroom. The sight of my old suits had no other effect on me than to show me how much thinner I had grown. I was happy to find clean underwear and decided to take a supply of it with me when I left. I was not touched by any sentiment. I had decided long before to think of exile not as a misfortune but as a kind of cold war, necessary to my development. That decision proved helpful now and then.

"The day passed in an emotional twilight. My impending departure depressed us both, but I was more used to this kind of thing than Helen. My experience had prepared me for it, while to Helen the thought that I was getting ready to leave again came almost as a personal insult. Before she had recovered from the shock of my arrival and before the wound to her pride had time to heal, here I was leaving her again. With both of us a reaction to the night had set in; the tide of feeling ebbed, baring submerged fragments of wreckage, trifles that took on enormous proportions. We were ever so careful not to touch sensitive spots; we had lost the habit of each other. I would have liked to be alone for an hour to collect my wits; but when it came to me that an hour meant the twelfth part of my remaining time with Helen, I abandoned the idea. Formerly, in peaceful years, I had occasionally entertained myself wondering what I would do if I knew I had only a month to live. I had never come to any definite conclusion. By a strange contradiction, whatever I thought I ought to do was at the same time something I wouldn't have done under any circumstances. It was the same now. Instead of embracing the day, of opening myself up to it wholeheartedly, instead of feeling Helen with every fiber of my being, as I longed to, I moved about as gingerly as if I were made of glass. She seemed to be having the same trouble. We suffered, we were all sharp edges, and only when the light began failing did our dread of losing each other become so intense that we knew each other again.

"At seven the doorbell rang. I started. To me bells meant the police. 'Who can it be?' I whispered.

" 'Let's be quiet and wait,' said Helen. 'It must be some friend; if I don't answer, he'll go away.'

"The bell rang again. Then came an authoritative pounding on the door. 'Go into the bedroom,' Helen whispered.

" 'Who is it?'

" 'I don't know. Go into the bedroom. I'll get rid of him. If he keeps on pounding, it will stir up the neighbors.'

"She pushed me away. I looked around quickly to make sure none of my belongings were lying about. Then I went into the bedroom. I heard Helen asking: 'Who is it?' and a man's voice answering. Then Helen said, 'Oh, it's you? What's wrong?' I pulled the door shut. The apartment had a second exit through the kitchen but I couldn't reach it. I'd have been seen. The only thing I could do was to hide in a big built-in closet, where Helen kept her clothes. It wasn't really a closet, just a big niche in the wall with a door across it. I had plenty of air.

"I heard the man going into the living room with Helen. I recognized his voice. It was her brother, Georg, who had sent me to the concentration camp.

"I looked at Helen's dressing table. The only available weapon was a paper cutter with a jade handle; I saw nothing else. Without stopping to think, I put the knife in my pocket and went back into the closet. If he discovered me, I'd have to defend myself; there was no other way. I'd try to kill him and to get away.

" 'The telephone?' I heard Helen say. 'I didn't hear anything. I was asleep. Is anything wrong?'

"There are moments of danger when you feel hot and dry inside, as though the slightest spark would set you on fire. You think so fast it's almost as if you were clairvoyant. Even before I heard Georg's answer, I sensed that he knew nothing of my presence.

" 'I tried to phone you several times,' he said. 'Nobody answered. Not even the maid. We thought something had happened. Why didn't you open?'

74

" 'I was asleep,' said Helen calmly. 'That's why I switched off the telephone. I had a headache; I still have. You woke me up.'

" 'A headache?'

" 'Yes, and it's worse than ever. I took two pills. I've got to sleep them off.'

" 'Sleeping pills?'

" 'No, headache pills. I'll have to put you out now, Georg. I've got to sleep them off.'

" 'Pills are ridiculous,' said Georg. 'Get dressed and come for a walk. It's beautiful out. Fresh air is better than pills.'

" 'But I've already taken them. I've got to sleep them off. I don't feel like running around.'

"They talked a while longer. Georg wanted to come back for Helen later, but she said no. He asked if she had enough to eat in the house. Yes, she had plenty to eat. Where was the maid? She had the afternoon off; she'd be back to make supper.

" 'Then there's nothing to worry about?' said Georg.

" 'Of course not.'

" 'Well, I just thought . . . sometimes people worry . . . even when there's no need to. After all . . .'

" 'After all, what?' asked Helen sharply.

" 'Well, there was once a time . . .'

" 'So what!'

" 'All right,' said Georg. 'Why talk about it? If everything is all right, so much the better. But after all, I'm your brother. It's only natural that I should worry. . . .'

" 'Yes.'

" 'Yes, what?'

" 'You're my brother.'

" 'I wish you really realized that.'

" 'I realize it very well,' said Helen impatiently.

" 'What's got into you today?'

" 'Nothing.'

" 'I hope it's not the old business starting up again.'

75

" 'Nothing is starting up. I've got a headache and that's that. And I don't like to be checked up on.'

" 'Nobody's checking up on you. I'm just concerned.'

" 'There's nothing to be concerned about. I'm fine.'

" 'Have you been to see the doctor?'

" 'Yes,' Helen replied after a moment's silence.

" 'What does he say?'

" 'Nothing.'

" 'But he must say something.'

" 'He says I should rest,' said Helen irritably. 'He says I should sleep when I'm tired and have a headache, and not argue, and not have to ask whether taking a nap is compatible with my duties as a national comrade and citizen of the glorious Thousand-Year Reich.'

" 'Did he say that?'

" 'No, he did not say that,' Helen answered in a loud voice. 'I put that in. He only told me not to work myself up unnecessarily. He committed no crime and there's no need to send him to a concentration camp. He's a sincere supporter of the government. Are you satisfied?'

"Georg muttered something. I assumed that he was preparing to leave, and since I had learned that this is a risky moment, because unexpected things can happen, I closed the door except for a slight crack. A moment later I saw him coming into the bedroom. I saw his shadow through the crack and heard his footsteps moving into the bathroom. It seemed to me that Helen had come in, too, but I didn't see her. I closed the door completely and stood there in the darkness, surrounded by Helen's clothes; the paper cutter was clenched in my fist.

"I knew that Georg had not discovered me and I knew that he would probably return from the bathroom to the living room and go away; just the same I had a tightening in my throat and the sweat trickled down my sides from my armpits. Fear of the unknown isn't the same as fear of something

76

you know. Something unknown may be dangerous, but it's undefined; you can check your fear with discipline or even with tricks. But when you know what's facing you, you can't do much with discipline or psychological handsprings. I had known the first kind of fear before they sent me to the concentration camp; I felt the second now, for I knew what was in store for me in the camp if I should be sent back there.

"Strange to say, I hadn't given the matter a thought in all the time since I had crossed the border; I hadn't wanted to. The thought would have stopped me, and I didn't want to be stopped. Besides, our memory falsifies things to help us survive. It glosses over the unbearable parts of the past. You know what I mean?"

"Yes, I know," I replied. "But they are not really forgotten, just lying dormant. A jolt can bring them back to life."

Schwarz nodded. "I stood in the dark, perfumed corner of the closet. The clothes pressed in on me like the soft wings of giant bats. I stood stock-still, scarcely breathing, for fear the silk would rustle or that I'd cough or sneeze. Fear rose up from the closet floor like a black gas. I thought it would asphyxiate me. My experience in the concentration camp could have been worse. I had suffered the usual mistreatment, but then I had been released, and in the end my memories had faded. But now it all came alive before me; what I myself had seen, what had happened to others, the things I had heard about or guessed from indications—it was beyond me how I could have been insane enough to leave the blessed countries where my only punishment for living would be imprisonment or expulsion. Such countries, it seemed to me now, were veritable havens of humanity.

"I heard Georg in the bathroom. The wall was thin and Georg was too much a member of the master race to do things quietly. He threw back the toilet lid with a crash and urinated with self-assurance. That should have comforted me; it showed that he had nothing on his mind, that he was untouched by suspicion, but later, strangely enough, this struck me as the worst humiliation of all: having to listen while he relieved himself, even if it reminded me of stories about burglars who soil the premises before leaving, to show their contempt or out of shame, because the urge was originally brought on by their fear.

"I heard the toilet flush and I heard Georg marching victoriously out of the bathroom and through the bedroom. Then came the muffled closing of the hall door and the closet was thrown open; I saw the light and in it Helen's dark silhouette. 'He's gone,' she whispered.

"I stepped out like an Achilles surprised in women's clothing. The change from terror to a feeling of ridiculousness and embarrassment was so quick that they merged into one. Such mixtures were nothing new to me; still, there is a difference whether that arm clutching at your throat means expulsion or death.

" 'You've got to leave right away,' Helen said.

"I looked at her. I don't know why I expected to see something akin to contempt in her face; perhaps it was because I myself, a moment after the danger was past, felt humiliated as a man, a feeling that would never have come to me with anyone but Helen.

"Her face showed nothing but naked terror. 'You've got to get away,' she repeated. 'It was insane of you to come here.'

"Although I had thought the same a moment before, I shook my head. 'Not now,' I said. 'In an hour. He might be taking a walk in the neighborhood. Will he come back?'

" 'I don't think so. He doesn't suspect anything.'

"Helen went into the living room, turned out the lamp, opened the curtains, and peered out. The light from the bedroom formed a golden cone on the floor. Just outside the beam, she stood there watching tensely, as though on the lookout for game. 'You can't walk to the station,' she whispered. 'Somebody might recognize you. But you've got to leave town. I'll borrow Ella's car and drive you to Münster. What fools we've been! You can't stay here!'

"I saw her standing at the window, only a few feet away, but even that was a separation, and I felt a twinge of pain. She herself seemed to realize for the first time that we would have to part again. All the barriers that had kept materializing during the day vanished. Now she had seen the danger with her own eyes and that had dispelled every other thought. She was all fear and love, and at the same moment crushed by a sense of loss. We would have to part; I saw it as clearly as she did, without evasion or pretense, and my intolerable grief transformed itself into an equally unbearable desire. I wanted to hold her—I reached out for her, I wanted her, I had to have her once more! 'Not now!' she whispered. 'I've got to call Ella! Not now. We have to . . .'

"Have to nothing, I thought. I had an hour, and then the world would collapse. Why hadn't I realized that before? I had sensed it, but why had I built up a glass wall between myself and my feeling? If it had been insane of me to come back, this had been even more so. I had to take something of Helen with me into the gray emptiness to which I would return, something more than a memory of cautious, devious behavior, more than that one union between sleep and sleep; I had to have her, lucidly, with all her senses, her mind, her eyes, her thoughts, entirely, not merely like an animal between night and morning.

"She resisted. She whispered that Georg might come back, and I don't know whether she really believed so. I had been in danger so often that I was able to forget it the moment it was past—now I wanted only one thing, in this room with the smell of Helen's perfume and clothes and the bed and the twilight: to possess her with everything that was in me, and if there was one thing that tormented me and pierced the flat dull sense of loss, it was the realization that nature wouldn't let me possess her even more fully and deeply. If only I could

79

spread myself over her like a blanket, if only I could have had a thousand hands and mouths, if only I could have held her in a perfect concave mold, skin to skin without intervening space—but even then there would be a last regret, for still it would be only skin to skin instead of blood in blood: we could be together, but never completely united."

CHAPTER 7

I had listened to Schwarz without interrupting. He was speaking to me, but I knew that as far as he was concerned I was little more than a wall that sent back an occasional echo. That, too, was how I regarded myself; otherwise I couldn't have listened without embarrassment, and I felt certain that otherwise he would have been unable to tell about these things that he wished to resurrect once again before they came to rest in the silent sands of memory. I was a stranger whose path crossed his for one night, that is why he was without reticence in my company. He had come to me wrapped in the anonymous cloak of a strange, dead name, Schwarz, and when he cast off the cloak, he would also cast off his personality and disappear in the anonymous crowd moving toward the black gate at the last border, where no papers are required and from which no one is ever sent back.

The waiter informed us that a German diplomat had arrived. He pointed him out to us. Hitler's emissary sat five tables away from us with three other persons, a man and two women. The ladies were rather on the hefty side; they had on silk dresses, both blue, but of different shades, which clashed. The German diplomat had his back turned to us; that struck me as fitting and proper; reassuring, too.

"I thought it would interest you gentlemen," said the waiter, "because I heard you speaking German."

Involuntarily Schwarz and I exhanged the refugee glance— an imperceptible lifting of the eyelids, followed by a look of blank indifference, as if we couldn't care less. The refugee glance is different from the German glance under Hitler— that cautious peering around in all directions, followed by a hurried exchange of whispers—but both, like the forced migration of innumerable Schwarzes from Germany and the displacement of whole populations in Russia, are a part of twentieth-century civilization. In a hundred years, when all the cries of anguish have died away, a clever historian will discover that all these miseries have served as a leaven to progress.

Schwarz looked up at the waiter without the slightest sign of interest. "We know who he is," he said. "Bring us some more wine. . . . Helen," he continued just as calmly, "went to get her friend's car. I waited alone in the apartment. Night had fallen, and the windows were open. I had turned out all the lights to make it look as if no one was there. If anyone rang, I wouldn't answer. If Georg came back, I could get away by the service entrance if necessary.

"For half an hour I sat near the window, listening to the street sounds. An immense feeling of loss came over me. It wasn't painful. More like a dark shadow slowly spreading until it blacked out the whole earth and swallowed up the horizon. And in the midst of all this desolation I seemed to see a pair of scales weighing an empty past against an empty future, and Helen between them, the shadow of the scales across her shoulders. It was as though I had come to the mid-point in my life; the next stop would throw the scales off balance; they would slowly incline toward the future, fill up with gray, and never be in balance again.

"I was awakened by the sound of the car. I saw Helen alight in the glow of the street lamp and disappear into the entrance. I went through the dark dead apartment and heard the key in the door. She came in quickly. 'We can go now,' she said. 'Do you have to go back to Münster?'

" 'I've left my suitcase there. I've registered under the name of Schwarz. Where else can I go?'

" 'Pay your bill and go to another hotel.'

" 'Where?'

" 'Yes, where?' Helen pondered. 'In Münster,' she said finally. 'You're right. Where else? That's the nearest place.'

"I had packed a suitcase with a few things that might come in handy. We decided it would be best for me not to get into the car in front of the house, but down the street on Hitler-Platz. Helen would take the suitcase.

"I reached the street unseen. A warm wind was blowing. The trees rustled in the darkness. Helen caught up with me on the square. 'Get in,' she whispered. 'Hurry.'

"The car was a closed cabriolet. Helen's face was illumined by the dashboard light. Her eyes sparkled. 'I'd better drive carefully,' she said. 'An accident means police—that's all we need.'

"I did not reply. Refugees don't speak of such things. It invites calamity. Helen laughed and drove along the ramparts. She was all keyed up, as though the whole thing were an adventure. She kept talking to herself or to the car. When she had to stop near a traffic policeman, she muttered words of prayer; and when there was a red light, she pleaded with it: 'Get a move on. Turn green. What are you waiting for?' Her levity baffled me. To me it was our last hour. I had no idea of the decision she had made.

"Once we were out of town, she calmed down. 'When are you planning to leave Münster?' she asked.

"I didn't know, because I had no place to go. I only knew

83

that I could not stay long. Fool's luck can't hold out forever; there comes a warning. You feel that your time is up. I felt that now. 'Tomorrow,' I said.

"For a while she said nothing. Then she asked, 'How do you think you'll go about it?'

"I had thought it over while sitting alone in the dark living room. It would be too risky to take the train and simply show my passport at the border. They might perfectly well ask me for other papers, an exit visa, proof that I had paid the emigration tax—I had no such papers. 'The same way I came,' I said. 'Through Austria. Across the Rhine into Switzerland. At night.' I turned toward Helen. 'Let's not talk about it,' I said. 'Or as little as possible.'

"She nodded. 'I've brought some money. You'll need it. If you sneak across the border, you can take it with you. Can it be changed in Switzerland?'

" 'Yes, but won't you need it yourself?'

" 'I can't take it with me. I'll be searched at the border. We're only allowed to take out a few marks.'

"I gaped at her. What was she talking about? It must have been a slip of the tongue. 'How much is there?' I asked.

"Helen gave me a quick look. 'Not as little as you think. I put it aside a long time ago. It's in the bag.'

"She motioned toward a small leather bag. 'It's mostly in hundred-mark notes. But there's a package of twenty-mark notes, too, for Germany, so you won't have to change any big ones. Take it. It's your money anyway.'

" 'Didn't the party confiscate my account?'

" 'Yes, but not soon enough. I was able to draw this out first. Someone in the bank helped me. I wanted to have it for you. I was going to send it, but I never knew where you were.'

" 'I didn't write you because I thought you were being watched. I didn't want them to send you to a camp, too.'

" 'That's not the only reason,' said Helen calmly.

" 'No, maybe not.'

"We drove through a village with white Westphalian houses and thatched roofs and black wooden beams. Young men in uniform were strutting about. The Horst Wessel song came roaring from a beer hall.

" 'There's going to be war,' said Helen. 'Is that why you've come back?'

" 'How do you know there's going to be war?'

" 'From Georg. Is that why you've come?'

"Why was she still so eager to know that, I wondered. Now that I was leaving again.

" 'Yes, Helen,' I said. 'That's one reason.'

" 'You came to get me?'

"I stared at her. 'Good Lord, Helen,' I said finally. 'Don't talk like that. You have no idea what it's like out there. It's not a lark. And if war breaks out, it will be awful. The Germans will all be locked up.'

"We had to stop at a grade crossing. Outside the gate-keeper's hut there was a little garden full of dahlias and roses. The rods of the gate sang in the wind like harp strings. Other cars stopped behind us—a small Opel containing four stout, solemn-looking men; an open green two-seater with an old woman in it; then, silently, a black Mercedes limousine that looked for all the world like a hearse drew up close beside us. The driver was wearing a black SS uniform, and in back sat two SS officers with pale faces. The car was so close to us I could have reached into it. The train was a long time in coming. Helen sat beside me in silence. Resplendent with chrome, the Mercedes pushed slightly forward until the radiator nearly touched the gate. It really did seem like a hearse transporting two corpses, like a symbol of the war we had just been talking about; the black uniforms, the cadaverous faces, the silver death's heads, the black car, and the silence that no longer seemed to smell of roses, but of evergreen and putrefaction.

"The train roared past like life itself. It was an express with sleeping cars and a brightly lighted dining car; you could even see the white tablecloths. When the gate went up, the Mercedes pushed ahead of the other cars into the darkness, like a black torpedo that seemed to make the night still darker and turn the trees to skeletons.

" 'I'm going with you,' Helen said.

" 'What? What's that you're saying?'

" 'Why not?'

"She stopped the car. The silence descended on us like a silent blow, and then we heard the sounds of the night. 'Why not?' Helen repeated. 'Were you going to leave me behind again?'

"In the blue glow of the dashboard light she looked as pale as those officers—as though she, too, had been marked by the death that was prowling through the June night. In that moment I knew what I had really feared deep down: that the war would come between us, that we'd never find each other again when it was over, because even with the greatest optimism you can't hope for so much private good luck after an earthquake that would destroy everything.

" 'If you didn't come to get me, it was a crime for you to come. Don't you see that?' said Helen, suddenly shaken with fury.

" 'Yes,' I answered.

" 'Then what's the good of being evasive?'

" 'I'm not being evasive. But you don't know what it means.'

" 'Do you? Why did you come then? Don't lie to me. To say good-by again?'

" 'No.'

" 'Then why? To stay here and commit suicide?'

"I shook my head. I knew there was only one answer that she would understand, and only one that it was permissible to give now, even if the whole thing was a pipe dream. 'I came to get you,' I said. 'Don't you know that yet?'

"Her face changed. Her anger vanished. She was very beautiful. 'Yes,' she murmured. 'But you have to tell me. Don't *you* know that yet?'

"I screwed up my courage. 'I'll tell you a hundred times, Helen; I'd like to tell you every second—it's what I want most in the world, even if it is impossible.'

" 'It's not impossible at all. I have a passport.'

"I said nothing for a moment. The word burst like a lightning flash upon the confusion of my thoughts. 'You have a passport? Valid for foreign travel?'

"Helen opened her handbag and took out her passport. She not only had it, she had it with her. I looked at it as one might look at the Holy Grail. A valid passport was just that. It was at once a declaration and a right. 'Since when have you had it?' I asked.

" 'I got it two years ago,' she said. 'It's good for another three. I've used it three times, once to go to Austria, when it was still independent, and for two trips to Switzerland.'

"I leafed through it. I had to collect my wits. Then the reality sank in. This piece of paper in my hands was a passport. It was no longer impossible for Helen to leave Germany. 'Perfectly simple, isn't it?' she said, watching me.

"I nodded stupidly. 'You can just take the train and leave.' I looked at the passport again. 'But you haven't a French visa.'

" 'They'll give me one in Zurich. You don't need a visa for Switzerland.'

" 'That's true. But what about your family? Will they let you go?'

" 'I won't ask them. And I won't tell them anything. I'll say I have to go to Zurich to see the doctor. That's what I did before.'

" 'Are you sick?'

" 'Of course not,' said Helen. 'I said that to get a passport, to get out of here. I was stifling.'

"I remembered that Georg had asked her if she had been

87

to see the doctor. 'You're sure you're not sick?' I asked her again.

" 'Don't be silly. But my family thinks I am. I convinced them; that was the only way I could have any peace. And leave the country. Martens helped me. It takes time to convince a hundred-per-cent German that there may be specialists in Switzerland who know more than the authorities in Berlin.'

"Helen laughed. 'Don't look so shaken. There won't be any danger. I won't be dodging border patrols in the dead of night. I'll say I have to see my doctor in Zurich and simply take the train, the same as I did before. And if you're there, why shouldn't we meet? Does that sound better?'

" 'Yes,' I said. 'But we'd better drive on. Things are beginning to look so good that I can't help expecting a whole brigade of SS men to come popping out of the woods. I never imagined that it could be so simple.'

" 'Darling,' said Helen very gently, 'it looks simple because we're desperate. It's a strange kind of compensation. I wonder if it's always that way.'

" 'I hope we never have to find out.'

"We left the dusty back road and returned to the highway. 'It's all right with me,' said Helen, without the slightest sign of desperation. 'I'm quite prepared to go on living like this.'

"She went to the hotel with me. It was amazing how quickly she adapted herself to my situation. 'I'll go into the lobby with you,' she said. 'A man alone always looks more suspicious.'

" 'You learn quickly.'

"She shook her head. 'I learned that long ago. After the National Awakening, when people were denouncing their neighbors right and left. It was as if someone had lifted up a big stone—all the vermin came scurrying out. At last they had found a lot of big words to make their meanness and vulgarity look like something else.'

"The hotel clerk gave me my key, and I went to my room. Helen waited in the lobby.

"My suitcase was on the stand beside the door. I looked around the anonymous room and tried to remember how I had got there, but already my memory was blurred. I realized that I was no longer hiding on some shore, despairing of ever crossing the river. I was already on a raft—and not alone.

"I put down the suitcase I had brought and hurried back to the lobby.

" 'How much time have you got?' I asked Helen.

" 'I'll have to return the car tonight.'

"I looked at her. I wanted her so much that for a moment I couldn't speak. I stared at the brown-and-green chairs in the lobby and at the brightly lighted reception desk with the key rack and mailboxes behind it, and realized that it would be impossible to take Helen to my room. 'We could eat together,' I said. 'Let's act as if we were going to see each other tomorrow.'

" 'Not tomorrow,' Helen replied. 'The day after.'

"The day after tomorrow! Maybe that meant something to her. To me it meant just about the same as 'never' or a very unpromising lottery ticket. I had experienced too many days after tomorrow, and they had all turned out differently from what I had hoped.

" 'The day after tomorrow,' I said. 'Or the day after that. It depends on the weather. Let's not think of it now.'

" 'I can't think of anything else,' said Helen.

"We went to the Domkeller, a restaurant furnished in German Gothic style, and found a table where our conversation could not be overheard. I ordered a bottle of wine, and we settled the details. Helen would go to Zurich next day. There she would wait for me. I would return to Switzerland as I had come, by way of Austria and the Rhine, and call her up when I got to Zurich.

" 'And what if you don't get there?' she asked.

" 'They let you write letters in Swiss jails. Wait a week. Then if you haven't heard from me, go back home.'

"Helen's eyes rested on me. She knew what I meant. In German prisons you don't write letters. 'Is the border closely guarded?' she asked.

" 'No,' I said. 'And don't worry about it. I got in—why shouldn't I be able to get out?'

"We tried to ignore this leave-taking but didn't quite succeed. It stood between us like a great black pillar. The best we could do was to look around it from time to time into each other's stricken faces. 'It's like five years ago,' I said. 'Except that this time we're both going.'

"Helen shook her head. 'Be careful!' she said. 'For God's sake be careful. I'll wait. More than a week. As long as you want me to. Don't take any chances.'

" 'I'll be careful. Let's not talk about it any more. Being careful doesn't work if you talk about it too much.'

"She laid her hand on mine. 'I'm just beginning to realize that you've come back. Now that it's time for you to leave. So late.'

" 'It's the same with me,' I said. 'But now we know.'

" 'So late,' she murmured. 'And now you're leaving again.'

" 'It's not too late,' I said. 'And we've known it all along. Would I have come otherwise, and would you have waited for me?'

" 'I wasn't always waiting,' she said.

"I didn't answer. I hadn't been either, but I knew that I must never admit it. Now least of all. We were both absolutely open and defenseless. If we should ever live together, we could always go back to this moment in a noisy restaurant in Münster for strength and reassurance. It would be a mirror; we could look into it, and it would show us two images: what fate had wanted us to be and what it had made of us.

" 'You'll have to go now,' I said. 'Be careful. Don't drive too fast.'

90

"We stood in the windy street between the rows of old houses. 'You be careful,' she whispered. 'You need it more.'

"I stayed in my room for a while, then I couldn't stand it any longer. I went to the station, bought a ticket to Munich, and made a note of the trains. There was one that night, and I decided to take it.

"The city was still. I passed the cathedral and stopped. In the darkness I could recognize only a few of the old buildings on the square. I thought of Helen and of what would happen, but my vision of the future became as enormous and indistinct as the great windows high up in the dark façade of the cathedral. Was I doing right in taking her away, I wondered, or would we come to grief? Was I frivolously committing a crime or merely accepting an unprecedented gift? Or maybe both?

"Near the hotel I heard subdued voices and steps. Two SS men came out of a house door, pushing a man ahead of them into the street. I saw his face in the light of a street lamp. It was narrow and waxen, and a black trickle of blood ran down over his chin from one corner of his mouth. The crown of his head was bald, but there was a growth of dark hair on the sides. His eyes were wide open and full of horror such as I had not seen in years. Not a sound escaped him. The SS men pushed and pulled him impatiently. They were quiet about it. There was something muffled and eerie about the whole scene. The SS men cast furious, challenging glances at me as they passed, and the prisoner stared at me out of paralyzed eyes, making a gesture that seemed to be a plea for help; his lips moved, but not a sound came out. It was a scene as old as humankind: the minions of power, the victim, the eternal third, the onlooker, who doesn't raise a finger in defense of the victim, who makes no attempt to set him free, because he fears for his own safety, which for that very reason is always in danger.

"I knew I could do nothing for the arrested man. The armed SS men would have overpowered me without difficulty. I remembered that someone had told me about a similar scene. He had seen an SS man arresting and beating a Jew and had come to the Jew's help; he had knocked the SS man unconscious and told the victim to run. But the arrested Jew had cursed his liberator; now, he said, he was really lost, because this, too, would be counted against him; sobbing, he had gone for water to revive the SS man, so that the SS man could lead him to his death. This story came back to me now, but, even so, I was thoroughly ashamed of my fear and helplessness. I felt that it was sinful and frivolous to be thinking of my own welfare while others were being murdered. I went to the hotel, gathered up my things, and took a cab to the station, although it was much too early. It was more dangerous to sit in the waiting room than to hide in my hotel room, but that was what I wanted. Pure childishness, but the risk restored my self-respect a little.

CHAPTER 8

"I traveled all night and the following day and reached Austria without any trouble. The newspapers were full of recriminations, protests, and the usual reports of frontier incidents—provoked, of course, by the weaker party—that always precede wars. I saw trains loaded with troops, but most of the people I spoke to didn't think there would be a war. They expected a new Munich; they were convinced that the rest of Europe was much too weak and decadent to risk a war with Germany. It was very different from France, where everyone knew that war was inevitable. But the threatened party always knows more, and knows it sooner, than the aggressor.

"I reached Feldkirch and took a room at a small hotel. It was summer, the tourist season, and I attracted no attention. The two suitcases made me respectable. I decided to abandon them and travel light—a knapsack would be the best thing;

the region was full of hikers. I paid my room rent for a week in advance.

"I started out next day. Until midnight I hid in a clearing not far from the border. I remember that the gnats bothered me at first and that I spent quite some time watching a blue salamander in a pool of water. A crested salamander. Every now and then he came up for air and I could see his spotted, yellowish-red belly. I reflected that for him the world stopped at this pool. As far as he was concerned, that little water hole was Switzerland, Germany, France, Africa, and Yokohama, all in one. He dove and bobbed up, dove and bobbed up, in complete harmony with the summer evening.

"I slept a few hours and made ready. I was full of confidence. Ten minutes later a customs guard appeared beside me as though he had shot out of the earth. 'Halt! Don't move! What are you doing here?'

"He must have been lurking a long while in the darkness. I protested that I was an innocent hiker, but that didn't help at all. 'You can tell them that at headquarters,' he said, cocked his rifle, and marched me ahead of him to the nearest village.

"I was crushed and stunned. Still, a small corner of my brain was wide awake, wondering how I could escape. But it was out of the question; this guard knew his business. He stayed exactly the right distance behind me; there was no chance of attacking him by surprise, and I couldn't have gone five steps without being shot.

"At the customs station he opened a little room. 'Go in. Wait here.'

" 'How long?'

" 'Until you're questioned.'

" 'Can't you do it right away? I haven't done anything.'

" 'Then you have nothing to worry about.'

" 'I'm not worried,' I said, taking off my knapsack. 'Let's begin.'

" 'We'll begin when we're ready,' said the guard, with a

smile that bared his uncommonly white teeth. He looked and behaved like a hunter. 'Tomorrow morning the officer in charge will be here. You can sleep in that chair. It's only for a few hours. *Heil* Hitler!'

"I looked around the room. The window was barred; the door was very solid and locked from outside. I could hear people moving about on the other side of the wall. Escape was out of the question. I sat and waited. It was dismal. At last the sky turned gray and then gradually blue and bright. I heard voices and smelled coffee. The door was opened. I pretended to be waking up, and yawned. A customs officer came in; he was stout and red-faced, and seemed more easygoing than the hunter. 'At last!' I said. 'This is a mighty uncomfortable place to sleep.'

" 'What were you doing by the border?' he asked, and opened my knapsack. 'Trying to sneak across? Smuggling?'

" 'Did you ever hear of smuggling old pants?' I asked. 'Or shirts, for that matter?'

" 'Maybe not. But what were you doing there at night?' He put my knapsack aside. I suddenly thought of the money I had on me. If he found it, I was lost. I prayed that he wouldn't search me.

" 'I was enjoying the view of the Rhine by night,' I said, smiling. 'I'm a tourist. It's so romantic.'

" 'Where'd you start from?'

"I named the town and my hotel. 'I was intending to go back this morning,' I said. 'My bags are still there. I've paid my rent a week in advance. Would a smuggler do that?'

" 'We'll look into it,' he said. 'I'll come for you in an hour. We'll go back and see what you've got in your bags.'

"It was a long way. The fat man pushed his bicycle along beside him and smoked. He, too, was as watchful as a police dog. We finally got there.

" 'There he is!' someone called out of the hotel window. Then the landlady rushed out, beet-red with excitement. 'Gracious, we thought something had happened to you. Where have you been all night?'

"Finding my bed unslept in, she had thought I had been murdered. Apparently there was a bandit loose in the region. She had called the police. The policeman followed her out of the house. He was the same type as the hunter. 'I got lost,' I said, as calmly as I could. 'And it was such a lovely night. I slept out in the open for the first time since I was a boy. It was wonderful. I'm sorry to have worried you. Unfortunately, I went too near the border by mistake. Won't you please tell this customs officer that I live here?'

"The landlady complied with my request. The customs officer was satisfied, but the policeman had perked up an ear. 'So you've been hanging around the border,' he said. 'Have you got papers? Who are you, anyway?'

"For a moment the breath went out of me. Helen's money was in my inside pocket; if it were found on me, they'd suspect me of trying to smuggle it into Switzerland and arrest me on the spot. And then what?

"I stated my name but did not show my passport; Germans and Austrians don't need one in their own country. 'How do we know you're not the bandit we're looking for?' asked the policeman who looked like the hunter.

"I laughed. 'There's nothing to laugh about,' he said angrily, and began to search my bags.

"I pretended to take the whole thing as a joke; but if they were to search my person, how was I to account for all that money? I decided to say that I was thinking of buying some property in the vicinity.

"The policeman found a letter in a side pocket of one of the suitcases. I was very much surprised; I couldn't remember any such letter. It was the suitcase I had brought from Osnabrück—I had tossed some of my former belongings into it, and Helen had taken it to the car. The policeman opened the letter and began to read. I watched him closely. I had no idea what the letter could be and only hoped there was nothing of any importance in it.

"The policeman grunted and looked up. 'Is your name Josef Schwarz?'

"I nodded. 'Why didn't you say so right away?' he asked.

" 'I did,' I answered, trying to read the printed letterhead through the paper.

" 'That's a fact,' said the customs officer. 'He told us.'

" 'Then the letter is about you?' the policeman asked.

"I stretched out my hand. He hesitated for a moment; then he handed it to me. I looked at the letterhead: National Socialist Party Headquarters, Osnabrück. Slowly I read: The Osnabrück authorities request whom it may concern to give all possible assistance to Party Member Josef Schwarz, traveling on important secret business. Signed 'Georg Jürgens, Obersturmbannführer,' in Helen's handwriting.

"I held on to the letter. 'And you are Mr. Josef Schwarz?' The policeman's tone had become a good deal more respectful.

"I produced my passport, pointed to the name, and put it away again. 'Secret government business,' I said.

" 'So that's it?'

" 'Yes, that's it,' I said gravely, and put the letter in my pocket. 'I hope you're satisfied.'

" 'Of course.' The policeman screwed up one pale-blue eye. 'I understand. Observation of the border.'

"I raised my hand. 'I must request you not to breathe a word. It's secret. That's why I didn't tell you before. But you've wormed it out of me. Are you a party member?'

" 'Naturally,' said the policeman. Only then did I notice that he had red hair. I gave him a pat on the shoulder. 'Good man! Here's a little something for the two of you. Have a good glass of wine after all your trouble.' "

Schwarz turned to me with a melancholy smile. "It's amazing how easy it is to hoodwink people whose job it is to be suspicious. Have you had that experience?"

"Not without papers," I said. "But I admire your wife. She figured that letter might come in handy."

"She must have thought I wouldn't take it if she mentioned it. On moral grounds. Or that I'd be afraid to. Actually, I would have taken it. Anyway, it saved me."

I had listened to Schwarz with mounting interest. Now I looked around. An Englishman and the German diplomat were on the dance floor. They were doing a fox trot, and the Englishman was the better dancer. The German needed more room; he danced with a dogged aggressiveness, pushing his partner ahead of him like a fieldpiece. In the half-darkness it seemed to me for a moment that a chessboard had come to life. From time to time the two kings, the German and the English, came dangerously together; but the Englishman always managed to dodge. "Then what did you do?" I asked Schwarz.

"I went to my room. I was exhausted and wanted to rest and think things over. The way Helen had saved me was so unforeseen, it was like the intervention of a *deus ex machina* —a theatrical twist that turns a hopeless muddle into a happy ending. But it was plain that I'd better be on my way before that policeman had too much time to talk or think. I decided to trust my luck while it held. I inquired about trains and found out there would be an express to Switzerland in an hour. I told the landlady I had to go to Zurich for a day and would be taking only one of my bags; could she keep the other until my return? Then I went to the station. Have you ever done that kind of thing? You've been careful for years, then you throw all caution to the winds."

"Yes," I said. "But sometimes you go wrong. You think fate owes you something. But the fact is that it doesn't owe you a thing."

"Of course not," said Schwarz. "But sometimes you lose

your confidence in the old methods and decide to try something new. Helen had wanted me to cross the border with her in the train. I hadn't done so, and I would have been lost if her inspiration hadn't saved me—so now I thought I'd better do things her way."

"Did you?"

Schwarz nodded. "I bought a first-class ticket; luxury always inspires confidence. I didn't think of the money I had on me until the train began to move. I couldn't hide it in the compartment; I was not alone. I had a traveling companion, a man—he was very pale and he seemed anxious. I tried the toilets; both were occupied. By this time the train had reached the border station. My instinct drove me to the dining car. I sat down, ordered a bottle of expensive wine, and asked for the menu.

" 'Have you baggage?' the waiter asked.

" 'Yes, in the next car.'

" 'Wouldn't you prefer to take care of the customs first? I'll hold your place for you.'

" 'That can take a long time. Bring me something to eat first. I'm hungry. I'll pay in advance, so you'll know I'm coming back.'

"I had hoped that the border guards would overlook the dining car, but no such luck. The waiter was just putting the wine and soup on the table when two men in uniform came through. I had meanwhile slipped my money under the felt table cover, and put Helen's letter into my passport.

" 'Passport!' said one of the guards crisply. I handed him mine. 'No baggage?' he asked before opening it.

" 'Just one suitcase,' I said. 'Right next door in first class.'

" 'You'll have to open it,' said the other guard.

"I stood up. 'Keep my place for me,' I said to the waiter.

" 'Of course I will, sir. You've paid in advance.'

"The customs guard looked at me. 'You've paid in advance?'

" 'Why yes. Otherwise I couldn't have afforded it. After the border you've got to pay in Swiss francs. I haven't got any.'

"The customs guard laughed. 'Not a bad idea,' he said. 'Funny more people don't think of it. You go ahead. I'll be checking the other passengers on my way.'

" 'What about my passport?'

" 'Don't worry. We'll find you.'

"I went to my car. My fellow traveler was sitting there, looking more worried than ever. From time to time he ran a moist handkerchief over his perspiring face and hands. I stared out at the station and opened the window. There would be no point in jumping out if I was caught; escape was impossible, but somehow it soothed me to have the window open.

"A guard stood in the doorway. 'Your luggage!'

"I took down my suitcase and opened it. He looked in. Then he searched my companion's bag. 'All right,' he said and saluted.

" 'My passport,' I said.

" 'My colleague has it.'

"His colleague came in a few moments later. It wasn't the officer who had taken my passport, but a uniformed party man with glasses and high boots." Schwarz smiled. "How the Germans love boots!"

"They need them," I said. "Wading through all the muck they've made."

Schwarz emptied his glass. He hadn't been drinking much. I looked at my watch: it was half past three. Schwarz noticed. "It won't be much longer," he said. "You'll have plenty of time to catch your boat. The rest is about happiness. There's never much to say about that."

"How did you get through?" I asked.

"The party man had read Helen's letter. He returned my passport and asked me if I knew anyone in Switzerland. I nodded.

" 'Whom?'

" 'Ammer and Rotenberg.'

"Those were two Nazis who were working in Switzerland. Every refugee who had ever lived there knew them and hated them.

" 'Anyone else?'

" 'Our people in Bern. I don't imagine there's any need to name them all?'

"He saluted. 'Lots of luck. *Heil* Hitler!'

"My companion was not so lucky. He had to show all his papers and was subjected to a cross-examination. He sweated and stuttered. I couldn't bear to look on. 'May I go back to the dining car?' I asked.

" 'Of course!' said the party comrade. 'I hope you enjoy your lunch.'

"The dining car had filled up in my absence. An American family had taken my table. 'I thought you were keeping my place for me,' I said to the waiter.

"He shrugged his shoulders. 'I tried, sir. But what can you do with Americans? They don't understand German and they sit down where they please. Why don't you sit over there? A table's a table. See, I've moved your wine.'

"I didn't know what to do. A family of four had occupied my table. A very pretty girl of sixteen was sitting next to my money. I couldn't insist on getting my table back. It might stir up a fuss. We were still on German soil.

"As I stood there trying to make up my mind, the waiter said: 'Do please sit down, sir. I'll move you back as soon as they leave. Americans eat quickly. Sandwiches and orange juice. Then I'll serve you a nice lunch.'

"There was nothing else to do. I took a seat where I was able to keep an eye on my money. It's funny when you think of it—a minute before, I'd have given all the money in the world just to get through. Now my only thought was to get that money back the moment we crossed the border, even if I had to assault the American family. I looked out and saw

101

the worried little man being led away. My first feeling, I have to admit, was one of immense relief at not being in his shoes—then came sympathy, but in such cases sympathy is only a hypocritical attempt to conjure bad luck. I was completely disgusted with myself, but there was nothing I could do about it, even if I had really wanted to. I wanted to cross that border safely and I wanted my money. It wasn't the money as such—it was security, Helen, the months to come; still, it was money, it was my own skin, my egotistical happiness. We never get away from it. But there's always that ungovernable, hypocritical ham actor inside us. . . ."

"Mr. Schwarz," I interrupted. "How did you get your money back?"

"You're right," he said. "But my tirade is part of the story. The Swiss customs officers came into the dining car, and the American family not only had hand baggage but trunks in the baggage car. They had to leave. The children went along. They had finished eating. The table was cleared. I moved over, laid my hand on the tablecloth and felt the slight thickening.

"Again the waiter transferred my wine.

" 'Make out all right with the customs?' he asked.

" 'Of course,' I answered. 'Bring me my pot roast. Are we in Switzerland now?'

" 'No,' he said. 'Not till we start moving.'

"He went off to the kitchen, and I waited for the train to move. I'm sure you know all about that last desperate feeling of impatience. I stared out the window at the people on the platform; a dwarf in a tuxedo, with trousers that were too short, wheeling a cart back and forth, trying frantically to sell Austrian wine and chocolate. The frightened man from my compartment was coming back. He was alone and in a great hurry. 'That's fast drinking,' said the waiter beside me.

" 'What?'

" 'It looks as if you were trying to put out a fire.'

"I glanced at the bottle. It was almost empty. I hadn't even known I was drinking. At that moment the dining car gave a lurch. The bottle reeled. I caught it in my hand. The train began to move. 'Bring me another,' I said. The waiter disappeared.

"I removed the money from under the tablecloth and put it in my pocket. A moment later the Americans came back, sat down at the table I had occupied a moment before, and ordered coffee. The girl began to take pictures of the landscape. Very wise of her, I thought; it was the most beautiful landscape in the world.

"The waiter came back with the bottle. 'We're in Switzerland now.'

"I paid for the wine and gave him a good tip. 'Keep the wine,' I said. 'I don't need it. I wanted to celebrate something, but I see that the first bottle was too much for me.'

" 'You were drinking on an empty stomach,' he explained.

" 'Yes, that's it.' I stood up.

" 'Is it your birthday?' the waiter asked.

" 'No,' I said. 'It's my golden wedding day.'

"The little man in my compartment sat silent for a few minutes; he had stopped perspiring, but it would be no exaggeration to say that his clothes were wringing wet. Then he spoke. 'Are we in Switzerland?'

" 'Yes,' I said.

"He fell silent again and looked out the window. We stopped at a station with a Swiss name. A Swiss stationmaster waved a flag. Two Swiss policemen stood chatting beside the baggage car. There was a stand selling Swiss chocolate and Swiss sausages. My companion reached out and bought a Swiss newspaper. 'Are we in Switzerland?' he asked the newsboy.

" 'Of course. Where else would we be? Ten rappen.'

" 'What?'

" 'Ten rappen. Ten centimes. For the paper.'

"The man paid as if he had just won in the lottery. The Swiss money must have convinced him. He hadn't believed me. He opened the newspaper, skimmed through it, and put it down. It was some time before I heard what he was saying. I was so full of my own new freedom that the wheels of the train seemed to be rattling in my head. Then I saw his lips moving and realized that he was speaking.

" 'At last I'm out,' he said, glaring at me, 'out of your God-damned country, Mr. Party Comrade, which you swine have turned into a barracks and a concentration camp. This is Switzerland; it's free; nobody takes any orders from you and your kind. I can say what I please here without having my teeth kicked in. You thieves, you murderers, you executioners, what have you made of Germany!'

"Small bubbles formed at the corners of his mouth. He stared at me as a hysterical woman might stare at a toad. After what he had heard, he thought I was a member of the party.

"I listened with unruffled calm. I was only glad to be safe.

" 'You're a brave man,' I said. 'I'm at least twenty pounds heavier than you and six inches taller. But get it off your chest. It will make you feel better.'

" 'Don't you dare to make fun of me!' he cried, more furious than ever. 'I won't stand for it. We're not in Nazi land any more. What have you done to my parents? What did my old father do to you? And now! Now you want to set the whole world on fire.'

" 'Do you think there's going to be a war?' I asked.

" 'As if you didn't know,' he said. 'What else can you do with your Thousand-Year Reich and your armaments? You murderers! If you don't make war, your phony prosperity will collapse and you with it.'

" 'I am of the same opinion,' I said, and felt the warm afternoon sun on my face like a caress. 'But what if Germany wins?'

"The man with the damp clothing stared at me and gulped. 'If you win, there's no God,' he said with difficulty.

" 'I quite agree with you.' I stood up.

" 'Don't touch me,' he hissed. 'You'll be arrested. I'll pull the emergency brake. I'll report you. You ought to be reported anyway, you spy! I heard what you said.'

"That's all I need, I thought. 'Switzerland is a free country,' I said. 'You can't get a man arrested just by denouncing him. You've picked up some bad ideas in Germany.'

"I took my bag and moved to another compartment. I thought it preferable not to explain myself to this hysterical man; but I also preferred not to sit with him. Hate is an acid that corrodes the soul, regardless of whether you or the other fellow does the hating. I had learned that in the course of my wanderings.

"And so I came to Zurich."

CHAPTER 9

The music stopped for a moment. Angry words could be heard from the dance floor. Then the band started up louder than before, and a woman in a canary-yellow dress, with a string of false diamonds in her hair, began to sing. The inevitable had happened: a German had collided with an Englishman. Each accused the other of doing it on purpose. The manager and two waiters played League of Nations, trying to mollify the contenders, but no one listened. The band was more clever: it changed rhythms. The fox trot gave way to a tango, and the diplomats had to choose between making themselves ridiculous by standing still or starting to dance again. But the German warrior didn't seem to know the tango, while the Englishman merely kept time, without stirring from the spot. Both began to be jostled by other couples, and the argument disintegrated. Glowering, the diplomats returned to their tables.

"Why don't the heroes challenge each other to a duel?" asked Schwarz contemptuously.

"So you arrived in Zurich," I said.

He smiled feebly. "Why don't we get out of here?"

"Where can we go?"

"There must be some ordinary bar that stays open all night. This place is full of corpses, dancing and playing war."

He paid and asked the waiter if there were somewhere else we could go. The waiter jotted an address on a slip of paper that he tore off his pad, and told us how to get there.

We stepped out into a glorious night. The stars were still shining, but on the horizon the sea and the morning met in a first blue embrace. The sky was higher than before, and the smell of salt and flowers still stronger. The day was going to be clear. By day Lisbon has a naïve theatrical quality that enchants and captivates, but by night it is a fairy-tale city, descending over lighted terraces to the sea, like a woman in festive garments going down to meet her dark lover.

We stood for a while in silence. "Isn't this the way we used to think of life?" said Schwarz finally. "A thousand lights and streets leading into the infinite . . ."

I did not answer. To me, life was the ship that lay down there on the Tagus, and it didn't lead to the infinite . . . it led to America. I had had my fill of adventures; the times had hurled adventures at us like rotten eggs. The only adventure for me was a valid passport, a visa, and a ticket. To a wanderer against his will, a normal life becomes the most romantic of dreams and adventure a torment.

"That day Zurich looked to me the way this city looks to you tonight," said Schwarz. "It was the beginning of what I thought I had lost. Time—you know that—is diluted death, a poison administered slowly, in harmless doses. At first it stimulates us and even makes us feel immortal—but drop by drop and day by day it grows stronger and destroys our blood. Even if we wanted to buy back our youth at the price of the years that are still ahead of us, we couldn't; the acid of time has changed us, the chemical combination isn't the same any more. It would take a miracle. That miracle happened in Zurich."

He stood still, looking down at the sparkling city. "This is the most terrible night in my life," he said slowly. "I want to remember it as the happiest. Shouldn't memory be able to do that? It must. A miracle is never perfect when it happens; there are always little disappointments. But once it's gone for good and nothing can change it, memory could make it perfect, and then it would never change. If I can just call it to life now, won't it always stay the same? Won't it stay with me as long as I live?"

He seemed almost moonstruck as he stood on the stairs, looking into the overpowering advancing dawn, a pitiful forgotten figure out of the night. I felt terribly sorry for him. "It's true," I said, trying to spare his feelings. "How can we be really sure of our happiness until we know how much of it is going to stay with us?"

"The only way," Schwarz whispered, "is to know that we can't hold it, and stop trying to. We frighten it away with our clumsy hands. But if we can keep our hands off it, won't it go on living fearlessly behind our eyes? Won't it stay there as long as our eyes live?"

He looked down at the city, where a pine coffin stood and a ship lay at anchor. A look of dead suffering decomposed his features; the mouth was a black hollow, the eyes were stones. Then his face came to life again.

We continued down the hill toward the harbor. After a time he began to speak. "Who are we?" he said. "Who are you? Who am I? And what about all those other people and those who are gone? Which is real, a man or his reflection in the mirror? A living human being or his memory, his image shorn of grief? Have my dead wife and I become a single person? Can it be that she was never completely mine before and that only the sinister alchemy of death has made her so? Is she completely mine now that she exists only as a phosphorescent shimmer under my skull, now that she can answer only when I want her to and as I want her to? Or, after losing her once, am I losing her a second time, a little more each moment as her memory pales?" He stared at me. "I've got to hold her, don't you see that?"

We came to a street in which long flights of stairs led down the hill. Some sort of festival must have been held here the day before. Wilted garlands, which made me think of a cemetery, were suspended from iron rods between the rows of houses, and strings of light bulbs punctuated by great tulip-shaped lanterns hung across the street. Higher up, at intervals of fifty or sixty feet, there were five-pointed stars composed of small electric-light bulbs. But the procession, or festival, had passed, and now the decorations lay bare and faded in the dawn. Far below us something seemed to have gone wrong with the electric circuit: only a single star burned with the strangely sharp, pale glow that electric lights take on at dawn and dusk.

"This is the place," said Schwarz, opening a door. A powerful, sunburned man received us. It was a low-ceilinged room with wine barrels along the wall and a few tables, one of them occupied by a couple. We ordered wine and cold fried fish. There was nothing else to be had.

"Do you know Zurich?" Schwarz asked.

"Yes. I've been arrested in Switzerland. Nice jails. Much better than in France. Especially in winter. Unfortunately, they never keep you more than two weeks, though you'd be glad to take a rest. Then they deport you and the border circus starts all over again."

"My decision to cross the border openly had somehow liberated me," said Schwarz. "I wasn't afraid any more. It no longer paralyzed me to see a policeman in the street; I still felt a shock, but it was mild, just enough to make me appreciate my freedom."

I nodded. "Danger increases our awareness of life. Perfect as long as the danger doesn't come too close."

"Do you think so?" Schwarz gave me a strange look. "I think it goes farther," he said. "It goes as far as what we call death, and still farther. Does a city stop existing because you've left it? Wouldn't it still be inside you even if it were destroyed? Who knows what death is? Maybe life is nothing more than a beam of light passing slowly over our changing faces. Maybe we had a face before we were born that will live on after all our perishable faces have passed away?"

A cat came slinking up to the table. I tossed it a piece of fish. It lifted its tail and turned away. "You met your wife in Zurich?" I asked cautiously.

"I met her at the hotel. The embarrassed temporizing I had sensed in Osnabrück was gone, and gone for good. She was no longer unhappy and offended, making strategic capital of her injury. I met a woman I did not know, a woman I loved. It seemed as though nine years of an uneventful past had knit us together, and yet the past had lost its power to hem her in. For her, too, the poison of time had evaporated when she crossed the border. We were no longer at the mercy of the past; it belonged to us. Usually the past is just a depressing reflection of the years; but our past became a mirror that reflected nothing but us. The decision to break away and the act of breaking away removed us so radically from everything that had gone before that the impossible happened: we were reborn."

Schwarz looked at me and again that strange expression passed over his face. "It stayed that way. It was Helen who kept it up. I couldn't—especially toward the end. But it was enough that she was able to carry it off. That was what mattered. Don't you agree? But now I've got to do it myself, just this once; that's why I am talking to you. Yes, that's the reason."

"Did you stay in Zurich?" I asked.

"We stayed for a week," said Schwarz, in a more normal tone. "We lived in that city and that country, the only one in Europe where the world hadn't begun to reel. We had money enough for a few months. Helen had brought some jewelry we could sell, and in France I still had the late Schwarz's drawings.

"That summer of 1939! It was as though God had wished to show the world one last time what peace can be and what it was going to lose. The days were brimful of carefree summer, and they became thoroughly unreal when we left Zurich for Lake Maggiore in the south.

"Helen had received letters and phone calls from her family. She had left word that she was leaving for Zurich to see her doctor. It was easy for her family to find out where she was; the Swiss registration system is very efficient. They left her no peace with their questions and reproaches. She could still go back. We had to decide.

"We lived in the same hotel, but not together. We were married, but our passports carried different names; it's pieces of paper that govern our lives at such times; we couldn't really live together. It was a strange situation, but it strengthened our feeling that time had been turned back for us. According to one law we were man and wife, according to another we were not. The new surroundings, the long separation, and especially the change that had come over Helen in Switzerland—all that created a strange state: everything seemed vague, but at the same time intensely real. And over this strange world of ours hovered the last vanishing mists of a dream we could hardly remember. At the time I didn't know what had produced this blessed state—I took it as an unexpected gift, as though a god were allowing me to repeat a stretch of existence that I had bungled the first time and to transform it into perfect life. The mole who had burrowed his way under borders without a passport became a bird who knew no frontiers.

* * *

"One morning when I called for Helen, I found her talking to a Mr. Krause, whom she introduced as a gentleman from the German consulate. She spoke to me in French when I came in and addressed me as Monsieur Lenoir. Krause misunderstood her and asked me in bad French if I were the famous painter's son. Helen laughed. 'Mr. Lenoir is from Geneva,' she said. 'But he speaks German. He's a great admirer of Renoir, though.'

" 'You like Impressionist painting?' Krause asked me.

" 'He even has a collection,' said Helen.

" 'I have a few drawings,' I said. To convert my inheritance from the late Schwarz into a collection seemed to be one of Helen's new caprices. But since one of her caprices had kept me out of a concentration camp, I played along.

" 'Do you know Oskar Reinhart's collection in Winterthur?' Krause asked me amiably.

"I nodded. 'Reinhart has a Van Gogh that I'd give a month of my life for.'

" 'Which month?' Helen asked.

" 'Which Van Gogh?' asked Krause.

" *The Garden of the Insane Asylum.*'

"Krause smiled. 'A magnificent painting.'

"He began to speak of painting, and when he got around to the Louvre, I was able to join in, thanks to the education I had received from the late Schwarz. I understood Helen's tactics now; she was trying to prevent Krause from recognizing me as her husband or as a refugee. The German consulates were not above reporting people to the Swiss police. I sensed that Krause was trying to ferret out my relationship to Helen, as she had known from the start. Now she dreamed up a wife for me—Lucienne—and two children, the elder being a girl who played the piano splendidly.

"Krause's eyes darted from one to the other. He took advantage of our common interest in art to suggest another meeting—why wouldn't we have lunch in one of the little restaurants on the lake, where the fish is so good?—it's so unusual to meet someone who really knows anything about painting.

"I agreed with equal enthusiasm—I'd be delighted to on my return to Switzerland. That would be in four to six weeks. He was surprised; didn't I live in Geneva? I told him I was a Genevan, but lived in Belfort. Since Belfort is in France, it would be harder for him to make inquiries there. On leaving, he couldn't resist the temptation to ask one last question: where had Helen and I met? Two such congenial people—it was unusual.

"Helen looked at me. 'At the doctor's, Mr. Krause. Sick people are often more congenial than'—this with a malicious smile—'people who are so healthy they have muscles instead of nerves, even in their heads.'

"Krause took Helen's gibe with a shrewd smile. 'I understand, Madame.'

"Not to be outdone by Helen, I asked: 'Don't the Germans nowadays regard Renoir as degenerate art? Van Gogh, for sure.'

" 'Not the connoisseurs among us,' said Krause, with another shrewd look, and slipped through the door.

" 'What did he want?' I asked Helen.

" 'To spy. I tried to warn you not to come, but you were already on your way. My brother sent him. How I hate all that!'

"The shadowy arm of the Gestapo had reached across the border to remind us that we were not entirely free. Krause had asked Helen to drop in at the consulate at her convenience. Nothing urgent, but her passport would have to have a new stamp. A kind of exit visa. That had been forgotten.

" 'He says it's a new regulation,' said Helen.

" 'He's lying,' I replied. 'I'd know about it. Refugees always get wind of these things. If you go, they're quite capable of taking your passport away.'

" 'And then I'd be a refugee like you?'

" 'Yes. Unless you decided to go back.'

" 'I'm staying,' she said. 'I'm not going to any consulate and I'm not going back.'

"We hadn't spoken about it before. This was the decision. I did not answer. I just looked at Helen. Behind her I saw the sky and the trees in the park and a narrow glittering strip of lake. Her face was dark in the bright light. 'You're not responsible,' she said impatiently. 'You didn't talk me into it and it has nothing to do with you. Even if you didn't exist, I wouldn't go back. Now are you satisfied?'

" 'Yes,' I said, surprised and rather ashamed. 'But that's not what I was thinking about.'

" 'I know that, Josef. So let's not talk about it any more. Never.'

" 'Krause will come back,' I said, 'or somebody else.'

"She nodded. 'They'll make trouble if they find out who you are. Why don't we go south?'

" 'We can't go to Italy. Mussolini's police are too chummy with the Gestapo.'

" 'Isn't there any other south?'

" 'Yes. The Swiss Ticino. Locarno, Lugano.'

"We took the train that afternoon. Five hours later we were sitting outside the Locanda Svizzera on the piazza in Ascona, in a world that was not five, but fifty, hours away from Zurich. The landscape was Italian, the town was full of tourists, and no one seemed to have a thought in his head except to swim, to lie in the sun, and to live it up while it was still possible. Do you remember those last months of peace? There was a strange feeling in the air all over Europe," said Schwarz.

"Yes," I said. "Everyone was hoping for a miracle. A second Munich. Then a third. And so on."

"It was a kind of twilight between hope and despair. Time

114

stood still. In the shadow of impending disaster everything else seemed unreal. It was as if an enormous medieval comet shared the sky with the sun. Everything was out of focus. And everything was possible."

"When did you go to France?" I asked.

Schwarz nodded. "You're right. Everything else was temporary. France is the uneasy home of the homeless. All roads lead back to France. A week later Helen received a letter from Herr Krause, telling her to report at once to the consulate in Zurich or Lugano. It was urgent.

"We had to leave. Switzerland was too small and too well organized. We'd be found wherever we went. And any day my papers could be checked; they'd see that my passport was phony and deport me. We went to Lugano, but steered clear of the German consulate. Instead we went to the French consulate. We received tourist visas good for six months. I had counted on three months at the most.

" 'When shall we go?' I asked Helen.

" 'Tomorrow.'

"We had our last dinner in the garden of the Albergo della Posta in Ronco, a village perched like a swallow's nest high up in the hills overlooking the lake. Japanese lanterns hung between the trees, cats crept over the walls, and from the terraces below came the smell of roses and wild jasmine. The lake with its islands—there was said to have been a temple of Venus on one of them in Roman times—lay motionless; the mountains roundabout were cobalt blue against the bright sky. We ate spaghetti and *piccata,* and drank the *nostrano* wine. It was an evening of almost intolerable sweetness and melancholy.

" 'It's too bad that we have to leave,' said Helen. 'I'd have been glad to spend the summer here.'

" 'You'll have plenty of chances to say that.'

" 'Is there anything better to say? I've said the opposite often enough.'

" 'The opposite?'

" 'It's too bad that I have to *stay* here.'

"I took her hand. Her skin was very brown—she tanned easily; two or three days did the trick—and that made her eyes look lighter. 'I love you very much,' I said. 'I love you and this moment and the summer that won't last and this countryside we are leaving, and for the first time in my life myself, because I am nothing but a mirror that reflects you, and that way I have two of you. God bless this evening and this hour!'

" 'God bless everything! Let's drink to it. And God bless you, because you've finally dared to say something that would normally make you blush.'

" 'I'm blushing,' I said. 'But only inside and I'm not ashamed. I've got to get used to it. Even a caterpillar has to get used to the light when it emerges from the darkness and discovers it has wings. How lucky the people are here! And how the wild jasmine smells! The waitress says there are whole forests full of it.'

"When the wine was gone, we walked through the narrow streets and took the old road that leads past the Ronco cemetery, with its flowers and crosses, and down along the hillside to Ascona. The south is a sorcerer; the palms and oleander blot out your thoughts and free your fancy. More and more stars appeared. The sky was like the flag of an ever-expanding United States of the universe. The cafés on the piazza in Ascona sent beams of light far out into the lake, and a cool breeze blew from the valleys.

"We came to the house we had rented on the lake shore. It was small, but there were two bedrooms. That seemed to be enough for local morality. 'How long can we live on the money we have?' Helen asked.

" 'For a year if we're careful. Maybe a year and a half.'

" 'And if we're not careful?'

" 'Just this summer.'

" 'Let's not be careful,' she said.

116

" 'A summer is short.'

" 'Yes,' she said with sudden violence. 'A summer is short, and life is short, but why? Because we know how short they are. Do those cats out there know that life is short? Do birds know? Or butterflies? For them it goes on forever. Nobody has told them. Why have we been told?'

" 'There are a number of answers to that.'

" 'Give me just one.'

"We were standing in the dark room. The doors and windows were open. 'One is that life would be unbearable if it went on forever.'

" 'You think we'd be bored? Like God? That's not true. Give me another.'

" 'That there's more unhappiness than happiness. And that it's merciful to have life end some time.'

"Helen was silent for a moment. Then she said: 'There's not a grain of truth in all that. We only say such things because we know we are not here to stay and there's nothing we can hold on to. There's no mercy in that. We just invent it. We invent it because it's our only hope.'

" 'Don't we believe in it all the same?' I asked.

" 'I don't.'

" 'You don't believe in hope?'

" 'I don't believe in anything. One day our number is up and that's all.' She threw her clothes on the bed. 'It's the same with everybody. A prisoner hopes to escape. Maybe he even succeeds. But next time he won't be so lucky.'

" 'That's all he hopes for. A surcease. That's all there is.'

" 'Yes, that's all there is. It's the same with the world and the war. It hopes for another surcease. But nothing can prevent the war.'

" 'Maybe war can be prevented,' I said. 'But not death.'

" 'Don't laugh!' she cried.

"I moved toward her. Recoiling, she slipped through the door into the open.

117

" 'What's the matter?' I asked in surprise. It was lighter outside, and I saw that her face was bathed in tears. She didn't
answer and I didn't ask again. 'I'm drunk,' she said finally.
'Can't you see that?'

" 'No.'

" 'I've had too much wine.'

" 'Not enough. There's another bottle.'

"There was a stone table in the meadow behind the house.
I put the *fiasco* on it and went inside for glasses. When I
came back, I saw Helen crossing the meadow in the direction
of the lake. I did not follow her at once. I filled the glasses;
the wine looked black in the soft glow of the lake and the
sky. Then I went slowly through the meadow to the palms
and oleanders by the shore. I was worried about Helen, and
heaved a sigh of relief when I saw her. She was standing by
the water, bowed and curiously passive, as though waiting for
something, a voice or perhaps a vision. I stood still, not so
much to watch her, but for fear of frightening her. After a while
she sighed and stood up straight. Then she stepped into the
water.

"When I saw her swimming, I went back for a towel and
her bathrobe. Then I sat down on a block of granite and
waited. Her head with its coil of hair looked very small in the
distance; she was all I had in the world, I thought, and my impulse was to call to her to come back. But at the same time I
sensed that she had something to settle with herself, something
unknown to me, and that this was the crucial moment; to her
the water was fate, question and answer. She had to fight this
out alone, as everyone must—the best someone else can do is
to be there and perhaps to supply a little warmth.

"Helen swam out in an arc, turned, and headed back toward me in a straight line. I saw her coming closer, her dark
head against the purple lake. And then she rose slender and
bright from the water and ran to me.

" 'It's cold. And spooky. The maid says there's a great big octopus living under the islands.'

" 'The biggest fish in this lake are old pike,' I said, wrapping her in the towel. 'No octopi. All the octopi are in the new Germany. But water is always spooky at night.'

" 'If we can think there are octopuses, there must be some,' said Helen. 'You can't think anything that doesn't exist.'

" 'That would be an easy way to prove the existence of God.'

" 'Don't you believe it?'

" 'I believe everything tonight.'

"She pressed against me. I dropped the wet towel and gave her her bathrobe. 'Do you think we live more than once?' she asked.

" 'Yes,' I said without hesitation.

"She sighed. 'Thank God. I wouldn't want to argue about that, not now. I'm tired and cold. I keep forgetting that this water comes down from the mountains.'

"Along with the wine, I had brought a bottle of grappa from the Albergo della Posta. Grappa is a clear brandy made of grape husks, strong and spicy and good for times like this. I went inside for it and poured her a large glassful. She drank it slowly. 'I hate to leave here,' she said.

" 'You'll have forgotten it by tomorrow,' I replied. 'We're going to Paris. You've never been there. It's the most beautiful city in the world.'

" 'The most beautiful city in the world is the one where you are happy. Is that a platitude?'

"I laughed. 'Let's not worry about style!' I said. 'If that's a platitude, we can't have too many of them. Do you want some more grappa?'

"She nodded, and I brought out another glass for myself. We sat at the stone table in the meadow until Helen grew sleepy. I took her to bed. She fell asleep beside me. I looked through the open door at the meadow, which slowly turned blue and then silvery. Helen woke up an hour later and went to the kitchen for water. She came back with a letter that had come while we were in Ronco. It must have been lying in her room. 'From Martens,' she said.

"She read it and put it down. 'Does he know you're here?' I asked.

"She nodded. 'He told my family that he had advised me to go to Switzerland to be examined again, and that I should stay a few weeks.'

" 'Did you go to him for treatment?'

" 'Off and on.'

" 'What for?'

" 'Nothing special,' she said, and put the letter in her bag. She did not give it to me to read.

" 'Where did you get that scar?' I asked.

"There was a thin white line across her abdomen. I had noticed it before, but her brown skin made it more conspicuous.

" 'A slight operation. Nothing of any importance.'

" 'What kind of operation?'

" 'The kind we don't talk about. Women have these things.'

"She put the light out. 'It's good you came for me,' she whispered. 'I couldn't have stood it any more. Love me! Love me and don't ask questions. Never.'

CHAPTER 10

"Happiness!" said Schwarz. "How its colors run in your memory! Like cheap shirts in the laundry. Only unhappy people can count. We went to Paris and found rooms in a small hotel on the Quai des Grands-Augustins, on the left bank of the Seine. There was no elevator, the stairs were warped and worn with age, and the rooms were small; but we had a view of the Seine, the bookstalls on the quay, the Palais de Justice and Notre-Dame. We had passports. We were human beings until September, 1939.

"We were human beings until September, and it made no difference whether our passports were genuine or not. But it made a difference when the 'phony war' began. 'What did you live on when you were here before?' Helen asked me one day. 'Were you allowed to work?'

" 'Of course not. I wasn't even allowed to exist. How would you expect a nonexistent person to get a work permit?'

" 'What did you live on then?'

" 'I don't remember,' I answered truthfully. 'I worked at various trades. None of the jobs lasted very long. The French are no great sticklers for legality. You can always find something to do if you'll accept low wages. I loaded crates at Les Halles; I waited on table; I peddled ties, socks, and shirts; I gave German lessons; once in a while the refugee committee gave me a little something; I sold my belongings; I wrote some short articles for Swiss newspapers.'

" 'Couldn't you get a newspaper job again?'

" 'No. For that you need working papers and a residence permit. My last job was addressing letters. Then came Schwarz and my apocryphal existence.'

" 'Why apocryphal?'

" 'Because I was supposed to be someone else, living under the cover of a dead man's name. I'd ceased to exist as myself.'

" 'I wish you'd call it something else,' said Helen.

" 'It doesn't much matter what I call it. A double life, a borrowed life. Or a second life. Yes, maybe that's the most accurate. We're like castaways who have no regrets, because they've lost their memory—it's memory that makes people feel that they've lost the good things without improving the bad ones.'

"Helen laughed. 'What are we now? Impostors, corpses, or ghosts?'

" 'Legally we are tourists. We are allowed to be here, but not to work.'

" 'Fine,' she said. 'Then we won't work. Let's go to the Ile Saint-Louis and sit on a bench in the sun. Then we'll go to the Café de France and eat on the sidewalk. How's that for a program?'

" 'It's a fine program,' I said. And we stuck to it. I stopped looking for odd jobs. For weeks on end we were together from early morning to early morning. Out in the world time stormed by: extras, troop movements, emergency sessions of the Chamber, but all that had nothing to do with us. It simply wasn't there. We were living in eternity. When your world is brimful of feeling, there's no room for time. You're on another shore, beyond time. Or don't you believe that?"

Schwarz turned to me with a look of desperate appeal. "You don't believe it?" he asked.

I was tired, and, I couldn't help it, impatient. Stories about happiness are without interest, and Schwarz's fantasies about eternity left me pretty cold, too. "I don't know," I answered absently. "Maybe happiness or eternity comes when we die; then the calendar stops and time with it. But if we go on living, there's no help for it—whatever we do takes place in time, and time passes."

"I won't let it die!" said Schwarz with sudden violence. "I want it to stand still like a marble statue. Not like a castle of sand that washes away in the tide! What would become of the dead whom we love? What would become of them? Wouldn't they die over and over again? Where else are they if not in our memory? Her face! I'm the only one who still knows it. Can I leave it to the ravages of time? I know it will fade even in my mind, it will be distorted and falsified, unless I can project it and set it up outside of me. The lies and fantasies of my mind will entwine it like ivy and destroy it and in the end there will be nothing left but ivy. I know that. That's why I have to save my memory from myself, from the corrosive egotism that will make me try to forget so that I can go on living. Don't you understand?"

"I understand, Mr. Schwarz," I said, treading as softly as I could. "That's why you are talking to me—to save your memory from yourself. . . ."

I was annoyed with myself for having spoken so bluntly before. The man was mad, with a logical madness, a Don Quixote, determined to battle the windmills of time, and I had too much respect for his grief to try to analyze his condition. "If I succeed—" Schwarz could not go on. Then he took a fresh start: "If I succeed, it will be safe against anything I can do. You believe me?"

"Yes, Mr. Schwarz. Our memory is not an ivory casket in

a dusty museum. It is an animal that lives and eats and digests. It consumes itself like the phoenix in the legend, so that we can go on living and not be destroyed by it. That's what you are trying to prevent."

"That's it!" Schwarz's eyes were full of gratitude. "You said that memory can turn to stone only if we die. That's what I am going to do."

"I was talking nonsense," I said wearily. I hated such conversations. I had known so many neurotics; exile produces them as rain produces mushrooms.

"I'm not going to take my life," said Schwarz, and smiled, as though he knew what I was thinking. "Human lives are too much needed right now. I'm only going to die as Josef Schwarz. Tomorrow morning when I leave you, Josef Schwarz will be dead."

A thought passed through my mind, and with it a wild hope. "What are you going to do?" I asked.

"Disappear."

"As Josef Schwarz?"

"Yes."

"Just the name?"

"Everything that was Josef Schwarz is going to disappear. My former self."

"What will you do with your passport?"

"I won't be needing it."

"Have you another?"

Schwarz shook his head. "I don't need one."

"Is there an American visa in it?"

"Yes."

"Would you sell it to me?" I asked, though I had no money.

Schwarz shook his head.

"Why not?"

"I can't sell it," said Schwarz. "I received it as a present. But I can give it to you. Tomorrow morning. Can you use it?"

124

"Good Lord!" I said breathlessly. "Use it! It would save my life. There's no American visa in mine, and I have no idea how I'd get one by tomorrow."

Schwarz smiled sadly. "How things repeat themselves. You remind me of the time when Schwarz was dying; I sat in his room, and I couldn't think of anything but that passport that would make me a human being again. Fine. I'll give you mine. You'll only have to change the picture. The age must be about right."

"Thirty-nine," I said.

"You'll be five years older. Have you got somebody who's good with passports?"

"Yes," I replied. "I know a man here. It's easy to change the picture."

Schwarz nodded. "Easier than a personality." He stared into space for a moment. "Wouldn't it be strange if you were to develop an interest in paintings? Like Schwarz—and then myself?"

A shudder ran through me. "A passport is a piece of paper," I said. "It's not magic."

"No?" said Schwarz.

"Well, yes," I answered. "But not that way. How long did you stay in Paris?"

I was in such a turmoil over Schwarz's promise to give me his passport that I didn't hear what he said. I could think only about what I would have to do to get a visa for Ruth. I could try to pass her off as my sister. But it probably wouldn't work; they were very strict at American consulates. I'd have to try though, unless a second miracle happened. Then I heard Schwarz speaking.

"One day he turned up in our room in Paris," he said. "It had taken him six weeks, but he found us. This time he didn't send somebody from the German consulate. He came in person and there he stood in the hotel room with the eighteenth-century pastoral prints—Georg Jürgens, Obersturmbannfüh-

125

rer, Helen's brother, tall, broad-shouldered, two hundred pounds or over, and ten times as German as in Osnabrück, despite his civilian clothes. He glared at us.

" 'So it was all lies,' he said. 'I thought there was something fishy.'

" 'That shouldn't surprise you,' I said. 'It stinks wherever you go. I wonder why.'

"Helen laughed. 'Stop laughing!' Georg shouted.

" 'Stop shouting!' I said. 'Or I'll have you thrown out.'

" 'Why don't you try to do it yourself?'

"I shook my head. 'Are you still playing the hero when there's no danger? You outweigh me by twenty pounds. Nobody would put us in the ring together. What do you want?'

" 'That's none of your business, you God-damned traitor. Get out. I want to talk to my sister.'

" 'Stay right here!' said Helen to me. She was bristling with rage. Slowly she rose from her chair and picked up a marble ash tray. 'One more word in that tone and you'll get this in your face,' she said very calmly. 'This isn't Germany.'

" 'No, unfortunately. But never mind. It soon will be.'

" 'Never,' cried Helen. 'Maybe you armed robots will conquer it for a while, but it will still be France. Is that what you've come here to talk about?'

" 'I've come here to take you home. Don't you know what will happen to you if the war catches you here?'

" 'Not much.'

" 'They'll put you in prison.'

"Helen was taken aback for a moment. 'Maybe they'll put us in a camp,' I said. 'But it will be an internment camp—not a concentration camp as in Germany. . . .'

" 'What do you know about it?' Georg sneered.

" 'Plenty,' I answered. 'I was in one of yours, thanks to you.'

" 'You worm. You were in a rehabilitation camp,' said

Georg contemptuously. 'But it didn't do you any good. The moment you were released, you deserted.'

" 'I admire your terminology,' I said. 'If anyone escapes from your clutches, it's desertion.'

" 'What else would you call it? Your orders were not to leave Germany.'

"I made a disparaging gesture. I had had enough talks of this kind with Georg before he had the power to lock me up.

" 'Georg always was an idiot,' said Helen. 'A weakling with big muscles. He needs his armored philosophy as a fat woman needs a corset, because without it he wouldn't have any shape at all. Don't argue with him. He makes a lot of noise because he's weak.'

" 'Cut it out!' said Georg more peaceably than I had expected. 'Pack your things, Helen. The situation is serious. We're taking the train tonight.'

" 'How serious?'

" 'There's going to be war. Otherwise I wouldn't be here.'

" 'You'd be here anyway,' said Helen. 'Just the same as you were in Switzerland two years ago when I didn't want to go back. It's upsetting to a loyal party man to have a sister who doesn't want to live in Germany. You persuaded me to go back. But this time I'm staying right here and there's no point in talking about it.'

"Georg glared at her. 'Because of this miserable scoundrel? I suppose he talked you into it.'

"Helen laughed. 'Scoundrel—I haven't heard that word in a long time. It sounds like the Middle Ages! No, this scoundrel, my husband, didn't talk me into anything. He actually did his best to send me back. For better reasons than yours.'

" 'I want to speak to you alone,' said Georg.

" 'It won't do you any good.'

" 'You're my sister.'

" 'I'm a married woman.'

" 'That's not a blood relationship,' said Georg. Then suddenly he took the tone of an offended child. 'You haven't even offered me a chair. Here I come all the way from Osnabrück and you don't even ask me to sit down.'

"Helen laughed. 'This isn't my room. My husband pays the rent.'

" 'Be seated, Obersturmbannführer and minion of Hitler,' I said. 'But don't stay too long.'

"Georg gave me an angry look and sat down with a crash on the decrepit couch. 'I'd like to speak to my sister alone. Can't you get that through your head?'

" 'Did you let me speak to her alone when you had me arrested?' I asked him.

" 'That was entirely different.'

" 'With Georg and his party comrades, what they do is always entirely different,' said Helen. 'When they kill or arrest people for disagreeing with them, when they send you to a concentration camp, they are defending the besmirched honor of the Fatherland—am I right, Georg?'

" 'Exactly.'

" 'He's always right,' Helen went on. 'Never any doubts, never any qualms of conscience. He's always on the right side, where the power is. He's like his Führer—the most peace-loving man in the world as long as everybody does what he says. The others are always the troublemakers. Am I right, Georg?'

" 'What has that to do with us?'

" 'Nothing,' said Helen. 'And everything. Don't you see how ridiculous your self-righteousness is in this city of tolerance? Even dressed as a civilian, you're always wearing boots to trample people with. But here you haven't any power. Not yet. Here you can't enroll me in your sweaty, flat-footed National Socialist Women's Association. Here you can't treat me like a prisoner. Here I can breathe, and I mean to stay here and keep on breathing.'

" 'You have a German passport. There's going to be a war. You'll be sent to prison.'

" 'Not right away. Anyway, I'd rather be in prison here than in Germany. Because you'd have to lock me up, too. It wouldn't be the same now that I've breathed the sweet air of freedom, now that I know what it's like to be away from you and your barracks and your human stud farms and your horrid shouting. I wouldn't be able to keep my mouth shut any more.'

"I stood up. I couldn't stand to see her laying herself bare before this National Socialist vulgarian, who would never understand her. 'It's all his fault!' Georg snarled. 'Damned cosmopolitan. He's corrupted you. You just wait, we'll settle your hash.'

"He stood up, too. He could easily have beaten me up. He was twice my size, and the course in national rehabilitation they had put me through in the concentration camp had left me with a stiff elbow. 'Don't you lay a finger on him!' said Helen very softly.

" 'The coward!' said Georg. 'Why do you have to defend him? Can't he look after himself?' "

Schwarz turned to me. "It's a curious thing about sheer physical brawn. We know it has nothing to do with courage or strength of character. A gun in the hand of a cripple can deflate the biggest bag of brawn and muscle. You know all that and even so you feel humiliated because you can't stand up to one of these stupid bruisers. You know that it's not a contest of courage, that this bully is probably a perfect coward —but it doesn't do a particle of good. You look for excuses, you want to justify yourself, you feel like a worm because you don't want to be beaten to a pulp. You know what I mean?"

I nodded. "We know how absurd it is. But that makes us feel even worse."

"If he had attacked me, I'd have defended myself," said Schwarz. "I swear I would have."

129

I raised my hand. "Why do you say that, Mr. Schwarz? You don't have to explain these things to me."

He smiled feebly. "I guess not. I'm still trying to justify myself. That shows how deep it goes. It's like a barb in the flesh. I wonder if we ever get over this male vanity?"

"What happened?" I asked. "Did you fight?"

"No. Helen began to laugh. 'Will you look at that fool,' she said to me. 'He thinks that if he beats you up, I'll see how unmanly you are; he thinks I'll repent and go back to the land where the fist reigns supreme.' She turned to Georg. 'You have the gall to call my husband a coward. He's shown more courage than you can even conceive of. He came for me. He came back to Germany to bring me out.'

" 'What?' Georg's eyes nearly popped out of his head. 'To Germany?'

"Helen recollected herself. 'Forget it. I'm here and I'm not going back.'

" 'He came to get you?' Georg asked. 'Who helped him?'

" 'Nobody,' said Helen. 'You'd like to arrest a few people, wouldn't you?'

"I had never seen her like that—trembling with revulsion, hatred, and blazing triumph at having escaped from his clutches. I felt the same way; but another thought struck me with blinding force—the thought of revenge. Georg had no power here. He couldn't whistle for his Gestapo. He was alone.

"I was completely shaken. I had to do something, but I didn't know what. I couldn't fight and I had no desire to. What I wanted was to blot this man out. To wipe him off the face of the earth. Without a trial. You don't try an incarnation of evil, and that was how I felt about Georg. It wasn't just revenge—to destroy him would be to save dozens of unknown victims. I went to the door. I had no idea of what I was going to do. My head was reeling and I was surprised that I didn't fall. I had to be alone. I had to think. Helen watched me closely, but said nothing. Georg eyed me with contempt and sat down again. 'At last,' he growled, when I closed the door behind me.

"I went down the stairs. Smells rose from the kitchen: fish for lunch. There was an Italian chest on the next landing. I had passed any number of times and never noticed it. Now I examined the carvings as if I were planning to buy it. Then I continued on like a sleepwalker. On the third floor a door was open. The room was painted light green, the windows were open, and the chambermaid was turning the mattress. Strange all the things you notice when you're so excited you think you can't see a thing. I knocked at the door of a man I knew on the second floor. His name was Fischer and he had once shown me his revolver. He kept it because it made life easier to bear. The possibility of putting an end to his God-forsaken refugee's existence any time he pleased gave him the illusion that he was keeping on of his own free will.

"Fischer was out, but his room wasn't locked. He had nothing to hide. I went in to wait for him. I had no definite plan, but I knew I had to borrow that gun. It would be absurd to kill Georg in the hotel, that was plain to me; it would have endangered Helen and myself and the other refugees who lived there. I sat down in a chair and tried to calm myself. I didn't succeed. I just sat there, staring into space.

"A canary began to sing. It was in a wire cage hanging between the windows. I hadn't noticed it before and started as though someone had bumped into me. Then Helen came in.

" 'What are you doing here?' she asked.

" 'Nothing. Where is Georg?'

" 'He's gone.'

"I didn't know how long I had been in Fischer's room. Not very long, it seemed to me. 'Will he be back?' I asked.

" 'I don't know. He's stubborn. Why did you go away? To leave us alone?'

" 'No, Helen,' I said. 'I just couldn't stand the sight of him any longer.'

"She stood in the doorway and looked at me. 'Do you hate me?'

" 'Hate you?' I asked in profound astonishment. 'Why?'

" 'The thought came to me after Georg had gone. If you hadn't married me, all this wouldn't have happened to you.'

" 'The same thing would have happened. Or worse. Maybe in his own way Georg was easier on me for your sake. They didn't drive me into the electric barbed wire, they didn't hang me on a meat hook. . . . I hate you? How could you even think of such a thing?'

"Suddenly I saw the green summertime through Fischer's windows. The room was in the rear; there was a chestnut tree in the court, and the sun filtered through the leaves. My hysteria seeped away like a hangover in the late afternoon. I was myself again. I knew what day of the week it was; I knew that it was summer outside, that I was in Paris, and that you don't shoot people down like rabbits. 'I could more easily imagine you hating me,' I said. 'Or despising me.'

" 'Despising you?'

" 'Yes. Because I can't keep your brother away. Because I . . .'

"I was silent. The minutes that had just passed were far away. 'What are we doing here?' I asked. 'In this room?'

"We went up the stairs. 'Everything Georg said is true,' I said. 'You must know that. If war comes, we will be enemy aliens; you even more than I.'

"Helen opened the windows and the door. 'It stinks of army boots and terror,' she said. 'Let the summer in. Let's leave the windows open and go out. Isn't it time for lunch?'

" 'Yes, and it's time to leave Paris.'

" 'Why?'

" 'Georg will try to make trouble for me with the police.'

" 'He doesn't know you have a false passport.'

" 'He'll figure it out. And he'll be back.'

" 'Maybe so. But I'll get rid of him. Let's go out.'

* * *

132

"We went to a little restaurant behind the Palais de Justice and ate at a table on the sidewalk. There was *pâté maison, boeuf à la mode,* salad, and Camembert. We drank Vouvray *en carafe* and ended up with coffee. I remember all that very clearly, even the golden crust of the bread and the chipped coffee cups. I was exhausted and at the same time full of gratitude, not toward anyone in particular; in general. I felt as if I had escaped out of a dark, dirty ditch and didn't even dare to look back because I myself had unconsciously been a part of the muck. But now I had escaped, and I was sitting at a table with a red-and-white-checkered tablecloth, feeling cleansed and safe. The sun shone yellow through the wine, sparrows were scolding on a heap of horse manure, the owner's cat was watching them with well-fed disinterest, a light breeze was blowing across the silent square, and life was as beautiful as it can only be in our dreams.

"Later we walked through the honey-colored Paris afternoon and stopped outside the window of a small dressmaking establishment. We had often stood there. 'You ought to have a new dress,' I said.

" 'Now?' Helen asked. 'With the war about to break out? Isn't that extravagant?'

" 'Yes,' I said. 'That's why we've got to buy it.'

"She kissed me. 'All right.'

"I sat quietly in an armchair near the door to the back room. The *couturière* brought in dress after dress, and soon Helen was so absorbed in trying them on that she almost forgot me. I heard the women's voices passing back and forth and saw the dresses flitting by in the opening of the door and caught an occasional glimpse of Helen's bare brown back. I was overcome by a gentle weariness, a kind of painless death without any idea of dying.

"I was slightly ashamed of myself when I realized why I had wanted to buy Helen a dress. It was a revolt against that day, against Georg, against my helplessness—a childish attempt to justify myself. I awoke from my lethargy when Helen

133

stood before me in a very wide, bright-colored skirt and a black, short, close-fitting sweater. 'Just the thing!' I said. 'We'll take it.'

" 'It's very expensive,' said Helen.

"The dressmaker assured us that it was a model from one of the big houses—a charming lie, but we didn't mind. We walked out happily with our parcels. It was good to buy something you couldn't afford, I thought. The frivolity of the thing dispelled the shadow of Georg. Helen wore the outfit that evening and put it on again when we got up at night to look out of the window at the moonlit city—insatiable as always, economizing on sleep, fully aware that there wasn't much time.

CHAPTER 11

"What's left of all that now?" said Schwarz. "Already the colors have begun to run. The time sequence is blurred; the landscape has lost its contours; there's nothing left but a flat picture under changing light. Not even a coherent picture—it's more like disconnected images rising from the dark stream of memory; the hotel window, a bare shoulder, whispered words that hover in the air like ghosts, the light above the green roof tops, the smell of the river at night, the moon on the gray stone of Notre-Dame, her face, full of love and devotion, another face in Provence and the Pyrenees, and then, that last rigid face I had never seen before, trying to crowd out all the others, as though all the rest had been a mistake."

He raised his head. Again his face had that tortured look, though he tried to force a smile into it. "What's left is in here," he said, pointing to his head. "And even in my mind it's no safer than a dress in a closet full of moths. That's why I'm telling you about it. You'll keep it safe, with you there's no danger. Your memory won't try to wipe it away to save you, as mine does to save me. With me it's in bad hands; even now, that last rigid face is crowding out the others like a cancer—" his voice rose—"but those others were the real faces; they were our life, not that unknown, terrible, last . . ."

"Did you stay on in Paris?" I asked.

"Georg came back once," said Schwarz. "He tried sentimentality and he tried threats. I was out when he came. I didn't see him until he was leaving the hotel. He stopped me. 'You rotter!' he said under his breath. 'You're ruining my sister. But just wait. We'll catch up with you. In a few weeks we'll have you both. And then, my friend, I'll attend to you personally. You'll get down on your knees to me and beg me to finish you off—if you can still speak.'

" 'I can easily imagine that,' I said.

" 'You can't imagine anything. If you could, you'd have stayed away. I'll give you one more chance. If my sister is back in Osnabrück in three days, I'll forget part of the score. In three days. Have I made myself plain?'

" 'You were never very subtle.'

" 'Is that so? Well, just don't forget that my sister has to go back. You know that yourself, you swine. She's sick. Don't pretend you don't know it. You can't pull the wool over my eyes.'

"I stared at him. I didn't know whether he was making this up, whether it was true, or whether he was only repeating what Helen had told him when she had first wanted to go to Switzerland. 'No,' I said. 'I don't know anything of the sort.'

" 'You don't, eh? That's convenient. You liar. She needs a doctor. And in a hurry. Write Martens and ask him. He knows.'

"Two men—dark forms against the white daylight—were passing through the open door of the lobby. 'In three days,' Georg said. 'Or you'll vomit out your God-damned soul ounce by ounce. I'll be back soon! In uniform!'

"The men were in the lobby now. He pushed between them and marched off. The two men passed around me and mounted the stairs. I followed them. Helen was standing at the window of her room. 'Did you meet him?' she asked.

" 'Yes. He says you've got to go home because you're sick.'

"She shook her head. 'What he won't think up!'

" 'Are you sick?' I asked.

" 'Nonsense!' she said. 'I just made that up to get a passport.'

" 'He says Martens knows it, too.'

"Helen laughed. 'Of course he knows. Don't you remember? He wrote me when we were in Ascona. I arranged the whole thing with him.'

" 'Then you're not sick, Helen?'

" 'Do I look sick?'

" 'No, but that doesn't prove a thing. You're really not sick?'

" 'No,' she said impatiently. 'Did Georg say anything else?'

" 'The usual threats. What did he want of you?'

" 'The same. I don't think he'll come back.'

" 'What did he come for in the first place?'

"Helen smiled strangely. 'He thinks I belong to him. He thinks I have to do everything he says. He has always been that way. Even when we were children. Brothers are often like that. He thinks he's acting for the good of the family. I hate him.'

" 'For that?'

" 'I hate him. That's enough. I told him so. But there's going to be war. He's sure.'

"We fell silent. The sound of traffic on the Quai des Grands-Augustins seemed to grow louder. Behind the Palais de Justice the spire of Sainte-Chapelle rose into the clear sky. We heard the cries of the newsboys, rising above the sound of motors as the cries of gulls rise above the roaring of the sea.

" 'I won't be able to protect you,' I said.

" 'I know that.'

" 'You'll be interned.'

" 'What about you?'

"I shrugged my shoulders. 'They'll probably intern me, too. We may be separated.'

"She nodded.

" 'French prisons are no rest homes.'

" 'And German prisons?'

" 'In Germany you wouldn't be locked up.'

" 'I'm staying here,' said Helen with a gesture of impatience. 'You've done your duty; you've warned me. Now forget about it. I'm staying. It has nothing to do with you. I simply won't go back.'

"I looked at her.

" 'To hell with safety!' she cried. 'I'm sick of being careful. I was fed up long ago.'

"I put my arm around her shoulder. 'That's easy to say, Helen. . . .'

"She pushed me away. 'Leave me then!' she screamed. 'Go away and you won't be responsible. Leave me alone! Leave me, I can manage alone.'

"She looked at me as if I were Georg. 'Stop acting like a mother hen! You don't understand a thing! Stop smothering me with your worries and your fear of responsibility! I didn't leave on your account. Try to get that through your head. It wasn't on account of you. I left for my own sake.'

" 'I know that.'

"She came back to me. 'You've got to believe me,' she said gently. 'In spite of appearances. I had to leave. It was only an accident that you turned up. You've got to understand. Safety isn't everything.'

" 'That is true,' I said. 'But you want it for others if you love them.'

" 'There is no such thing as safety,' she said. 'Don't contradict me. I know! I know better than you. I've thought the

138

whole thing over. You'll never know how much I've thought about it. Let's not discuss it any more, my darling. The evening is waiting for us. There won't be many more for us in Paris.'

" 'If you won't go back to Germany, what about Switzerland?'

" 'Georg says the Nazis are going to overrun Switzerland the way the Kaiser overran Belgium in the First World War.'

" 'Georg doesn't know everything.'

" 'Let's stay here for the present. Maybe the whole thing is a lie. How can he know exactly what's going to happen? It looked like war before. And then came Munich. Why shouldn't there be a second Munich?'

"I didn't know whether she believed what she was saying or was only trying to ease my mind. It's so easy to believe what falls in with your hopes; that's what I did that evening. How could France go to war? It wasn't prepared. It had to give in. Why should the French go to war for the Poles? They hadn't raised a finger for Czechoslovakia.

"Ten days later the borders were closed. The war had begun."

"Were you arrested right away, Mr. Schwarz?" I asked.

"We had another week. We were forbidden to leave the city. It was ironic. For five years they had been throwing me out—then all of a sudden they wouldn't let me leave. Where were you?"

"In Paris," I said.

"Were you shut up in the Vélodrome, too?"

"Of course."

"I don't recall your face."

"There were hundreds of refugees in the Vélodrome, Mr. Schwarz."

"Do you remember the last few days before war was declared, when Paris was blacked out?"

"Yes, of course. It was as though the world had gone dark."

"The little blue lights on street corners," said Schwarz. "They reminded me of night lights in hospitals. In that cold blue darkness, the whole city seemed to be sick. The shivers ran through you. I thought we'd better have some ready cash and sold one of Schwarz's drawings. It was a bad time to be selling. The dealer I went to offered me a pittance. I turned it down and took the drawing back. Finally I sold it to a rich refugee, somebody formerly connected with the movies in Germany. He distrusted the currency and was buying up everything he could lay hands on. I left my last drawing with the hotel owner for safekeeping. Then the police came for me. It was in the afternoon. There were two men. They told me to say good-by to Helen. She stood there pale, with flashing eyes. 'It's not possible,' she said.

" 'Yes, it is,' I said. 'It's perfectly possible. They will come for you later. We'd better not throw our passports away. Keep yours, too.'

" 'That's right,' said one of the policemen in good German. 'Better hold on to them.'

" 'Thank you,' I answered. 'Can you leave us alone to say good-by?'

"The policeman looked toward the door. 'If I had wanted to run away, I could have done it several days ago,' I said.

"He nodded. I went with Helen to her room. 'When it really happens,' I said, 'it's not the same as when you're just talking about it.' And I took her in my arms.

"She broke away. 'How will I get in touch with you?'

"We had the usual last-minute discussion. We had two addresses, the hotel and in care of a French friend. The policeman knocked at the door. I opened. 'Take a blanket with you,' he said. 'It will only be a day or two, but take a blanket anyway and something to eat.'

" 'I haven't got a blanket.'

" 'I'll bring you one,' said Helen. She quickly packed up what edibles we had on hand. 'Is it really only for a day or two?' she asked.

" 'At the most,' said the policeman. 'Just to check your identity and that kind of thing. *C'est la guerre,* Madame.'

"We were often to hear that."

Schwarz took a cigarette from his pocket and lighted it. "You know how it was—the wait at the police station, other refugees pouring in, rounded up as if they were dangerous Nazis, the ride in the paddy wagon to the Préfecture, the endless wait at the Préfecture. Were you in the Salle Lépine, too?"

I nodded. The Salle Lépine was a large room at the Préfecture, a kind of movie theater, where they ordinarily showed training films for the police. There was a screen and a few hundred seats. "I spent two days there," I answered. "At night they took us to a big coal cellar with benches to sleep on. In the morning we looked like chimney sweeps."

"We sat on those chairs for days," said Schwarz. "We were filthy. It wasn't long before we looked like the criminals they took us for. Georg had his revenge on me, though he hadn't planned it. It was through the Préfecture that he had learned our address. Someone had consulted the files for him. He had made no secret of his party membership—that was brought up now. They thought I was a spy. I was questioned four times a day about my relations with Georg and the National Socialist party. At first I laughed; it was too absurd. But then I discovered that absurdities can be very dangerous—take the party in Germany—and now, under the impact of bureaucracy and war, even France, the land of reason, seemed to have gone mad. Without knowing it, Georg had left a time bomb behind him; it's no joke to be taken for a spy in wartime.

"Every day new batches of terrified people were brought in. Not one man had been killed at the front—this was *la drôle de guerre,* as the wits called it—but an atmosphere of war had settled over the country like a plague. The life and welfare of the individual counted for nothing. People had ceased to be human beings—they were classified according to military criteria as soldiers, fit for military service, unfit for military service, and enemies.

"By the third day in the Salle Lépine, I was thoroughly exhausted. Some of our number had been taken away. The rest were engaged in whispered conversation, sleeping, or eating. Life was reduced to the barest essentials. Still, we were not too downcast. Compared to a German concentration camp, this was nothing. At the worst you might be kicked or pushed a little if you were slow in responding to orders. But power is power, and a policeman is a policeman the world over.

"I was very tired from all the questioning. Under the screen on the platform, our armed guards sat in a row with legs outstretched. The dimly lighted room, the bare, soiled screen, and we down below—a dismal picture that seemed to symbolize life itself: you were always either a prisoner or a guard, free only to decide what kind of film you wanted to see on the empty screen—an educational film, a comedy, or a tragedy. Ultimately there was nothing but this empty screen, a hungry heart, and the stupid representatives of power, who behaved as if they were eternal and always right, though the screens had been blank for years. It would always be like this, I thought, nothing would ever change. One day I'd disappear and no one would be the wiser. You know those hours— when hope dies—you've been through it."

I nodded. "The hour of silent suicide. Your resistance is gone; you take the last step without thinking, almost by accident."

"The door opened," Schwarz went on, "and with the yellow light from the corridor Helen came in. She had a basket and a couple of blankets and was carrying a leopard-skin coat over her arm. I recognized her by her walk and by the way she carried her head. She stood still for a moment. Then she passed down the rows, searching. She passed close to me and did not see me. It was almost like the time in the Osnabrück cathedral. 'Helen!' I said.

"She turned around. I stood up. She looked at me. 'What have they done to you?' she asked angrily.

" 'Nothing much. We sleep in a coal cellar. It's bad for the complexion. How did you get here?'

" 'I've been arrested,' she said with a note of pride. 'Just like you. And much sooner than the other women. I was hoping to find you here.'

" 'Why did they arrest you?'

" 'Why did they arrest *you*?'

" 'They think I'm a spy.'

" 'Me too. Because my passport is in order.'

" 'How do you know that?'

" 'I've just been questioned. They told me so. I'm not a bona fide refugee. They haven't arrested the women yet. A little man with pomade on his hair told me. Is he the one who questions you? He smells of snails.'

" 'I don't know. Everything smells of snails in this place. Thank God you've brought blankets.'

" 'I brought all I could.' Helen opened the basket. Two bottles clinked. 'Cognac,' she said. 'No wine. It's the strength that counts. How's the food?'

" 'About what you'd expect. They let us send out for sandwiches.'

"Helen bent down and inspected me. 'You look like a cargo of African slaves. Can't you wash?'

" 'Not so far. But it's not meanness. Just disorder.'

"She took out the cognac. 'The corks have been pulled,' she said. 'The hotelkeeper did it; he was very kind. He said I wouldn't find a corkscrew here. Have a drink.'

"I took an enormous gulp and passed the bottle back to her. 'I even have a glass,' she said. 'It's my tribute to civilization. Let's keep it up while we can.'

"She filled the glass and drank. 'You smell of summer and freedom,' I said. 'What's it like on the outside?'

" 'Like peacetime. The cafés are full. The sky is blue.' She looked at the row of policemen on the platform and laughed. 'It makes me think of a shooting gallery. You shoot at those dummies up there, and if one of them tips over, you get a bottle of wine or an ash tray.'

" 'Here it's the dummies that have the guns.'

"Helen fished into her basket and produced a *pâté*. 'From the *patron*,' she said. 'With best greetings and a message: *Merde à la guerre*. It's *pâté de volaille*. I've got forks and a knife. I say it again: *Vive la civilisation!*'

"Suddenly I felt gay. Helen was there; nothing was lost. There was still no fighting, and maybe it was true that we would soon be released.

"The following afternoon we heard that we were going to be separated. I would be sent to the transit camp in Colombes, Helen to La Petite Roquette prison. Even if they had believed we were married, it wouldn't have helped. Married couples were separated, too.

"We sat up all night in the cellar with the permission of a kindhearted guard. Someone had brought a few candles. Some of our number had already been shipped out; there were still about a hundred of us left. Quite a few Spanish refugees, too. There was something ironical about the thoroughness with which antifascists were being rounded up in an antifascist country. It made you think of Germany.

" 'Why do they want to separate us?' Helen asked.

" 'I don't know. It's not cruelty, just stupidity.'

" 'If they put men and women in the same camp,' said a little old Spaniard, 'there'd be nothing but jealousy and fights. That's why you're being separated. *C'est la guerre!*'

"Helen slept beside me in her leopard coat. There were a few comfortable padded benches, but they had been set aside for some elderly women. One of them offered Helen her bench to sleep on from three to five; she refused. 'I'll have plenty of time to sleep alone later on,' she said.

"It was a weird night. The voices gradually died down. The old women stopped whimpering; now and then one of them would wake up sobbing, but soon drift off into sleep as though

144

smothered in black wool. The candles went out one by one. Helen slept on my shoulder. She put her arms around me in her sleep, and when she woke up, she whispered to me. Sometimes she spoke like a child and sometimes like a woman in love—words that people don't say in the daytime, or even at night under normal circumstances—words of suffering and parting, words of the body, which rebels against parting, words of the skin, of the blood, words of plaint, the oldest plaint in the world: why can't we stay together, why must one always go first, why is death forever tugging us by the hand, making us move on, even when we are tired, even when we are trying, for one short hour, to keep up the illusion of eternity? Later her head slid slowly down my shoulder to my knees. I held her head in my hands and saw her breathing in the light of the last candle. I heard men stand up and grope their way among the piles of coal, looking for a place to urinate. The feeble light flickered and enormous shadows danced about. Then the last light went out, and there was nothing but stuffy snoring darkness. Once she started up with a short high-pitched cry. 'I'm here,' I whispered. 'Don't be frightened. Everything is all right.'

"She lay back and kissed my hands. 'Yes, you're here,' she murmured. 'Stay with me always.'

" 'I'll always be with you,' I whispered. 'Even if we're separated for a little while, I'll always find you.'

" 'You'll find me?' she murmured, slipping into sleep.

" 'I'll always find you. Always! Wherever you are. Same as I found you last time.'

" 'That's good,' she sighed, and turned her face so that it rested in my hands as in a bowl. I didn't sleep. From time to time I felt her lips on my fingers, and once I thought I felt tears; but I said nothing. I loved her very much, and it seemed to me that I had never loved her more, even when possessing her, than in this sordid night full of snoring, punctured by the strange hissing sound of urine falling on coal. I was very still,

145

my self was extinguished by love. Then came the morning, the pale early grayness that steals every color away and discloses the skeleton under the skin. Suddenly it seemed to me that Helen was dying and that I must wake her to keep her alive. She awoke and opened an eye. 'Do you think we could get some coffee and *croissants?*' she asked.

"I was filled with happiness. 'I'll try to bribe one of the guards,' I said.

"Helen opened her other eye and looked at me. 'What has happened?' she asked. 'You look as if you'd won first prize in the lottery. Are we going to be released?'

" 'No,' I said. 'I've released myself.'

"She moved her head sleepily in my hands. 'Can't you give yourself any peace?'

" 'Yes,' I said. 'I'll have to, in fact. For quite a while, I'm afraid. I won't have much chance to make my own decisions. It's a comfort if you look at it that way.'

" 'Everything's a comfort,' said Helen with a yawn. 'As long as we live, everything is comforting, didn't you know that? Do you think they will shoot us as spies?'

" 'No. They'll lock us up.'

" 'Will they lock up the refugees they don't regard as spies?'

" 'Yes, they'll arrest everyone they lay hands on. They've arrested the men already.'

"Helen half raised herself. 'What's the difference then?'

" 'Maybe the others will be let out sooner.'

" 'You never can tell. Maybe we'll get better treatment just because they take us for spies.'

" 'That's nonsense, Helen.'

"She shook her head. 'It's not nonsense. It's experience. Don't you know that in this century innocence is the worst crime and that the innocent are always punished the most severely? It seems to me you'd know that after being arrested in two countries. You and your dreams of justice! Is there any more cognac?'

146

" 'Cognac and *pâté*.'

" 'Give me both,' said Helen. 'It's an odd breakfast, but I'm afraid we have an adventurous life ahead of us.'

" 'That's a good way to look at it,' I said, and gave her the cognac.

" 'It's the only way. Would you rather die of bitterness? Once you discard the idea of justice, it's not so hard to take the whole business as an adventure. Don't you agree?'

"The glorious smell of the old cognac and the succulent *pâté* hovered around Helen like an aura of happiness. She ate with gusto. 'I didn't know it would be so simple for you,' I said.

" 'Don't worry about me,' she said, taking some white bread from her basket. 'I'll get by. Justice doesn't mean as much to women as to you.'

" 'What do women care about?'

" 'This.' She pointed to the bread and the bottle and the *pâté*. 'Eat, darling. We'll come through all right. In ten years it will be a great adventure, and we'll tell our friends about it until they are bored stiff. Eat, man with the false name. What we eat now we won't have to carry later on.'

"I won't tell you all the details," said Schwarz. "You know how it was with the refugees. I only spent a few days in the stadium at Colombes. Helen was sent to La Petite Roquette. On the last day, our hotelkeeper turned up in the stadium. I only saw him from a distance; we weren't allowed to speak to visitors. The *patron* left a small cake and a large bottle of cognac. In the cake I found a note: 'Madame is well and cheerful. She is not in danger. Expects to be sent to a women's camp that is being set up in the Pyrenees. Write via hotel. *Madame est formidable!*' Folded up inside was a tiny note in Helen's handwriting. 'Don't worry. The danger is past. It's still an adventure. See you soon. Love.'

"She had succeeded in breaking the blockade—a very

147

sloppy blockade, but still! I couldn't imagine how. She told me about it later. She had carried on about some important papers left behind in her room, and they had sent her to the hotel with a policeman. She had slipped the *patron* the note and told him in a whisper how to deliver it. The policeman, who had a soft spot for lovers, had closed an eye. She had brought back no papers, but perfume, cognac, and a basket full of food, instead. She loved to eat. I was never able to understand how she managed to stay slim. When in the days of our freedom I woke up and found her place in bed empty, I only had to go to the corner where we kept our food—she would be sitting there with a blissful smile in the moonlight, gnawing at a ham bone or stuffing on some dessert she had saved from dinner. And drinking wine out of the bottle. She was like a cat that gets hungry at night. The *patron,* she told me, was just baking the *pâté* when she was arrested; she had made the policeman wait till it was done. It was her favorite kind of *pâté* and she just had to take it along. She flatly refused to go without it. The policeman had grumbled but capitulated. They dislike dragging people to the paddy wagon. Helen even remembered to take a package of paper napkins.

"Next day we were loaded into cars headed for the Pyrenees. This was the beginning of an epic of terror, comedy, escape, bureaucracy, despair, and love.

CHAPTER 12

"Some day, perhaps," said Schwarz, "our time will be known as the age of irony. Not the witty irony of the eighteenth century, but the stupid or malignant irony of a crude age of technological progress and cultural regression. Hitler keeps shouting that he is an apostle of peace and that other countries have forced war upon him; he not only tells the whole world, he believes it himself. Fifty million Germans believe it with him. The fact that they alone have been arming for years, and that no other country was prepared for war doesn't affect their opinion in the least. It was just one more irony that those of us who had escaped the German camps should have landed in French ones. You couldn't even be too indignant about it—a country that's fighting for its life has more important things to worry about than perfect justice for refugees. We weren't tortured, gassed, or shot, just interned; what more could we expect?"

"When did you see your wife again?" I asked.

"Not for a long time. Were you at Le Vernet?"

"No, but I know it was one of the worst of the French camps."

Schwarz smiled ironically. "That's a question of degree. Do you know the story about the crabs who were thrown into a pot of cold water to be boiled? When the temperature of the water rose to 120 degrees, they screamed that it was unbearable, and moaned for the happy time when it was only 100; when it went up to 140, they moaned for the time when it was only 120, when it was 160, for the time when it was only 140, and so on. Le Vernet was a thousand times better than the best German concentration camp; just as a concentration camp without gas chambers is better than one with gas chambers."

I nodded. "What happened to you?"

"Soon the cold weather came on. Naturally we didn't have enough blankets and there was no coal. The usual mismanagement. But unhappiness is harder to bear when you're freezing. I won't bore you with a description of winter in the camp. It's too easy to be ironical. If Helen and I had admitted we were Nazis, we would have fared better—we'd have been sent to a special camp. While we starved and froze and suffered from diarrhea, I saw pictures in the papers of interned German prisoners who were not refugees; they had knives and forks, chairs and tables, beds, blankets, and even their own mess hall. The papers wrote with pride of how well France was treating enemy aliens. There was no need to treat us refugees with kid gloves; we weren't dangerous.

"I adapted myself. I took Helen's advice and discarded the idea of justice. In the evening after work, I sat on my 'bunk,' a straw pallet, three feet wide and six feet long, and worked on my state of mind. I trained myself to consider this period as a time of transition that had nothing to do with my personal self. Certain things happened in my environment and I learned to react like a clever animal. Heartbreak can

150

kill you as easily as dysentery, and justice was a peacetime luxury."

"Did you really believe that?" I asked.

"No," said Schwarz. "I had to keep dinning it into my head. It was the little injustices—the smaller slice of bread, the heavier work load—that were hardest to take. You've got to learn to ignore these daily irritations or your resentment of the little things will black out the big ones."

"So you lived like a clever animal."

"Yes, until Helen's first letter came. That was two months later. It was sent by way of our hotel in Paris. I felt as if a window had been opened in a dark stuffy room. Life is still outside, but at least it exists again. Her letters came irregularly; sometimes there was none for weeks. It was strange how they changed and strengthened my image of Helen. She wrote that she was doing all right, that she had finally been sent to a camp and had been working, first in the kitchen, then in the camp store. Twice she managed to send me a package of food, how, with the help of what dodges and bribes, I can't imagine. I began to see a new face in the letters. How much of that was due to absence, my own desires, the caprices of imagination, I don't know. Everything takes on almost supernatural proportions when you're isolated and reduced to a few letters; you know that. A word dropped at random, that would mean nothing if written in other circumstances, can become a thunderbolt that shatters your existence; and another, just as meaningless as the first, can give you weeks of warmth. You spend whole months mulling over things that the writer forgot the moment the letter was sealed. A photograph came; Helen standing outside her barracks with another woman and a man. They were French members of the camp staff, she wrote."

Schwarz looked up. "How I studied that man's face! I borrowed a magnifying glass from a watchmaker. I couldn't make out why Helen had sent me the picture. She had probably thought nothing at all when she sent it. Or had she? I don't know. Have you ever felt that way?"

"Everybody has," I said. "Prisoner's psychosis. There's nothing exceptional about it."

The bar owner brought us our check. We were the last guests. "Is there some place else we can go?" Schwarz asked.

He told us of a place. "They've got girls," he said. "Nice and fat. Not expensive."

"Isn't there anywhere else?"

"Not that I know of at this time of night." He put on his jacket. "I'll take you there if you want. I've got nothing to do. Those girls are pretty sly. I'll see you don't get cheated."

"Can't we sit there without the girls?"

"Without the girls?" The man looked baffled. Then a grin spread over his face. "No girls? Oh, I see. Sure, of course. But that's all they've got, just girls."

He looked after us as we stepped out into the street. It was a wonderful dawn. The sun wasn't up yet, but the salt smell had grown stronger. Cars crept through the streets; the smell of coffee and sleep was wafted from open windows. The lights were all out. We heard the rumbling of an invisible cart a few streets away; fishing boats blossomed like yellow and red water lilies on the restless Tagus, and below, pale and still and without artificial light, lay the ship, the ark, the last hope. We went toward it down the hill.

The brothel was pretty dismal. Four or five fat, slovenly women sat smoking and playing cards. After a listless attempt to engage our interest, they left us in peace. I looked at my watch. "It won't be much longer," Schwarz said. "And the consulates don't open until nine."

I knew that as well as he did. What he didn't seem to know was that telling and listening aren't the same.

"A year seems like an eternity," said Schwarz. "And then it doesn't seem long at all. I tried to escape in January when we were working outside the camp. I was caught two days

152

later. The notorious Lieutenant G. lashed me across the face with his riding whip, and I was given three weeks in solitary on bread and water. On my second attempt I was caught right away. I gave up. It was just about impossible to move without ration cards and papers. Any gendarme could pick you up. And it was a long way to Helen's camp.

"Then our situation changed. In May the real war started, and four weeks later it was over. We were in the Unoccupied Zone, but word went around that an Army commission or even the Gestapo was going to inspect the camp. I guess you remember the panic that broke loose?"

"Yes," I said. "The panic, the suicides, the petitions to release us first, and the bureaucratic incompetence that often prevented this from being done. Not always. Sometimes there was an intelligent camp commander, who released the refugees on his own responsibility. Some of them, it's true, were picked up later in Marseille or at the border."

"In Marseille! By that time Helen and I had the poison," Schwarz broke in. "Little capsules. They gave you a fatalistic peace of mind. A pharmacist in my camp sold them to me. Two capsules. I don't know exactly what it was, but I believed him when he said that you'd die quickly and almost painlessly if you took one. He said the poison was enough for two. He sold it to me because he was afraid he'd take it himself some night, in the hour of despair, just before daybreak.

"We were lined up like clay pigeons. The defeat had come too fast. No one had expected it so soon. We didn't know yet that England would not make peace. All we could see was that everything was lost—" Schwarz made a gesture of weariness—"and even now we can't be sure it isn't. We were pushed back to the coast. Ahead of us there was only the sea."

The sea, I thought. And ships that still cross it.

In the doorway appeared the owner of the bar we had just left. He greeted us with a grin and a mock military salute. Then he whispered something to the fat whores. One of them, a woman with an enormous bosom, came up to us. "Tell us how you do it."

"What?"

"It must hurt like hell."

"What?" asked Schwarz absently.

"The way sailors do it on the high seas!" shouted the bar owner from the doorway, laughing so hard I expected him to spit out his teeth.

"The professor has been kidding you," I said to the woman, who gave off a wholesome smell of olive oil, garlic, onions, sweat, and life. "We're not fairies. We were in the Ethiopian war; the natives castrated us."

"You're Italians?"

"We used to be," I replied. "Eunuchs have no nationality. We're cosmopolitans."

She thought it over a little while. *"Tu es comique,"* she then said solemnly, and wagging her giant posterior she went back to the door, where the bar owner took her in hand.

"It's a strange thing about hopelessness," said Schwarz. "Your ego's gone. You don't even know who you are any more. But still there's something in you that clamors to live. And how obstinately it clings to sheer, naked existence! Sometimes you feel a perfect stillness like the dead calm sailors tell about at the heart of a typhoon. You give up—you're like a bug playing dead—but you're not dead. You've only abandoned all effort to concentrate on sheer survival for its own sake. You are wide awake but absolutely passive. You have no strength to waste. The typhoon is raging all around you, but you are becalmed. Fear and despair are gone; even they are luxuries you can no longer afford. The energy you spent on them would detract from your will to survive—so you block it off. You're nothing but eyes and detached, passive readiness. A strange, serene clarity comes over you. In those days I sometimes felt like a yogi, who casts off everything that has to do with the conscious ego, in order to . . ."

Schwarz faltered. "To seek God?" I asked, half mockingly.

Schwarz shook his head. "To find God. We're always look-ing for Him. But we look for Him as if we were trying to swim with all our clothes on and a full field pack. You've got to be naked. As naked as in the night when I left a safe foreign country to go back to my dangerous homeland, and crossed the Rhine as though it were a stream of destiny, a narrow strip of moonlit life.

"In the camp I sometimes thought of that night. It didn't sap my strength to think of it—it made me stronger. I had done what my life had demanded. I hadn't failed, I had gained a second, heaven-sent life with Helen—and even the despair that had come to me and still haunted my sleep from time to time was possible only because there had been some-thing else: Paris, Helen, and the unbelievable feeling of not being alone. Somewhere Helen was alive; maybe she was liv-ing with somebody else, but she was alive. It's horrible to think how much that can mean in times like these, when a man is less than an ant under a boot."

Schwarz fell silent. "Did you find God?" I asked. It was a crude question, but all at once I was very eager to know.

"A face in the mirror," Schwarz answered.

"Whose face?"

"It's always the same. Do you know your own? The face you had before you were born?"

I looked at him with consternation. He had used the same words before. "A face in the mirror," he repeated. "And the face that looks over your shoulder and behind it another— but then suddenly you yourself are the mirror with its endless repetitions. No, I didn't find Him. What would we do with Him if we did find Him? We'd have to stop being human be-ings. Just to look for Him—that's something else."

He smiled. "And then I didn't even have time and strength enough for that. I was too low. I could think only of what I loved. That's what kept me alive. I stopped thinking of God.

Or justice. The circle had closed. It was the same situation as in the river. Repeated. Once again I was on my own. When that state sets in, there's nothing much you can do. You can't even think. And it's not necessary; thinking would only confuse you. Things happen by themselves. From the ridiculous isolation of a human being you've returned to a world of anonymous events. All you need is to be ready. Ready to go when the invisible hand taps you on the shoulder. You only have to follow; as long as you don't ask questions, you'll be all right. You probably think I'm talking mystical nonsense."

I shook my head. "I know that feeling. People sometimes get it in times of great danger. Soldiers have told me about it. For no reason, something makes you walk out of a dugout that had all the appearance of safety; a moment later a direct hit turns it into a mass grave."

"What I finally did," said Schwarz, "was impossible. But it seemed like the most natural thing in the world. I packed up my belongings. Then one morning I walked out of the camp. Most attempts were made at night. I went to the main gate in broad daylight and told the sentries I had been discharged. There were two of them. I waved Schwarz's passport. At the same time I reached into my pocket, gave them some money, and told them to have a drink to my health. They didn't even ask to see my discharge. How could it occur to those two young peasants in uniform that anyone would have the nerve to leave by the main gate if he wasn't supposed to?

"I walked slowly down the white road. After the first few steps I felt as if the camp gate had turned into a dragon and was sneaking up behind me. But I didn't run. Calmly I put Schwarz's passport away and went on. There was a smell of rosemary and thyme in the air—the smell of freedom.

"After a time I pretended my shoelace had come undone. I bent down and looked back. No one was following me. I began to walk faster.

"I had none of the many papers you could be asked for in

156

those days. My French was fairly good; I hoped people would mistake it for some dialect. The whole country was on the move. The towns were full of fugitives from the Occupied Zone, and the roads were swarming with vehicles of all kinds, many of them piled high with bedding, household utensils, and escaping soldiers.

"I came to a little inn. Off to one side a few tables had been set up, bordered by a kitchen garden and a small orchard. The taproom was floored with tiles and smelled of spilled wine, fresh bread, and coffee.

"The girl who waited on me had bare feet. She laid a tablecloth and put down a coffeepot, a cup, a plate, and bread and honey. What luxury! I hadn't seen anything like it since Paris.

"Outside, behind the dusty hedge, the shattered world moved by—here in this privileged spot beneath the trees, there was peace, the buzzing of bees, the trembling golden light of late summer. I drank it all in as a camel stores up water for a trek through the desert. I closed my eyes and basked in the light and drank.

CHAPTER 13

"There was a gendarme standing near the station. I turned back. I doubted that my disappearance could have been noticed so soon, but still it seemed advisable to keep away from the railroad for the present. As long as an internee is safe behind the barbed wire, no one gives him a thought, but the moment he escapes, he becomes hugely important. In camp a crust of bread is too good for him; to catch him when he runs away, no expense is spared. Whole companies are mobilized.

"I hitched a ride in a truck. The driver cursed the war, the Germans, the French government, the American government, and God; but he shared his lunch with me before letting me off. I walked about an hour and finally reached the next railroad station. I had learned not to arouse suspicion by trying to be inconspicuous. I walked right in and asked for a first-class ticket to the next town. The ticket seller hesitated. Fear-ing that he was going to ask for my papers, I bawled him out for being so slow. Puzzled and intimidated, he gave me my ticket. I went to a café and waited for the train. It was an hour late, but at least it was running.

"It took me three days to get to Helen's camp. Once, a gendarme stopped me, but I shouted at him in German and brandished Schwarz's passport. He was scared stiff and only too glad when I left it at that. Austria was part of Germany; an Austrian passport was as good as the Gestapo's visiting card. It was amazing how much that dead man's passport, a piece of paper with some printing on it, could accomplish. Much more than any man.

"To reach Helen's camp you had to climb a mountain; first there was a heath full of heather and gorse and rosemary, then a forest. It was late afternoon when I got there. The camp had the usual barbed-wire fence, but it didn't seem as dismal as Le Vernet, probably because it was a women's camp. I could look in from the woods and see women in colored dresses and bright headcloths or turbans. The atmosphere seemed almost carefree.

"That deflated me. I had expected a place of utter gloom, which I would invade like a Don Quixote or a St. George. As it was, there seemed to be no need for me. If Helen was in such a nice place, she'd have forgotten me long ago.

"I remained hidden, trying to get the lay of the land. At nightfall a woman approached the fence. Others joined her. Soon there was a whole group of them. They stood still, hardly speaking to one another. They peered through the wire with unseeing eyes. What they wanted to see was not there— freedom. The sky turned violet, the shadows crept up from the valley, here and there one could see screened lights. The women became shadows that had lost their colors and even their shapes. Pale, formless faces hovered in an uneven row over the flat black silhouettes behind the wire. Then the ranks thinned; one after another the women went back into the camp. The hour of despair had passed. That was their name for it, as I later found out.

"Only one woman was still standing by the fence. I approached cautiously. 'Don't be afraid,' I said in French.

" 'Afraid?' she asked after a time. 'Of what?'

" 'I'd like to ask a favor of you.'

" 'You can save your breath, you swine,' she answered. 'Isn't there anything else in your rotten bones?'

"I gaped at her. 'What do you mean?'

" 'Don't pretend to be dumber than you are. You're nothing but a lot of pigs. Haven't you any women in your village? Why do you have to hang around here?'

"At last I understood. 'You've got me wrong,' I said. 'I've got to speak to a woman who's here in the camp.'

" 'That's what you all want. Why one? Why not two? Or the whole lot?'

" 'Listen to me!' I said. 'My wife is here. I've got to speak to her.'

" 'You, too?' the women laughed. She didn't seem angry, only tired. 'That's a new dodge. Every week you fellows think up something new.'

" 'I've never been here before.'

" 'You've learned fast. Go to hell.'

" 'Won't you listen to me,' I said in German. 'I just want you to tell a woman in the camp that I'm here. I'm a German. I was in a camp myself. In Le Vernet.'

" 'That's a good one,' said the woman calmly. 'He knows German, too. Damned Alsatian! I hope you die of syphilis. You and your damn friends that line up here every night with your merchandise. I wish you'd get cancer in your merchandise. Haven't you any feelings, you damn pigs? Don't you know what you're doing? Leave us alone. Leave us alone! You've locked us up. Isn't that enough? Leave us alone!' In the end she was screaming.

"I heard others coming and jumped back from the fence.

I spent the night in the woods. I didn't know where to go. I lay among the trees. The light faded and the moon rose over a countryside pale as white gold and already swathed in the cool mists of autumn. In the morning I went back down the mountain and managed to exchange my suit for a set of mechanic's overalls.

"I returned to the camp. At the sentry post I said I had come to check the electric wiring. My French stood the test; they let me in without any questions. Who would want to go into an internment camp?

"Cautiously I explored the streets of the camp. The barracks were like big crates, partitioned with curtains. Two stories. There was a corridor down the middle with curtains on both sides. Many of the curtains were open; you could look in and see how the cubbyholes were furnished. Most contained only the barest essentials, but some of the occupants had achieved a pathetic personal note with a piece of cloth, a photograph, or a postcard or two. I strolled through the half-dark barracks. The women stopped working and looked at me. 'News?' one of them asked me.

" 'Yes—for somebody called Helen. Helen Baumann.'

"The woman reflected. Another woman came up. 'Isn't that the Nazi bitch that works in the store? The one that whores around with the doctor?'

" 'She's not a Nazi,' I said.

" 'Neither is the one in the store,' said the first woman. 'I think her name is Helen.'

" 'Are there Nazis here?' I asked.

" 'Of course. It's all mixed up. Where are the Germans now?'

" 'I haven't seen any.'

" 'A military commission is supposed to be on its way. Have you heard anything about it?'

" 'No.'

" 'They're supposed to be coming to let the Nazis out. But

I've heard the Gestapo is coming, too. Do you know anything about it?'

" 'No.'

" 'They say the Germans aren't going to bother with the Unoccupied Zone.'

" 'That sounds just like them.'

" 'You haven't heard anything?'

" 'Just rumors.'

" 'From whom is the news for Helen Baumann?'

"I hesitated. 'From her husband. He's free.'

"The second woman laughed. 'He's got a surprise coming to him.'

" 'Can I go to the store?' I asked.

" 'Why not? You're French, aren't you?'

" 'Alsatian.'

" 'Are you afraid?' asked the second woman. 'Why? You got something to hide?'

" 'Who hasn't nowadays?'

" 'You can say that again,' said the first woman. The second said nothing. She looked at me as if I were a spy. She gave off a cloud of perfume—lily of the valley.

" 'Thank you,' I said. 'Where is the store?'

"The first woman told me the way. I passed through the half-darkness of the barracks as though running the gauntlet. At both sides faces appeared and inquiring eyes. I felt as if I had dropped in on a colony of Amazons. Then I was out in the street again, surrounded by sunlight and the tired smell of captivity that covers every camp like a gray glaze.

"I felt as if I had gone blind. I had never given Helen's fidelity or infidelity a thought. The question was beside the point, insignificant. Too much had happened; the only thing that mattered was to stay alive. Even if such a thought had come to me at Le Vernet, it would have been an abstraction, an idea that I myself had invented, wiped away, and taken up again.

"But now I was among her companions. I had seen them by the fence the night before, and now I saw them again, these starved women, who had been alone for months. They were women in spite of their captivity; in fact it made them all the more aware of their womanhood. It was all they had.

"I went to the store. A pale, red-haired woman was standing at a counter, selling what food there was to a group of inmates. 'What do you want?' she asked. I closed my eyes and motioned with my head. Then I stepped aside. She made a quick count of her customers. 'I'll be through in five minutes,' she whispered. 'Good or bad?'

"I understood that she meant good or bad news. I shrugged my shoulders. 'Good,' I said, and went outside.

"A little while later the woman came out and motioned to me. 'We have to be careful,' she said. 'Whom have you news for?'

" 'Helen Baumann. Is she here?'

" 'Why?'

"I said nothing. I saw the freckles on her nose and her uneasy eyes. 'Does she work in the store?' I asked.

" 'What do you want?' the woman asked back. 'Information? For whom? You're an electrician?'

" 'For her husband.'

" 'Not so long ago,' she said bitterly, 'a man asked the same question about another woman. Three days later someone came for her. She promised to let us know how things went. We never heard from her. You're no electrician.'

" 'I'm her husband,' I said.

" 'And I'm Greta Garbo,' said the woman.

" 'Why else would I be asking about her?'

" 'A lot of people have come around asking questions about Helen Baumann,' said the woman. 'Weird people. Do you want to know the truth? Helen Baumann is dead. She died and was buried two weeks ago. That's the truth. I thought you had news from outside.'

163

" 'She's dead?'

" 'Yes. And now leave me alone.'

" 'She's not dead,' I said. 'That's not what they say in the barracks.'

" 'They talk a lot of nonsense in the barracks.'

"I stared at the red-haired woman. 'Could you give her a letter? I'll be going, but I'd like to leave you a letter.'

" 'What for?'

" 'Why not? A letter can't hurt anybody.'

" 'No?' asked the woman. 'Were you born yesterday or the day before?'

" 'I don't know. I've grown in fits and starts. Can you sell me something to write a letter with?'

" 'You'll find paper and pencil on the desk over there,' she said. 'But what's the good of writing to a dead woman?'

" 'It's the latest style.'

"I took a sheet of paper and wrote: 'Helen, I am here. Out by the fence. Tonight. I'll be waiting.'

"I didn't seal the letter. 'Will you give it to her?' I asked the woman.

" 'There's a lot of lunatics in the world nowadays.'

" 'Yes or no?'

"I held the letter out to her, and she read it. 'Yes or no?' I repeated.

" 'No,' she said.

"I laid the letter on the table. 'At least don't destroy it,' I said.

"She made no reply. 'I'll come back and kill you if you prevent this letter from reaching my wife,' I said.

" 'Is that all?' the woman asked, and stared at me out of flat green eyes in a worn face.

"I shook my head and went to the door. 'She's not here?' I asked, turning around again.

"The woman stared and said nothing. 'I'll be in camp for another ten minutes,' I said. 'I'll come back and ask again.'

164

"I went down the camp street. I didn't believe her; I decided to wait a little while and go back to the store for another look around. But all at once I felt that my invisible protective cloak was gone—suddenly I was enormous and very conspicuous. I'd have to hide.

"I stepped into a door at random. 'What do you want?' a woman asked.

" 'I've been sent to check the wiring,' said someone beside me who was myself. 'Is anything out of order?'

" 'Not any more than usual.'

"The woman had on a white smock. 'Is this the hospital?' I asked.

" 'Yes. Is that where you were supposed to go?'

" 'My boss sent me up from town. To check the circuits.'

" 'Go ahead and check,' said the woman.

"A man in uniform came in. 'What's going on?'

"The woman in the white smock explained. I looked at the man. It seemed to me that I knew him from somewhere. 'Electricity?' he said. 'Medicine and vitamins would be a damn sight more useful.'

"He tossed his cap on the table and left the room.

" 'Everything's all right in here,' I said to the woman in white. 'Who was that?'

" 'The doctor, of course. The rest of them don't give a damn about anything.'

" 'Have you a lot of patients?'

" 'Plenty.'

" 'And deaths?'

"She looked at me. 'Why do you ask?'

" 'Just like that,' I replied. 'Why is everybody so suspicious around here?'

" 'Just like that,' the woman repeated. 'Pure caprice, you innocent angel with a home and a passport! No, there hasn't been a death in four weeks. But there were quite a few before that.'

165

"Four weeks before, I had received a letter from Helen. So she must still be here. 'Thank you,' I said.

" 'Don't thank me,' the woman said. 'Thank God that your parents gave you a country you can love, even if it has fallen on hard times—even if it persecutes the unfortunate and hands them over to the wolves—the same wolves that are responsible for all your trouble. Get along now. Go on making light. If you could only make a little light in some people's heads!'

" 'Has a German commission been here?' I asked hurriedly.

" 'Why do you want to know that?'

" 'I've heard that one is expected.'

" 'Do you find such information particularly fascinating?'

" 'No, but I've got to warn somebody.'

" 'Whom?' asked the woman, visibly on her guard.

" 'Helen Baumann,' I said.

"The woman looked at me. 'Warn her about what?' she asked.

" 'Do you know her?'

" 'Why?'

"Again that wall of distrust—it was explained to me later. 'I am her husband,' I said.

" 'Can you prove it?'

" 'No. My papers are in a different name. But maybe you'll be convinced when I tell you that I'm not French.'

"I brought out Schwarz's passport. 'A Nazi passport,' said the woman. 'Just what I thought. Why are you doing this?'

"I lost my patience. 'To see my wife again. She's here. She wrote me so herself.'

" 'Have you got the letter?'

" 'No. I destroyed it when I escaped from Le Vernet. Why is everybody so mysterious?'

" 'That's what I'd like you to tell me.'

"The doctor came back. 'Are you needed here?' he asked the woman.

" 'No.'

" 'Then come with me. Finished?' he asked me.

" 'Not yet. I'll be back tomorrow.'

"I went back to the store. The redhead was behind the counter, selling underwear. There were two customers. I waited. Again I had the feeling that my luck was running out; I'd better be going, or I might have trouble at the gate. The guards would be changed and I'd have to explain everything all over again. I saw no sign of Helen. The woman avoided my gaze. It was clear that she was dragging things out. Then some more customers arrived, and I saw an officer passing outside the window. I left the building.

"The guards hadn't been changed. They remembered me and let me pass. I had the same feeling as at Le Vernet: that they would crawl up behind me and capture me. I broke out in a sweat.

"An old truck was coming toward me. There was no place to hide. I kept on walking, my eyes to the ground. The truck passed me by and then stopped. I resisted the temptation to run. The truck had room to turn around in, and I wouldn't have had a chance. I heard quick steps behind me. Someone cried out: 'Heigh, mechanic!'

"I turned around. A middle-aged man in uniform came up to me. 'Do you know anything about motors?'

" 'No. I'm an electrician.'

" 'Maybe it's the ignition. Take a look.'

" 'Yes, please have a look,' said the driver. I looked up. It was Helen. She stood behind the soldier, staring at me and holding her finger to her lips. She was wearing pants and a sweater and was very thin.

" 'Yes, please have a look,' she repeated, and let me pass. 'Be careful,' she whispered. 'Pretend to know what you're doing. There's nothing wrong.'

"The soldier ambled along behind us. 'Where have you come from?' she whispered.

167

"I opened the hood with a clatter. 'Escaped. How can we meet?'

"She peered into the motor beside me. 'I buy for the store. Day after tomorrow. Be in the village. First café on the left as you come in. At nine in the morning.'

" 'And meanwhile?'

" 'Is it going to be long?' the soldier asked.

"Helen took a pack of cigarettes from her pants pocket and held it out to him. 'Only a couple of minutes. It's nothing serious.'

"The soldier lit up and sat down by the side of the road. I tinkered with the engine, and Helen looked on. 'Where?' I asked her. 'In the woods? By the fence? I was there yesterday. Can you come tonight?'

"She hesitated a moment. 'All right. Tonight. But I can't make it before ten.'

" 'Why not?'

" 'Because all the others should have left by then. If I'm not there at ten, it'll be tomorrow. Be careful.'

" 'How are the gendarmes here?'

"The soldier approached. 'Not so bad,' said Helen in French. 'It'll be done in a minute.'

" 'It's an old car,' I said.

"The soldier laughed. 'The Boches have the new ones. And the ministers. Finished?'

" 'Yes,' said Helen.

" 'Lucky we met you,' said the soldier. 'All I know about cars is that they need gas.'

"He climbed in. Helen followed. She shifted into gear. Probably she had just turned off the switch. The motor ran. 'Thank you,' she said, leaning out to me. Her lips formed inaudible words. 'You're a first-class mechanic,' she said then, and drove off.

"I stood there for a few seconds in the blue oil fumes. I felt as though I had passed from extreme heat to extreme

168

cold; that is, I felt nothing. I just walked along mechanically. Then little by little I began to think, and with thought came anxiety and the recollection of what I had heard, and the twitching, gnawing torment of doubt.

"I lay in the woods and waited. The wailing wall, as Helen called the row of women staring blindly into the dusk, thinned out. Soon most of them had drifted inside the camp. It grew darker. I stared at the fence posts. They turned to shadows, and then in among them a new dark shadow appeared.

" 'Where are you?' Helen whispered.

" 'Here.'

"I groped my way to her. 'Can you come out?' I asked.

" 'Later, when they've all gone. Wait.'

"I crept back into the woods, just far enough not to be seen if someone should direct a flashlight at the woods. I lay on the ground, breathing in the heady smell of dead leaves. A light breeze came up; all around me there was a rustling as though a thousand spies were crawling toward me. My eyes grew accustomed to the darkness; I saw Helen's shadow and above it, vaguely, her pale face. I couldn't make out her features. She hung on the barbed wire like a black plant with a white flower. Then she seemed like a dark nameless figure out of the dark past. Her face—because I couldn't distinguish the features—became the face of all the sufferers in the world. A little farther on I made out a second woman, who was standing just like Helen, and then a third and a fourth—they stood there like a row of caryatids supporting a canopy of grief and hope.

"The sight was almost intolerable, and I looked away. When I looked again, the other three had silently disappeared, and I saw that Helen had bent down and was tugging at the barbed wire. 'Hold it apart,' she said.

"I stepped on the lowest strand and lifted the next one.

" 'Wait,' Helen whispered.

" 'Where are the others?' I asked.

" 'They've gone back. One is a Nazi; that's why I couldn't come through sooner. She would have given me away. She's the one who was crying.'

"Helen took her blouse and skirt off and handed them to me through the wire. 'I mustn't tear them,' she said. 'They are the only ones I have.'

"I was reminded of a poor family: it's all right if the children bark their knees as long as they don't tear their stockings, because wounds heal, whereas stockings have to be bought.

"I felt her clothes in my hands. Helen bent down and crawled carefully between the strands of wire. She scratched her shoulder. The blood was like a thin black snake on her skin. She stood up. 'Do you think we can escape?' I asked.

" 'Where to ?'

"I didn't know. 'To Spain,' I said. 'To Africa.'

" 'Come,' said Helen. 'Come and we'll talk about it. It's impossible to get away from here without papers. That's why they're not very careful.'

"She went into the woods ahead of me. She was almost naked—and mysterious and very beautiful, with only a faint hint of the Helen who had been my wife in Paris, barely enough for a sweet, painful recognition that made my skin tingle with expectancy. The woman who had stepped out of the frieze of caryatids was almost nameless, still immersed in nine months of a strange life that outweighed twenty years of normal existence."

CHAPTER 14

The bar owner came over to us. "The fat one is magnificent," he informed us with dignity. "French. Knows all the tricks. I recommend her highly. Our women have fire, but they're in too much of a hurry." He smacked his lips. "I'll be going now. Nothing better than a French girl to clean the blood. They know about life. You don't have to lie to them as much as to our women. I hope you get home all right, gentlemen. Don't take Lolita or Juana. They're neither of them any good, and Lolita steals if you don't keep your eyes open."

He left us. As he opened the door, the morning leapt in with its sounds and light. "We'd better be going, too," I said.

"I've almost finished," said Schwarz, "and we still have some wine." He ordered wine and coffee for the three girls, to make them leave us alone.

"We didn't talk much that night," he went on. "I spread out my jacket on the ground, and when it grew cooler, we covered ourselves with Helen's skirt and blouse and my sweater. Helen fell asleep and woke up again; once when I was half asleep, it seemed to me that she was crying. A moment later she was wildly affectionate. There was something new, unfamiliar, in the way she caressed me. I asked her no questions and made no mention of what I had heard in the camp. I loved her very much, but felt removed from her in some strange, inexplicable way. My tenderness was mingled with a sadness that only made it stronger. We clung to one another at the edge of another world. There was no going back and no destination, just flight, flight together, and despair—a silent, otherworldly despair that drank up our tears of happiness and the unshed shadow tears of a knowledge that there is only passing and no return or arrival at any destination.

" 'Couldn't we escape?' I asked again, before Helen slipped back through the barbed wire.

"She answered only after reaching the other side. 'I can't,' she whispered. 'I can't. Others would be punished. Come back. Come back tomorrow night. Can you come tomorrow night?'

" 'If I'm not caught first.'

"She stared at me. 'What has become of our life?' she said. 'What have we done that our life should come to this?'

"I passed her her blouse and skirt. 'Are these your best things?' I asked.

"She nodded.

" 'Thank you for wearing them,' I said. 'I'll make it tomorrow night. I'm sure. I'll hide in the woods.'

" 'You'll have to eat. Have you got anything?'

" 'Yes, of course. And maybe I'll find berries in the woods. Or mushrooms or nuts.'

" 'Can you hold out until tomorrow night? Then I'll bring you some food.'

" 'Of course. It's almost morning now.'

" 'Don't eat any mushrooms. You don't know them. I'll

172

bring you plenty to eat.' She put on her skirt. It was wide and light blue, with white flowers. She threw it around her and buttoned it as though girding herself for a battle. 'I love you,' she said desperately. 'I love you much more than you can ever know. Don't forget that. Never!'

"She said that almost every time she left me. In those days we were everybody's game. The French gendarmes hunted us down in a misdirected passion for law and order. The Gestapo tried to poke its nose into the camps, although there was said to be an agreement to the contrary with the Pétain government. You never knew who might pick you up, and every morning we said good-by as if for the last time.

"Helen brought me bread and fruit and an occasional piece of sausage or cheese. I was afraid to stay in the village. Not far from the camp I came across the ruins of an old monastery, and there I set up housekeeping. In the daytime I slept or read the books and papers that Helen brought me, or watched the road from a thicket where I could not be seen. Helen also brought me the news and rumors: the Germans were coming steadily closer and not letting any agreements interfere with their activities.

"Even so, our life was almost idyllic. Fear gripped me from time to time, but the habit of living from hour to hour pulled me through. The weather was good; the sky at night was full of stars. Helen had brought a piece of tent cloth. We spread it out amid the ruins of the monastery and filled it with dry leaves. 'How do you manage to get out?' I asked her once. 'And so often?'

" 'I have a special job,' she said after a while, 'and a certain amount of pull. They even let me go to the village. I was coming back when you saw me the other day.'

" 'Is that where you get the food?'

" 'No. In the camp store. We can buy things if we have money and there's anything to buy.'

" 'Aren't you afraid of being seen here and reported?'

"She smiled. 'Only for you. Not for myself. What can happen to me? I'm a prisoner already.'

"The next night she did not appear. The wailing wall disintegrated, I crept up to the fence, the barracks lay black in the faint light. I waited, but she did not come. All night I heard the women on their way to the latrines, I heard sighing and moaning, and suddenly I saw the blackout lights of cars on the road. I spent the day in the woods. I was worried; something must have happened. For a while I thought of what I had heard in the camp, and, by a strange reversal, it was a comfort to me. Anything was better than that Helen should be sick, shipped out, or dead—three possibilities that merged in my mind. Our life was so hopeless, only one thing mattered: to stay together and try, when the time came, to escape to a quiet harbor. One day perhaps we'd be able to forget all this.

"But it can't be done," said Schwarz. "Not with all the love, compassion, kindness, and tenderness in the world. I knew that, but I didn't care. I lay in the woods and stared at the dead leaves, red and yellow and brown, as they fell from the branches, and my one thought was: Let her live! Let her live, oh God, and I'll never ask her anything. The life of a human being is so much more than all the situations it can get mixed up in; let her live, just live, without me if need be, but let her live.

"Helen didn't come the next night either. But I saw two cars on the road to the camp. I crept around in a wide arc and watched the road. I distinguished uniforms. Whether SS or Army I couldn't make out, but they were definitely German. It was an agonizing night. The cars arrived at about nine and didn't leave until after one. It must be the Gestapo, I thought, or they wouldn't have come at night. When they left, I couldn't see whether anyone from the camp was being taken along. I roamed around all night, along the fence and on the road. In the morning I thought of posing as an electrician again, but then I saw that the guard had been doubled and that a civilian was sitting by the gate with lists.

"The day seemed endless. As I passed the barbed wire for the hundredth time, I caught sight of a package wrapped in newspaper a few paces from the fence on my side. I picked it up. It contained a piece of bread, two apples, and an unsigned note saying: 'Tonight.' Helen must have tossed it over between my rounds. I felt so weak that I ate the bread on my knees. Then I went to my hiding place and slept. It was afternoon when I awoke. It was a clear day; the golden light was like wine. The colors of the leaves had deepened. In the rays of the warm afternoon sun that fell into my clearing, the beeches and lindens stood there yellow and brown, as if an invisible painter had transformed them during my sleep into torches, motionless in a motionless light. Not a leaf stirred."

Schwarz broke off. "Please don't be impatient if I seem to be giving you superfluous descriptions of nature. In all that time nature was as important to us as it is to animals. Nature was what never turned us away. It demanded no passport, no certificate of Aryanism. Nature gave and took but she was impersonal, and that was like a balm. That afternoon I lay still for a long while. I was afraid I might overflow like a pitcher brimful of water. Then, in the perfect stillness, hundreds of leaves detached themselves from their branches and came floating down, as though in answer to a mysterious command. They glided serenely through the clear air, and some of them fell on me. In that moment I saw the freedom, the boundless consolation of death. I made no decision, but I knew that I had the power to end my life if Helen should die, that I wouldn't have to stay behind alone. And I knew that this power is a boon, a compensation, for those who love too much, whose love is more than human. I knew all that without thinking, and once I knew it, it was somehow, in some remote way, no longer wholly necessary for me to die.

"Helen was not in the wailing wall. She appeared only after the others had gone. She had on shorts and a blouse. She handed me a bottle of wine and a package through the wire. She looked very young in her unaccustomed attire. 'The cork has been pulled,' she said. 'Here, I have a cup.'

"She slipped deftly between the wires. 'You must be almost starved. I found something in the store that I hadn't seen since Paris.'

" 'Cologne,' I said. She smelled of it, fresh in the fresh night.

"She shook her head. I saw that her hair had been cut; it was shorter than before. 'What on earth has been happening?' I asked, suddenly furious. 'Here I thought they'd taken you away or you were dying, and you come out looking as if you'd been to the beauty parlor. Have you had a manicure, too?'

" 'I did that myself.' She showed me her hands and laughed. 'Let's drink the wine.'

" 'What happened? Was the Gestapo there?'

" 'No. An Army commission. But they had two Gestapo men with them.'

" 'Did they take anyone away?'

" 'No,' she said. 'Give me a drink.'

"I saw that she was very upset. Her hands were hot, and her skin was so dry I expected it to crackle. 'They came,' she said, 'to draw up a list of the Nazis in the camp. They'll be sent back to Germany.'

" 'Are there many?'

" 'Plenty. We didn't think there were so many. Some didn't admit it. There was one I knew—all of a sudden she stepped forward and said she belonged to the party, that she had obtained important information, that she wanted to go back to the fatherland, that she had been treated disgustingly— couldn't they take her with them right away? I knew her well. Too well. She knows . . .'

176

"Helen drank quickly and gave me the cup. 'What does she know?' I asked.

" 'I don't remember exactly. There were so many nights when we talked and talked. She knows who I am. . . .' She raised her head. 'I'm never going back! Never! I'll kill myself if they try to make me.'

" 'You won't kill yourself,' I said, 'and they won't take you back. Heaven knows where Georg is; he doesn't know everything. And why should this woman want to tell them about you? What good can it do her?'

" 'Promise you won't let them take me back.'

" 'I promise,' I said. She was so frantic I couldn't help myself—of course there was nothing I could do, but I had to talk like God Almighty.

" 'I love you,' she said in her hoarse, agitated voice. 'I love you, and, whatever happens, you've got to believe me.'

" 'I believe you,' I said, believing and not believing.

"She leaned back exhausted. 'We've got to get out of here,' I said. 'This very night.'

" 'Where to? Have you a passport?'

" 'Yes. Someone who worked in the office where the internees' papers were kept returned it to me. Who has yours?'

"She did not reply. She stared into space for a while. 'There's a Jewish family here,' she said then. 'Husband, wife, and child. They just got here a few days ago. The child is sick. They stepped forward with the Nazis. They want to go back to Germany. Weren't they Jews? the captain asked them. The husband answered that they were Germans and wanted to go home. The captain wanted to say something else, but the Gestapo men were there. "You really want to go back?" he repeated.

" ' "Put them on the list, Captain," said one of the Gestapo men laughing. "If you're really so homesick, we'll do you the favor." Their names were taken. It's no use talking to them. They say they can't go on; they say the child is very sick, that

177

all the Jews here will be rounded up anyway, so they may as well come forward now. They say we are trapped here and they may as well go voluntarily. They act like deaf mules. Would you talk to them?'

" 'I? What can I say?'

" 'You've been there. You've been in a German camp. You went back. And escaped again.'

" 'Where would I speak to them?'

" 'Here. I'll get the husband. I know where he is. We'll be right back. I told him about you. We can still save him.'

"A few minutes later she reappeared with a sickly-looking man who refused to crawl through the barbed wire. He stood across from me on the camp side, and listened to me. A little later his wife came out. She was very pale and didn't say a word. They had been picked up about ten days before. They had been in different camps; they had escaped, and by a miracle they had found each other. They had written their names on walls, on sidewalks, wherever they went."

Schwarz looked at me. "You've heard of the Via Dolorosa?"

"Who hasn't? It reaches from Belgium to the Pyrenees."

The Via Dolorosa dated back to the first days of the war. But the great exodus began after the Germans had overrun Belgium and broken through the Maginot Line. First came automobiles piled high with household goods and bedding, later vehicles of every kind, horse carts, handcarts, baby carriages, and, as time went on, endless streams of people on foot, all headed south in the lovely summer weather, pursued by dive bombers. And the refugees joined the general exodus. Members of separated families took to writing names and messages in coal, chalk, paint, or anything that was handy on walls, house fronts, road markers. It got to be something like a roadside gazette. In addition, the refugees who had already been on the run for years and were hiding from the police had developed a kind of underground railway, a network of addresses extending from Nice to Naples and from Paris to

Zurich: reliable friends on whom they could count for news, information, and advice, and who could put you up for a night or two when necessary. Thanks to the gazette and this secret network, the Jew had found his wife and child, who would otherwise have been lost like the proverbial needle in the haystack.

"They were afraid," Schwarz went on, "that if they stayed in the camp they would be separated again. It was a women's camp. They had been brought in together, but had already been informed that the husband would soon be removed to a men's camp. 'We couldn't bear it,' he said. He had thought the whole thing over and was convinced that there was nothing else to do. Escape was impossible; they had tried and had nearly starved. Now the child was sick and the mother completely exhausted—and he himself was at the end of his strength. 'The rest of you,' he said, 'are no better off than cattle in a slaughterhouse yard. They'll come and get you whenever they feel like it. Why,' he asked finally, 'couldn't the French have let us go when there was still time?' He was a frail gentle man with a thin face and a little dark mustache.

"No one knew the answer. They didn't want us, but they wouldn't let us go—but who can worry about an absurdity more or less when a whole nation has collapsed? In any case those who might have done something about it hardly gave it a thought.

"On the following afternoon two trucks came driving up the road. At the same moment I saw the barbed wire come to life. A dozen or more women helped each other crawl through and dashed into the woods. I kept hidden until I caught sight of Helen. 'We've received a warning from the Préfecture,' she said. 'The Germans have come for the ones who want to go back. The French authorities don't know what else the Germans are going to do, so they've given us permission to hide in the woods until the Germans are gone.'

"It was the first time I had seen her by daylight except for the moment on the road. Her long legs and her face were tanned, but she was very thin. Her eyes were too big and too bright, and her face seemed haggard. 'You've been giving me your food and you yourself are starving,' I said.

" 'I have plenty to eat,' she said. 'That's all taken care of. Here—' she put her hand in her pocket—'there's even a piece of chocolate. Yesterday we were able to buy *pâté de foie gras* and sardines. But no bread.'

" 'Is the man I spoke to going?' I asked.

" 'Yes.'

"Suddenly Helen's whole face trembled. 'I'll never go back,' she said. 'Never. You've promised. I don't want them to catch me.'

" 'They won't catch you.'

"The cars drove off again an hour later. The women were singing and the sound came to us on the breeze: *Deutschland, Deutschland über alles.*

"That night I gave Helen half the poison I had brought from Le Vernet.

"Next day she knew that Georg had found out where she was. 'Who told you?' I asked.

" 'Someone who knows.'

" 'Who?'

" 'The camp doctor.'

" 'How does he know?'

" 'From the camp commander. There had been inquiries.'

" 'Did the doctor tell you what to do?'

" 'He can hide me a few days in the camp hospital. Not very long.'

" 'Then you'll have to leave. Who was it who warned those who were in danger to hide in the woods?'

" 'The Prefect.'

" 'Good,' I said. 'Get your passport back and wangle a discharge from here. Maybe the doctor can help you. If not, we'll just leave. Don't breathe a word. Not to anybody. I'll try to speak to the Prefect. He seems to be human.'

" 'Don't do it. Be careful. For heaven's sake, be careful.'

"I cleaned my overalls as best I could and emerged from the woods in the morning. I fully expected to run into German patrols or French gendarmes, but I'd have to count on that from now on.

"I managed to reach the Prefect. I bluffed a gendarme and one of the clerks, passing myself off as a German technician who needed information about putting up a power line for military purposes. I'd learned from experience that sheer gall often brings results. If that gendarme had taken me for a refugee, he would have arrested me on the spot. Instead, I shouted at him. His kind reacts best to shouting.

"When I got to the Prefect, I told him the truth. His first impulse was to throw me out. Then he was amused by my impudence. He gave me a cigarette and told me to go to hell, he had seen nothing and heard nothing. Ten minutes later, he told me there was nothing he could do, because the Germans probably had lists and would hold him responsible if anyone was missing. He didn't want to end his days in a German concentration camp.

" *'Monsieur le Préfet,'* I said. 'I know you have protected prisoners. And I know that you have to obey orders. But you and I also know that France is in a state of chaos, that today's orders can be tomorrow's disgrace, and that if confusion degenerates into senseless cruelty, it will be hard to find excuses later on. Why should you, against your will, hold innocent people in a barbed-wire cage, to be sent to the gas chambers and torture camps? It's conceivable that while France was still defending itself there was some justification for shutting up foreigners in internment camps, regardless of whether they were for or against the enemy. But the war's over now. A few days ago the victors took back their people; all you have left in the camps is victims, who live in terror of being dragged off to their death. I ought to ask you to intercede for them all—but I've come to plead for only one. If you are afraid of lists, put my wife down as escaped—or dead, for all I care. Say she committed suicide, if you like, that clears you of all responsibility.'

"He looked at me for a long moment. 'Come back tomorrow,' he said then.

"I didn't budge. 'By tomorrow somebody may have arrested me,' I said. 'Do it today.'

" 'Come back in two hours.'

" 'I'll wait outside your door,' I said. 'That's the safest place I can think of.'

"Suddenly he smiled. *'Quelle histoire d'amour!'* he said. 'You're married, and you've got to live as if you weren't. Usually it's the other way around.'

"I sighed with relief. An hour later he called me in. 'I've phoned the camp commander,' he said. 'It's true that inquiries have been made about your wife. We'll follow your suggestion and put her down as dead. That should set your mind at rest, and ours, too.'

"I nodded. All at once a strange, cold fear invaded me, a vestige of superstition. I was tempting fate. But hadn't I myself died long ago, and wasn't I living with a dead man's papers?

" 'We'll fix it up tomorrow,' said the Prefect.

" 'Do it today,' I answered. 'I spent two years in a concentration camp because I was a day late in deciding to clear out.'

"I was exhausted. He must have noticed it. My face went ashen; I was on the point of fainting. He sent out for cognac. 'Coffee,' I said, and fell into a chair. The room revolved in gray and purple shadows. I mustn't fall, I thought, when the buzzing in my ears began. Helen is free. We've got to get out of here.

"A face and a voice mingled with the flitting and the buzzing. The voice was shouting, indistinctly at first, then loud

182

and plain. I tried to follow the voice and the face, and then I heard: 'Do you think this is fun for me, *merde alors?* What the devil is all this? I'm not a jailer. I'm a decent, charitable man; to hell with them all—let them go, the whole lot of them!'

"Then I lost track of the voice, and I'm not sure whether it had really shouted like that or had only rung so loud in my ears. The coffee came; I staggered out and sat on a bench. A little while later a clerk came out and told me to wait a few minutes more—I had had no intention of leaving.

"Then the Prefect came out and told me everything was arranged. My fainting fit, it seemed to me, had done much more good than all my words. 'Do you feel better?' the Prefect asked. 'You don't have to be afraid of me. I'm just a little French provincial prefect.'

" 'That's more than God,' I said happily. 'All God gave me was a general residence permit for the earth, and it's perfectly useless. What I really need is a residence permit for this district, and no one can give me that but you, *Monsieur le Préfet.*'

"He laughed. 'But if they look for you, this is where you'll be most in danger.'

" 'If they're looking for me, Marseille is worse than here. That's where they'll expect to find me, not here. Give us a permit for one week. By that time we'll have started across the Red Sea.'

" 'The Red Sea?'

" 'That's a refugee expression. We live like the Jews on their way out of Egypt. Behind us the German Army and the Gestapo, on both sides the sea of French and Spanish police, and ahead of us the Promised Land of Portugal with the Port of Lisbon, the gateway to the still more Promised Land of America.'

" 'Have you got American visas?'

" 'We'll get them.'

" 'You seem to believe in miracles.'

" 'I have no choice. And hasn't one happened today?' "

Schwarz smiled at me. "It's amazing how calculating you can be when you're desperate. I knew exactly why I had said those last words and why I had flattered the Prefect by comparing him to God. I had to get a short residence permit out of him. When you're entirely dependent on another man, you get to be a psychologist, even if you're so frightened you can hardly breathe, and perhaps for that very reason. Fear and caution are separate functions, the one doesn't interfere with the other. Your fear is genuine, your misery is genuine, and so is your calculation. All have the same aim: salvation."

Schwarz had grown perceptibly calmer. "I'll be finished soon," he said. "We actually did get residence permits for a week. I was standing at the camp gate, waiting for Helen. It was late in the afternoon. A light rain was falling. The doctor was with her. I saw her speaking with him a moment before she saw me. She spoke with animation, her face showed more emotion than usual; I felt like an unseen passer-by, looking into a room from the street. Then she caught sight of me.

" 'Your wife is very ill,' the doctor said to me.

" 'That's right,' said Helen laughing. 'I'm being discharged so I can go to a hospital to die. That was the agreement.'

" 'I am speaking seriously.' The doctor's tone was hostile. 'Your wife really should be in a hospital.'

" 'Why wasn't she sent to one long ago?' I asked.

" 'What is all this?' said Helen. 'I'm not sick and I'm not going to any hospital.'

" 'Can you put her into a hospital where she would be safe?' I asked the doctor.

" 'No,' he replied after a pause.

"Helen laughed again. 'Of course not. What an absurd discussion! *Adieu,* Jean.'

"She started down the road ahead of me. I wanted to ask the doctor what was wrong with her, but I couldn't. He

184

stared at me, then turned quickly and went back to the camp. I followed Helen.

" 'Have you got your passport?' I asked.

"She nodded. 'Give me your bag,' I said.

" 'There isn't much in it.'

" 'Give it to me anyway.'

" 'I still have the evening dress you bought me in Paris.'

"We trudged on. 'Are you sick?' I asked her.

" 'If I were really sick, I'd be flat on my back, wouldn't I? I'd have a fever. I'm not sick. He's lying. He wanted me to stay. Look at me. Do I look sick?'

"She stood still.

" 'Yes,' I said.

" 'Don't be sad,' she said.

" 'I'm not sad.'

"I knew now that she was sick, and I knew that she would never admit it. 'Would it help you to be in a hospital?' I asked.

" 'No,' she said. 'Not in the least. You've got to believe me. If I were sick and a hospital could help me, I'd try to get into one. Believe me.'

" 'I believe you.'

"What could I have done? Suddenly I was hopelessly discouraged. 'Maybe you'd rather have stayed in the camp,' I said finally.

" 'I'd have killed myself if you hadn't come.'

"We walked on. It began to rain harder. The spray blew round us like a gray veil. 'We'll try to get to Marseille,' I said. 'And then to Lisbon and America.'

"There are good doctors in America, I thought. And hospitals where no one comes to arrest you. And maybe they will let me work. 'We'll forget Europe like a bad dream,' I said.

"Helen did not answer.

CHAPTER 15

"That was the beginning of our odyssey," said Schwarz. "The march through the desert and the Red Sea. I guess you know all about it."

I nodded. "Bordeaux. The Pyrenees. You feel out the border crossings. Retreat to Marseille. The battle to move sluggish hearts as the barbarian hordes come closer. Through it all the lunacy of bureaucracy gone wild. No residence permit, but no exit permit either. They won't let you stay and they won't let you leave. Finally you get your exit permit, but your Spanish transit visa has meanwhile expired. You can't get another unless you have a Portuguese visa, and that's contingent on something else again. Which means that you have to start all over again—your days are spent waiting outside the consulates, those vestibules of heaven and hell! A vicious circle of madness!"

"First we entered a zone of calm," said Schwarz. "That evening Helen had a crying jag. I had found a room in an out-of-the-way hotel. For the first time in months we were like a real married pair with our own room, together and alone—that was what brought on her fit of tears. Afterward we sat silent in the little garden. It was very cool, but we didn't feel like going to bed. We drank a bottle of wine and looked out at the road leading to the camp. A feeling of gratitude surged up in me, so deep and intense that it was almost painful. That night it crowded out everything else, even my fears for Helen's health. After her jag she seemed detached and very calm, like a landscape after the rain, and as lovely as certain faces on old cameos. I'm sure you understand," said Schwarz. "In an existence like ours, sickness has a different meaning. It means that you've got to stop running."

"I know," I said bitterly.

"The following evening we saw the blacked-out lights of a car crawling up the road to the camp. Helen became uneasy. All day we had scarcely stirred from our room. To have a bed and a room of our own was something so wonderful we didn't want to lose a minute of it. Both of us also realized how exhausted we were, and I would have been glad not to stir from that hotel for weeks. But Helen wanted to leave. She couldn't bear the sight of that road leading to the camp. She was afraid that the Gestapo would still be looking for her.

"We packed up our few belongings. It made sense to get started while we still had a residence permit for our district; if we were picked up somewhere else, the worst they could do was send us back; they wouldn't lock us up—or so we hoped.

"My idea was to head for Bordeaux; but on the road we heard that it was too late. A little Citroën four-seater picked us up, and the driver advised us to hide somewhere else. He told us of a small château not far from where he was going. He knew it was empty; perhaps we could camp there for the night.

"We had little choice. Late in the afternoon the driver dropped us off. Ahead of us in the gray light lay the little château, actually more of a country house. The windows were dark; there were no curtains. I mounted the stone steps and tried the door. It was unlocked; the lock seemed to have been forced. My steps resounded in the half-dark vestibule. I shouted, and the only answer was a broken echo. The rooms were bare. Everything removable had been removed. But it was still a fine eighteenth-century interior, with its paneled walls, nobly proportioned windows, beautiful ceilings, and graceful staircases.

"We slowly explored the house. No one answered our cries. I looked for light switches; there were none. There was no electricity; the château remained as it was built. The small dining room was done in gilt and white; the first bedroom we entered was gilt and light green. Not a stick of furniture; the owners must have removed it for safekeeping.

"In the attic room we found a chest containing masks, some cheap gaudy costumes, left over from a party, no doubt, and a few packages of candles. Better still, we found an iron bedstead and a mattress. In the kitchen we found some bread, a few cans of sardines, a bunch of garlic, a half-full jar of honey, and in the cellar a few pounds of potatoes, a few bottles of wine, and a wood pile. In short, fairyland.

"There was a fireplace in almost every room. We picked one of the bedrooms to settle in and curtained the windows with some of the costumes. I went out again and found the garden, a patch of vegetables and some fruit trees. There were still some apples and pears on the trees. I picked them and brought them in.

"When it was so dark that smoke would no longer be visible I made a fire in the fireplace and we began to eat. The atmosphere was spectral, enchanted. The firelight glowed on the beautiful paneling, and our shadows played over the walls like spirits from a happy world.

"The roof warmed up, and Helen took off her clothes to

dry them. She took out her Paris evening dress and put it on. I opened a bottle of wine. We had no glasses and drank out of the bottle. Later Helen changed clothes again. In a domino and a half-mask she had taken from the chest, she flitted up and down the dark stairs. She called from above and below, and her voice came echoing from all directions; I couldn't see her, I only heard her footfalls. All at once she was standing behind me in the darkness and I felt her breath on my neck. 'I thought I had lost you,' I said, and held her fast.

" 'You'll never lose me,' she whispered through the slit of her mask. 'And do you know why not? Because you've never tried to hold me, as a peasant holds his field. The most fascinating man is a bore without that quality.'

" 'I know I'm not fascinating,' I said in surprise.

"We stood on the stair landing. The bedroom door was ajar, and through the opening a flickering strip of light from the fireplace fell on the bronze ornaments of the banister and on Helen's mouth and shoulders.

" 'How would you know what you are?' she murmured. Behind the mask her eyes were fixed, fiery and whiteless, like those of a snake. 'But if you only knew how dismal all these Don Juan types are! Like a dress you can only wear once. You—you're different; you are my heart.'

"Perhaps it was our disguise that encouraged us to talk like that. Though with some reluctance, I, too, had put on a domino to let my overalls dry by the fire. The flickering firelight, the strange clothes, the *belle-époque* surroundings conspired to put unusual words in our mouths. Familiar words changed their meanings. 'Faithful' and 'unfaithful' lost their middle-class weight and intransigence, became ambivalent and interchangeable. There were so many degrees and shadings.

" 'We are dead,' Helen whispered. 'Both of us. There are no laws for dead people. You are dead with your dead passport, and I died in the hospital today. Look at our clothes.

We are like gaudy bats flitting through a dead century. It was a beautiful century, with its minuets, its grace, and its rococo heaven—but the festivities ended with the guillotine, shining and merciless in the cold morning. I wonder where our guillotine will be.'

" 'Helen,' I said. 'Don't talk like that.'

" 'It won't be anywhere,' she whispered. 'There's no guillotine for dead people. They can't cut our heads off; you can't cut the heads off light and shade. Hold me, here in this enchanted golden darkness, and perhaps some of it will stay with us, to light up the pitiful hour of our last breath.'

"A light shudder ran through me. 'Helen,' I pleaded, 'don't talk like that.'

" 'Remember me always as I am now,' she whispered. 'Who knows what will become of us. . . .'

" 'We'll go to America,' I said, 'and some day the war will be over.'

" 'I'm not complaining,' she said, her face pressed to mine. 'What have we to complain of? What would have become of us otherwise? A dull, mediocre couple, leading a dull, mediocre life in Osnabrück, with dull, mediocre emotions, and a few weeks' vacation in the summer . . .'

"I couldn't help laughing. 'That's one way to look at it.'

"She was very merry and festive that night. Holding a candle, she ran down the stairs in the little golden slippers she had bought in Paris and saved through thick and thin, and brought a fresh bottle of wine from the cellar. I waited on the landing as she rose through the darkness, pursued by a multitude of shadows, her face looking up at me in the candlelight. I was happy, if the word is applicable to a mirror that reflects a beloved face, pure and perfect against innumerable shadows.

"The fire died down. She fell asleep under a pile of costumes. It was a strange night. Later I heard the roar of planes, and the rococo mirrors began to rattle softly.

"We stayed there alone for four days. Then I went to the nearest village for provisions and heard that two ships were leaving Bordeaux. 'Haven't the Germans taken over yet?' I asked.

" 'Yes and no. It depends on who you are.'

"I talked it over with Helen. To my surprise, she wasn't too much interested. 'Ships, Helen!' I said, beside myself with excitement. 'Maybe we can get out of here. To Africa. To Lisbon. Anywhere.'

" 'Why not stay here?' she said. 'There are fruit and vegetables in the garden. I can cook as long as the wood holds out. We can get bread in the village. Is there any money left?'

" 'Some. And I still have a drawing. I can sell it in Bordeaux for the fare.'

" 'Who buys drawings nowadays?'

" 'People with money to invest.'

"She laughed. 'Then sell it and we'll stay here.'

" 'I wish we could.'

"She had fallen in love with the house. Off to one side there was a little park; behind it lay the orchard and vegetable plot. There were even a pond and a sundial. Helen loved the house, and the house seemed to love her. The setting suited her; it was a change from hotels and barracks. Our costumed life in this dwelling place of a serene past gave me an enchanted hope and sometimes even a belief in a life after death —as if this were our dress rehearsal. I, too, would have been glad to go on living like this for a hundred years.

"Nevertheless, I went on thinking about Bordeaux. It struck me as unlikely that ships would be putting out if the city was already partially occupied—but those were days of twilight war. France had an armistice, but the peace treaty hadn't been signed yet; there was supposed to be an occupied zone and a free zone, but France was powerless to enforce any agreements, and besides, the Germans were represented by both the Army and the Gestapo, which did not always work hand in hand.

" 'I've got to find out,' I said. 'You stay here and I'll try to get through to Bordeaux.'

"Helen shook her head. 'I won't stay here alone. I'll go with you.'

"This was not unreasonable. There were no longer any clearly defined areas of safety and danger. You could escape with your life from an enemy headquarters and be caught by Gestapo agents on some remote island; there were no rules you could bank on.

"We reached Bordeaux in a very haphazard way. I guess you're familiar with that mode of travel. When you think about it afterward, you don't see how it was possible. On foot, in a truck—we even rode part of the way on two broad-backed, good-natured farm horses that a hired man was taking away to sell.

"There were already troops in Bordeaux. The city was not occupied, but there were troops. It came as a shock; we expected to be arrested at any moment. Helen had on an inconspicuous suit; apart from the evening dress, a pair of pants, and two sweaters, it was all she possessed. I had a second suit in my knapsack.

"We left our bags at a café. People with baggage attracted attention, although there were quite a few Frenchmen on the move with suitcases. 'We'll go to a travel bureau and ask about the ships,' I said. We didn't know a soul in the city.

"We actually found one bureau open. There were old posters in the windows: 'Spend the Autumn in Lisbon'—'Algiers, Pearl of Africa'—'Vacation in Florida'—'Sunny Granada.' Most of them were thoroughly faded, but the colors of Lisbon and Granada were still resplendent.

"We hadn't long to wait at the window. A fourteen-year-old expert told us what was what. Ships? Nonexistent. Rumors of that kind had been going around for weeks. Long before the Germans arrived, an English ship had come to pick up Poles and other volunteers for the Polish Legion that was being organized in England. At the moment no ships were leaving.

"I asked what all the other people in the place had come for.

" 'Same thing as you, most of them,' said the expert.

" 'And what about you?'

" 'I've given up the idea of leaving,' he said. 'There's a living in this for me. I'm an interpreter, adviser, specialist in visas and housing. . . .'

"That was no surprise. Hard times make for precocity, and young people aren't befogged by sentimentality or preconceived ideas. We went to a café, and the expert gave me a survey of the situation. It was possible that the troops would leave; but it was hard to get a residence permit for Bordeaux, and for visas it was very bad. At the moment, Bayonne was said to be good for Spanish visas, but it was overcrowded; Marseille seemed to be the best place, but that was a long way. We all took that road sooner or later. You, too?" Schwarz asked me.

"Yes," I said. "That was our Calvary."

Schwarz nodded. "Of course I tried the American consulate. But Helen had a valid German passport, issued by the Nazis; how could we prove that we were in mortal peril? The terrified Jews without papers of any kind, who lay on the sidewalk outside the doors, seemed to be in much greater danger. Our passports were witnesses against us. Even old Schwarz's passport.

"We decided to go back to our château. Twice we were stopped by gendarmes; both times my foul humor came in handy—I growled at the gendarmes, held the passports under their noses, and said something about the military authorities. Helen laughed; it struck her as very comical. I had thought of this new tack when I went back to the café for our bags. The *patron* said he had never heard of any bags. 'Call the police if you feel like it,' he had said with a smile. 'But I guess you wouldn't want to do that.'

" 'I don't need the police,' I replied. 'Just give me my things.'

"The *patron* motioned to the waiter. 'Henri, monsieur wishes to leave.'

"Henri rolled up his sleeves and came closer. 'I'd think it over, Henri, if I were you,' I said to him. 'Or are you dying to know what a German concentration camp looks like on the inside?'

" '*Ta gueule,*' said Henri, and raised his fists.

" 'Okay, sergeant, fire!' I shouted, looking past Henri.

"Henri fell for it. He looked around, but his fists were still up, so I kicked him with all my might in the groin. He fell to the ground with a roar. The *patron* picked up a bottle and came out from behind the bar.

"I picked up a bottle of Dubonnet, knocked off the neck against a corner of the bar, and brandished my murderous weapon. The *patron* stood still. Behind me a second bottle crashed. I didn't look around; I couldn't leave the *patron* out of my sight.

" 'It's me,' said Helen, and shouted at the *patron:* '*Salaud!* Give us our things or you won't have any face left!'

"Her broken bottle in hand, she went into a crouch and approached the *patron*. I grabbed her with my free hand. Her bottle must have been Pernod, because suddenly the whole place reeked of anise. A stream of longshoreman's curses poured over the *patron*. Still crouching, Helen tried to struggle free from my hand. The *patron* retreated behind the bar.

" 'What's going on here?' asked a voice from the door in German.

"The *patron* began to grin. Helen turned around.

194

"The German sergeant whom I had invented for Henri's benefit was there in person.

" 'Is he hurt?' the sergeant asked.

" 'That swine?' Helen pointed to Henri, who was still lying doubled up on the floor with his fists between his legs. 'That's not blood. Just Dubonnet.'

" 'You're Germans?' asked the sergeant.

" 'Yes,' I replied. 'And we've been robbed.'

" 'Have you papers?'

"The *patron* grinned. He seemed to understand some German.

" 'Of course we have papers,' Helen fumed. 'And I must ask you to help us.' She held up her passport. 'I am Obersturmbannführer Jürgens' sister. See—' She pointed at the date in the passport. 'We're staying at the Château de ——' She gave a name that I had never heard in all my life. 'We've just come to Bordeaux for the day. We left our things here, with this thief. Now he claims he never saw them. Would you kindly help us.'

"She started for the *patron* again. 'Is that true?' the sergeant asked him.

" 'Of course it's true. A German woman does not lie!' said Helen.

"That was one of the idiotic slogans of the National Socialist regime.

" 'And who are you?' the sergeant asked me.

" 'The chauffeur,' I said, plucking at my overalls.

" 'All right! What are you waiting for?' the sergeant roared at the *patron*.

"The man behind the counter had stopped grinning.

" 'Do you want us to close your joint?' the sergeant asked.

"Helen translated with relish, adding a few '*salauds*' and '*sales étrangers*' of her own. I had been called those names so often that it gave me a special kick to hear her calling this Frenchman a dirty foreigner in his own country.

" 'Henri!' the *patron* bellowed. 'Where did you leave the stuff? It's all news to me,' he said to the sergeant. 'He must have taken it.'

" 'He's lying,' said Helen. 'He's just trying to put the blame on his gorilla. Go on, give us our things,' she shouted at the *patron,* 'or we'll call the Gestapo!'

"The *patron* gave Henri a kick. Henri slunk away. 'I beg your pardon,' said the *patron* to the sergeant. 'It's all a misunderstanding. Will you have something on me?'

" 'Cognac,' said Helen. 'The best.'

"The *patron* set a glass on the counter. Helen glared at him. He added two more. 'You're a brave woman,' said the sergeant.

" 'A German woman fears nothing,' Helen quoted from the Nazi manual, and put down the broken Pernod bottle.

" 'What kind of car do you drive?' the sergeant asked.

"I looked straight into his innocent gray eyes. 'A Mercedes, of course. That's the Führer's car.'

"He nodded. 'Beautiful place here, isn't it? Not like home, but pretty nice. How do you like it?'

" 'Lovely. But not like home, of course.'

"We drank. The cognac was excellent. Henri came in with our things and put them on a chair. I looked through the knapsack. Nothing was missing.

" 'Everything in order,' I said to the sergeant.

" 'It was the waiter's fault,' said the *patron.* 'You're fired, Henri. Clear out.'

" 'Thank you, sergeant,' said Helen. 'You're a German soldier and a gentleman.'

"The sergeant saluted. He was less than twenty-five. 'There's still the bill for those broken bottles of Pernod and Dubonnet,' said the *patron,* regaining his courage.

"Helen translated. 'He's not a gentleman,' she added. 'Nothing doing. It was self-defense.'

"The sergeant took the next bottle from the bar. 'Allow

196

me,' he said with an air of gallantry. 'The victor's got to have some privileges.'

" 'Madame doesn't drink Cointreau,' I said. 'Take the cognac, sergeant, even if it has been opened.'

"The sergeant presented Helen with the bottle. I put it into the knapsack. Once outside, we said good-by. I had been afraid the soldier would want to take us to our Mercedes, but Helen handled that adroitly. His parting words were: 'Such things don't happen in our country. We have order.'

"I looked after him. Order, I thought. With torture, bullets in the neck, and mass murder. Give me a million petty crooks like that café owner.

" 'How do you feel?' Helen asked.

" 'Fine. I didn't know you could curse like that.'

"She laughed. 'I learned it in the camp. What a relief! It's taken a year of internment off my back. But where did you learn to fight with broken bottles and kick people in the family jewels?'

" 'Fighting for the rights of man,' I answered. 'We are living in an age of paradoxes. To preserve peace, we wage war.'

"That was almost true. The only way we could keep alive was to lie and cheat. In the weeks that followed I stole fruit off the peasants' trees and milk out of their barns. It was a happy time. It was dangerous, ridiculous, sometimes heartbreaking, and often funny—but there was never any bitterness. I've just told you about the incident with the café owner. Those things began to happen all the time. You've probably had the same experience?"

I nodded. "Yes, it was funny all right, if you could look at it that way."

"I learned to," said Schwarz. "Through Helen. She had ceased to store up the past. What I had experienced only occasionally was her daily radiant reality. Every day the past crumbled away behind her. All her experience crowded into the present. What for others spread out over a whole life was for her concentrated in the moment; but there was nothing frantic or hysterical about this concentration. It was perfectly relaxed, as serene as Mozart and as inexorable as death. Morality and responsibility in the earth-bound sense had ceased to exist, replaced by higher, almost ethereal motivations. There was no time for the commonplace. She sparkled like fireworks, but her fireworks left no ashes. I didn't know it then, but she had lost the desire to be saved; she knew it was impossible. But since I insisted, she played along—and I, like a fool, dragged her with me from one station of the Cross to the next, all twelve of them, from Bordeaux to Bayonne and all the way to Marseille, and finally here.

"When we reached the château, it was occupied. We saw uniforms, soldiers bringing up wooden workbenches, officers in Air Force breeches and polished high boots, strutting about like strange peacocks.

"Hidden behind a beech tree and a marble goddess in the park, we watched. It was a silken late afternoon. 'Did we leave anything?' I asked.

" 'The apples on the trees, the air, the golden October, and our dreams,' said Helen.

" 'We've left them everywhere,' I answered. 'Like flying cobwebs in the autumn.'

"An officer on the terrace barked a command. 'The voice of the twentieth century,' said Helen. 'Let's get out of here. Where will we sleep tonight?'

" 'Somewhere in the hay,' I said. 'Or maybe even in a bed. In any case, together.'

CHAPTER 16

"Do you remember the square outside the consulate in Bayonne?" Schwarz asked. "The refugees would line up in columns of four, but after a while the ranks would disintegrate; the refugees would panic and block the entrance, weeping and groaning and fighting for a place."

"I remember," I said. "There were place tickets that entitled you to stand outside. But the crowd blocked the entrance just the same. When a window opened, the moaning became a screaming and a howling. They had to throw the passports out of the windows. A hundred arms shot up. The crowd looked like a forest."

The girls had gone off to bed except for two. One of them, who was rather pretty, sauntered over to our table with a yawn. "You're funny. All you do is talk and talk. It's our bedtime now. But the cafés are all open if you want to talk some more."

She opened the door. White and strident, the morning burst

in. The sun was shining. She closed the door behind us. I looked at my watch. "The ship won't be sailing today," said Schwarz. "Not until tomorrow night."

He saw that I didn't believe him. "Let's go and see," he said.

After the silent brothel, the noise at first was almost unbearable. Schwarz stood still. A crowd of children ran by, carrying baskets full of fish. "Watch them all running and shouting," he said. "As if no one were missing."

We went down to the harbor. The water was choppy, a cool wind was blowing, the sun was harsh and without warmth; sails fluttered in the breeze. Everyone was furiously busy with the morning, his work, and himself. We drifted through the bustle like two withered leaves. "You don't believe the ship isn't sailing until tomorrow?" Schwarz asked.

He looked very tired and worn in the merciless light. "I can't," I said. "You told me that it was sailing today. Let's ask. It means too much to me."

"As much as it did to me. And then all of a sudden it means nothing at all."

I did not reply. We walked on. A desperate impatience seized hold of me. Life called me with its cries and colors. The night was over. Must we go on conjuring up shadows?

We stopped outside a shop covered with posters. In the window a white sign announced that the sailing had been postponed until the following day.

"I'm almost done," said Schwarz.

I had gained a day. But in spite of the sign, I tried the door. It was still locked. Ten or a dozen people were watching me. From all sides they came a few steps closer as I pressed the door handle. They were refugees. When they saw that the door was still locked, they turned away and pretended to be looking into shop windows.

"You see that you still have time," said Schwarz, and suggested that we have some coffee in the port.

He drank the hot coffee quickly, cradling the cup in his hands as though to warm them. "What time is it?" he asked.

"Half past seven."

"One hour," he murmured. "They'll be coming in an hour." He looked up. "I didn't want to tell you a sob story. Is that what it sounds like?"

"No."

"What does it sound like?"

"Like the story of a love."

His features relaxed. "Thank you," he said. He pulled himself together. "The awful part began in Biarritz. I had heard that a small ship was putting out from Saint-Jean-de-Luz. There was nothing to it. When I arrived back at the pension, I found Helen lying on the floor. Her face was convulsed. 'A cramp,' she whispered. 'It will pass. Leave me alone.'

" 'I'll go for a doctor.'

" 'No doctor,' she panted. 'I don't need one. It will pass. Come back in five minutes. Leave me alone! Do what I say. No doctor. Go away!' she cried. 'I know what I'm doing. Come back in ten minutes. Then you —'

"She waved me away. She was unable to speak. But her eyes were so full of a terrible, incomprehensible plea that I left. I stood in front of the house, staring at the street. Then I inquired about a doctor and was told that a Dr. Dubois lived a few streets away. I ran to his place. He put on his things and came along with me.

"When we returned, Helen was lying on the bed. Her face was damp with sweat, but she was quieter. 'You've brought a doctor,' she said as reproachfully as if I had been her worst enemy.

"Dr. Dubois approached the bed with little mincing steps. 'I'm not sick,' she said.

" 'Madame,' said Dubois with a smile, 'suppose we let the doctor decide that.'

201

"He opened his bag and took out his instruments. 'Leave us alone,' Helen said to me.

"I left the room in confusion. I remembered what the camp doctor had said. I walked up and down the street, staring at the Michelin tire ad on the garage across the street. The fat man made of tires became a dark symbol, compounded of entrails and crawling white worms. I heard hammering from the garage, as though someone were making a sheet-iron coffin, and all at once I knew that this threat had long been with us, a livid background against which our life had taken on sharper contours, like a sunlit forest against a wall of storm clouds.

"I don't know how long it was before Dubois came out. He had a little goatee, and I guessed that his practice consisted chiefly in prescribing mild remedies for the coughs and hangovers of the summer people. That mincing walk of his threw me into despair. This was the dead season in Biarritz; he was grateful no doubt for any ailment that turned up. 'Your wife . . .' he said and paused.

"I glared at him. 'Just tell me the truth or don't say anything.'

"For a moment a thin, very touching smile changed him completely. 'Take this,' he said, pulling out a prescription pad and writing something illegible. 'Go to a drugstore and have it filled. Make sure they return the prescription. You can use it as often as you have to. I've put that down.'

"I took the white paper. 'What is it?' I asked.

" 'Nothing you can do anything about,' he answered. 'Remember that. Nothing you can do anything about.'

" 'What is it? Don't be so mysterious. I want the truth.'

"He did not reply. 'When you need it, go to a drugstore,' he said. 'They'll give it to you.'

" 'What is it?'

" 'A powerful sedative. You can only get it with a doctor's prescription.'

202

"I took the prescription. 'How much do I owe you?'

" 'Nothing.'

"He minced away. At the corner he turned around. 'Get it and leave it somewhere where your wife can find it. Don't talk to her about it. She knows. She's wonderful.'

" 'Helen,' I said to her. 'What does all this mean? You are sick. Why won't you tell me about it?'

" 'Don't torture me,' she replied very feebly. 'Let me live in my own way.'

" 'You don't want to talk about it?'

"She shook her head. 'There's nothing to talk about.'

" 'Isn't there anything I can do to help you?'

" 'No, dearest,' she said. 'This time you can't help me. If you could, I'd tell you so.'

" 'I still have the little Degas. I can sell it here. There are rich people in Biarritz. It will bring in enough money to put you in a hospital.'

" 'And have me arrested? Besides, it wouldn't do any good. Believe me.'

" 'Is it as bad as all that?'

"The look in her eyes was so harried and miserable that I asked her no more. I decided to drop in on Dubois and ask him again."

Schwarz fell silent. "Did she have cancer?" I asked.

He nodded. "I should have suspected it long before. In Switzerland they had told her that she could be operated on again but that it would do no good. She had had one operation; that was the scar I had seen. The specialist had told her the truth. She could choose between a few more useless operations that would keep her permanently in the hospital and a short life outside. He had also told her that there was no assurance that she would live any longer in the hospital. She had decided against the operations."

"She didn't want to tell you?"

"No. She hated her sickness. She tried to ignore it. She felt soiled, as though worms were crawling around inside her. She had the feeling that the disease was a kind of jellyfish, living and growing inside her. She thought I would be repelled if I knew about it. Perhaps she even hoped to make her cancer go away by ignoring it."

"And you never spoke to her about it?"

"Very little. She spoke to Dubois, and later on I made Dubois tell me the truth. He gave me more drugs. He told me the pain would increase; but it was also possible, he said, that the end would be quick and merciful.

"I didn't speak of it to Helen. She didn't want me to. She threatened to kill herself if I didn't leave her alone. After that I pretended to believe her—to believe that it was harmless cramps.

"We had to leave Biarritz. We deceived each other. Helen watched me and I watched her, but soon the deception acquired a strange power. First it destroyed what I feared most: the notion of time. The notion of weeks and months faded away. It still terrified us to think how little time we had ahead of us, but our fear became as transparent as glass. It was no longer a cloud over our days; it became a shield that deflected all disturbing thoughts; they simply couldn't come in. I had my fits of despair when Helen was asleep. I stared at her face as she lay there breathing gently, and at my sound hands, and I understood the terrible forlornness that our skin imposes on us, the gulf that can never be bridged. My healthy blood was powerless to cure the sick blood of my beloved. That was beyond understanding. And so is death.

"The moment became everything. Tomorrow was an eternity away. When Helen woke up, the day began, and when she slept and I felt her beside me, my thoughts hovered between hope and despair. I hatched fantastic plans based on miracles, or dreamed up a philosophy of the moment, blind to everything else. But all my fantasies were dispelled by the early light, swallowed up in the morning mists.

"The weather turned cold. I went about with the Degas; it should have brought in the fare to America, and I would have been glad to sell it. But there was no one willing to pay a reasonable price in the small towns and villages we passed through. Here and there we worked. I learned to work in the fields. I dug and hoed; I was glad to be busy. We were not the only ones. I saw professors sawing wood and opera singers hoeing beets. The peasants behaved like—peasants; they took advantage of the cheap labor. Some paid a little; others provided food, and a place to spend the night. And some chased you away. So we made our way to Marseille. Have you been there?"

"Who hasn't?" I said. "It was the hunting ground of the gendarmes and the Gestapo. They rounded up the refugees like rabbits outside the consulates."

"They almost caught us," said Schwarz. "The Prefect in charge of the *Service des étrangers* in Marseille did everything in his power to save the refugees. I was still possessed by the idea of getting an American visa. An American visa, it seemed to me, might even arrest cancer. To get a visa—you know all that—you had to prove that you were in extreme danger or you had to be on a list of well-known artists, scientists, or intellectuals that was drawn up in America. As if the whole lot of us weren't in danger—and as if man didn't equal man! Doesn't the distinction between ordinary and valuable men smack a little of the Nazi concept of the superman as opposed to subhuman vermin?"

"They can't take everybody," I said.

"No?" Schwarz retorted.

I did not answer. What answer was there? Yes and no were the same.

"Why not the most dispossessed?" Schwarz asked. "Those without a name and fame?"

Again I said nothing. Schwarz had two American visas—what more did he want? Didn't he know that the Americans gave anyone a visa provided someone over there made out an affidavit guaranteeing that he would not become a public charge?

He said as much the next moment. "I don't know a soul over there. But someone gave me an address in New York; I wrote a letter. I wrote to other people, too. I described our situation. Then a friend told me that I had gone about it all wrong; invalids were not admitted to the United States. Incurables were not even considered. I would have to say that Helen was in perfect health. Helen had overheard a part of the conversation. That was inevitable; no one spoke of anything else in Marseille. It was like a swarm of bees gone mad.

"That evening we were sitting in a restaurant off the Canebière. The wind swept through the streets. I was not discouraged. I hoped to find a humane doctor who would give Helen a health certificate. We were still playing the same game, pretending to believe each other, pretending that I knew nothing. I had written to the Prefect of her camp for an attestation that we were endangered. We had found a small room; I had obtained a residence permit for one week and was working nights illegally in a restaurant as a dishwasher; we had some money, and a druggist had given me ten ampoules of morphine on Dubois' prescription—so for the moment we had everything we needed.

"We sat at a table by the window, looking out at the street —for us a rare luxury, for a whole week there was no need to hide. Suddenly Helen gave a start and grasped my hand. She was staring into the windy darkness. 'Georg!' she whispered.

" 'Where?'

" 'In that open car. He just drove by.'

" 'Are you sure?'

"She nodded.

"It struck me as next to impossible. I made several attempts to distinguish the features of people in passing cars and found that I couldn't. But I was not reassured.

" 'Why should he be in Marseille of all places?' I asked. But the next instant I realized that Marseille was the most natural place in the world for him to be—the last haven of all the refugees in France.

" 'We'll have to leave Marseille,' I said.

" 'Where can we go?'

" 'Spain.'

" 'Isn't that even more dangerous?'

"There were rumors that the Gestapo had made itself at home in Spain and that refugees had been arrested by the Spanish police and turned over to the German authorities; but all sorts of rumors were going around in those days; you couldn't believe them all.

"I had another try at the old rat race: the Spanish transit visa which was granted only if you had a Portuguese visa, which in turn was contingent on a visa for some other country. Not to mention the worst bureaucratic chicanery of all: the French exit visa.

"One night we had a stroke of luck: a young American spoke to us. He was a little tipsy and was looking for someone to talk English to. A few minutes later he was sitting at our table, buying us drinks. He was about twenty-five and was waiting for a ship to take him back to America. 'Why don't you come along?' he asked.

"I said nothing for a moment. The naïve question seemed to open a rift in the table between us. He was living on another planet. What for him was as natural as a drink of water was for us as inaccessible as the Pleiades. 'No visas,' I said finally.

" 'That's no obstacle. We have a consulate here in Marseille. Real nice people.'

"I knew the nice people. They were demigods; you waited for hours in the street just to see their secretaries. Later we were allowed to wait in the cellar, because refugees were often picked up in the street by Gestapo agents.

" 'I'll take you there tomorrow,' said the American.

" 'Fine,' I said, not believing him for one moment.

" 'Let's drink on it.'

"We drank. His fresh, guileless face was almost more than I could bear. He told us about the sea of lights on Broadway. Fairy tales in a dark city. I watched Helen's face as he dropped the names of actors, plays, night clubs, as he evoked the innocent hubbub of a city that had never known a war; I was wretched and at the same time glad to see that she was listening, because up until then she had received every mention of America with a strange silent lethargy. Her face lit up; she smiled through the cigarette smoke and promised to let the man take her to see his favorite play. We drank and knew that the whole thing would be forgotten next day.

"We were mistaken. The young American called for us at ten o'clock sharp. I had a hangover, and Helen refused to go along. It was raining. The usual knot of refugees had formed outside the consulate. It was like a dream. The crowd parted before us as the Red Sea parted before the Jews fleeing from Pharaoh. The American's green passport was the Golden Key that opened all doors.

"The incredible happened. When the situation was explained to the young man, he announced very nonchalantly that he would vouch for us. It sounded preposterous; he was so young. It seemed to me that to vouch for me he'd have had to be older than I. We spent about an hour at the consulate. Some weeks before, I had filed a statement explaining why we were in danger. Through intermediaries in Switzerland—it had cost me no end of trouble—I had obtained letters proving that I had been in a German concentration camp. I had also presented proof that Georg was looking for both of us to take us back to Germany. I was told to come back in a week. Outside, the American shook hands with me. 'It's been swell meeting you. Here—' he produced a visiting card—'call me up when you get there.'

"He waved his hand and was about to leave. 'But what if something goes wrong? What if I need you?' I asked.

" 'What can go wrong? It's all settled.' He laughed. 'My father's pretty well known. I've heard there's a boat going to Oran tomorrow; I think I'll shoot over there before I go back. Who knows when I'll be here again? Better see as much as I can right now.'

"He vanished. Half a dozen refugees surrounded me, asking for his name and address; they guessed what had happened and wanted to get in on it. When I told them I didn't know where he was staying in Marseille, they called me some very unflattering names. I actually didn't know. I showed them the card with his American address. They wrote it down. I told them it would do no good, the man was going to Oran. They said they'd wait for him on the dock, before his boat left. I started home with mixed feelings. Maybe I had ruined everything by showing his card; but bewilderment had destroyed my presence of mind. And anyway, as I became more convinced at every step, the whole situation was hopeless.

"I told Helen all about it. She smiled. She was very gentle that evening. We had sublet our little room from a subtenant —you know about those addresses that pass from mouth to mouth. The green canary we had promised to take care of was singing like mad in his wire cage; he never stopped. Now and then a cat would step in from the nearby roofs and sit in the window devouring the bird with its yellow eyes. It was cold, but Helen wanted the windows open. She always did when she was in pain.

"The house didn't quiet down until very late. 'Do you remember the little château?' Helen asked.

" 'I remember as if someone had told me about it,' I said. 'As if it weren't myself but someone else who had been there.'

"She looked at me. 'Maybe that's how it is,' she said. 'Everyone has several people inside him. All different. And some-times one of them becomes independent and takes over for a while. Then you become somebody else, somebody you'd never known. But we come back.' She turned to me with an air of urgency: 'Don't we?'

" 'I never had different people inside me,' I said. 'I've al-ways been monotonously the same.'

"She shook her head violently. 'You're wrong. Some day you'll find out.'

" 'What do you mean?'

" 'Forget it. Look at that cat in the window. And that silly bird. So unsuspecting. The jubilant victim!'

" 'The cat will never get him. He's safe in his cage.'

"Helen burst out laughing. 'Safe in his cage,' she repeated. 'Who wants to be safe in a cage?'

"We awoke toward morning. The concierge was scream-ing and cursing. Fully dressed and ready to run for it, I opened the door, but there was no sign of police. 'The blood!' the woman screamed. 'Couldn't she do it some other way? What a mess! And now we'll have the police. That's what comes of having a kind heart. People take advantage. And the five weeks' rent she owes me!'

"The other tenants had gathered in the gray light of the hallway and were staring into the room next to ours. A woman of sixty had committed suicide by cutting the veins of one wrist. The blood had run down the side of her bed. 'Get a doc-tor,' said Lachmann, a refugee from Frankfurt, who made his living in Marseille selling rosaries and pictures of saints.

" 'A doctor!' fumed the concierge. 'She's been dead for hours. Can't you see that? That's what comes of taking you people in. Now we'll have the police. They can arrest the lot of you, for all I care. And the bed—how will I ever get it clean?'

" 'We'll clean it up,' said Lachmann. 'But don't bring the police into it.'

" 'And her rent? What about her rent?'

" 'We'll take up a collection,' said an old woman in a red kimono. 'Where else can we go? Take pity on us.'

" 'I took pity on her and she took advantage. If at least she had any valuables!'

"The concierge rummaged about. The one naked bulb gave off a pale yellow light. Under the bed there was a cheap fiber suitcase. The concierge knelt down at the end of the iron bed, the end with no blood on it, and pulled it out. Under her striped house dress she presented the posterior of a great obscene insect pouncing on its prey. She opened the suitcase. 'Nothing! Rags. Old shoes.'

" 'Look here!' said the old woman in the red kimono, pointing at a little box. Her name was Lucie Löwe; she sold discard stockings on the black market and mended broken china.

"The concierge opened the box. On a bed of pink cotton lay a small chain and a ring with a little stone in it.

" 'Gold?' asked the concierge. 'Must be plated.'

" 'Gold,' said Lachmann.

" 'If it were gold,' said the concierge, 'she'd have sold it before doing what she did.'

" 'It's not always hunger that makes you do those things,' said Lachmann calmly. 'It's gold, all right. And the little stone is a ruby. Worth at least seven or eight hundred francs.'

" 'Don't make me laugh.'

" 'I can sell it for you if you like.'

" 'And swindle me, eh? Oh no, my friend, you've come to the wrong address.'

"She had to call the police. There was no getting around it. Meanwhile, the refugee tenants disappeared. Most of them started on their daily activities—waiting at the consulates or trying to sell something or looking for work. The rest of us went to the nearest church. We posted a lookout on the corner to tell us when the coast was clear. Churches were safe.

"Mass was being said. In the aisles sat women in black dresses, stooped over like dark hillocks. The candles burned impassively, the organ played, and the light glittered on the upraised golden chalice which contained the blood of Christ, who with it had redeemed the world. What had it led to? To bloody crusades, religious fanaticism, the tortures of the Inquisition, witch hunts and the burning of heretics—all in the name of charity.

" 'Why don't we go to the railroad station?' I asked Helen. 'It's warmer.'

" 'All right, but wait just a moment.'

"She went to a pew below the pulpit and knelt down. I don't know whether she prayed and to whom, but I thought of the day when I had waited for her in the cathedral in Osnabrück. I had found a woman whom I had not known, and who from day to day had grown stranger to me, yet closer. Now she seemed to be slipping away from me again, into a realm where all names are forgotten, where there is only darkness and perhaps certain unknown laws of darkness. She rejected that dark realm; she came back, but she no longer belonged to me as I had tried to believe. Perhaps she had never belonged to me; who, after all, belongs to whom, and what is it to belong to someone, to belong to one another? Isn't it a forlorn illusion, a convention? Time and again she turned back, as she called it, for an hour, for the duration of a glance, for a night. And always I felt like a bookkeeper who is not allowed to audit. I could only accept without question whatever this unaccountable, unhappy, damned, and beloved creature chose to be and to tell me. I know there are other names for it, cheap, easy, disparaging names—but they are for other circumstances and for people who mistake their selfish desires for votive tablets. Loneliness demands a com-

212

panion and does not ask who it is. If you don't know that, you may have been alone, but you were never lonely.

" 'What did you pray for?' I asked, and was sorry I had asked.

"She gave me a strange look. 'For an American visa,' she answered, and I knew she was lying. Maybe the exact opposite. I thought for a moment—I had often been struck by her passive resistance to my American projects. 'America?' she had said one night. 'What will you do in America? Why run so far? When you get there, there will be some other America to run to, and then another, don't you see that?' She wanted no more changes. She had abandoned all belief in a future. The death that was consuming her had no wish to run away. It governed her like a vivisectionist who looks on to see what will happen when one organ and then another, one cell and then another, is modified and destroyed. It played a cruel game of masks with her, not so very different from our innocent masquerade at the castle. From one minute to the next this woman, looking at me out of tremulous eyes, could be all hatred for me or all devotion; at times she was a gambler, losing with heartbreaking courage, and at times she was all hunger and desperation. But always she was a human being who had nothing but me to return to from out of the darkness, and who was grateful for that in her last, brave, frightened tremor.

"Our lookout came in to announce that the police had gone. 'We should have gone to the museum,' said Lachmann. 'It's heated.'

" 'Is there one here?' asked a hunchbacked young woman, whose husband had been taken away by the police and who had been waiting for him for six weeks.

" 'Of course.'

"I couldn't help thinking of old Schwarz. 'Would you like to go?' I asked Helen.

" 'Not now. Let's go back.'

213

"I didn't want her to see the dead woman again; but she insisted. The concierge had calmed down when we got back. Perhaps she had had the chain and the ring appraised. 'Poor woman,' she said. 'Now she hasn't even got a name.'

" 'Had she no papers?'

" 'She had a *sauf-conduit*. The others drew lots for it before the police came. The little redhead won.'

" 'That's good. She had no papers at all. I'm sure the dead woman wouldn't have minded.'

" 'Would you like to see her?'

" 'No,' I said.

" 'Yes,' said Helen.

"I went with her. The dead woman had stopped bleeding. When we came in, two refugee women were washing the body. They turned it over like a white plank. The hair hung down to the floor. 'Get out!' one of them hissed at me.

"I went. Helen stayed. A little while later I came back to get her. She was standing alone in the narrow room at the foot of the bed, staring at the white sunken face, in which one eye was not quite closed. 'Come now,' I said.

" 'So that's how one looks,' she whispered. 'Where will they bury her?'

" 'I don't know. Where the poor are buried. If there's a charge, the concierge will take up a collection.'

"Helen did not answer. Cold air blew in through the open window. 'When will she be buried?' she asked.

" 'Tomorrow or the day after. Maybe they'll want to do an autopsy.'

" 'Why? Won't they believe it was suicide?'

" 'Oh, I guess they will.'

"The concierge came in. 'They're taking her to a hospital tomorrow for an autopsy. That's how the young doctors learn to operate. It makes no difference to her, and that way it's free of charge. Would you care for a cup of coffee?'

" 'No,' said Helen.

" 'I need one,' said the concierge. 'I'm all upset, though I don't see why. We've all got to go some day.'

" 'Yes,' said Helen. 'But no one wants to believe it.'

"I awoke in the middle of the night. She was sitting up in bed and seemed to be listening. 'Do you smell it, too?' she asked.

" 'What?'

" 'The corpse. I smell it. Close the window.'

" 'There isn't any smell, Helen. It doesn't happen so quickly.'

" 'I do smell it.'

" 'Maybe it's the leaves.' The roomers had set some laurel boughs and a candle by the deathbed.

" 'What's the good of that?' Helen asked. 'Tomorrow she'll be dissected; when they're through, they'll toss the pieces in a bucket and sell them to the zoo.'

" 'They won't sell anything,' I said. 'After the autopsy the body will be cremated or buried.' I tried to put my arms around Helen's shoulders, but she pushed me away. 'I don't want to be cut up,' she said.

" 'Why should you be cut up?'

"She didn't hear me. 'Promise not to let them cut me up.'

" 'I promise.'

" 'Close the window. I smell it again.'

"I got up and closed the window. The moon was bright, and the cat was sitting on the sill. It hissed and jumped away when the window grazed it. 'What was that?' Helen asked behind me.

" 'The cat.'

" 'See, she smelled it, too.'

"I turned around. 'She sits here every night waiting for the canary to come out of the cage. Go back to sleep, Helen. You've been dreaming. Really there's no smell coming from her room.'

215

" 'Then it must be me.'

"I stared at her. 'Nobody smells, Helen; you've been dreaming.'

" 'If it's not the corpse, it must be me. Stop lying!' she replied angrily.

" 'Good Lord, Helen. Nobody smells. If there's any smell, it's garlic from the restaurant downstairs. Here.' I took a little bottle of Cologne—one of the articles I was selling on the black market—and sprinkled a few drops on the bed. 'See, now everything smells fine.'

"She was still sitting bolt upright. 'So you admit it,' she said, 'or you wouldn't have sprinkled the Cologne.'

" 'I don't admit anything. I did it to comfort you.'

" 'I know what you think,' she said. 'You think I smell. Like the corpse. Don't lie! I can see it by the way you look at me. I've seen it for weeks. Do you think I don't notice how you look at me when you think I'm not looking? I know that I disgust you; I know it, I see it, I can feel it every day. I know what you think. You don't believe what the doctors say. You think I've got something else, and you think you can smell it. I disgust you. Why don't you admit it?'

"I stood perfectly still. If she had more to say, let her say it. But she stopped. I could feel that she was trembling. Propped up on her arms, she was leaning forward, a pale, indistinct shape. Her eyes were too big for their sockets and her lips were heavily made up. She had taken to putting on make-up before going to bed. She glared at me like a wounded animal ready to spring at my throat.

"It was a long time before she calmed down. In the end I knocked on Baum's door on the second floor and bought a flask of cognac from him. We sat on the bed drinking and waited for morning. The men came early for the body. We heard their heavy boots on the stairs, and the stretcher bumped, colliding with the walls of the narrow hallway. Their jokes could be heard indistinctly through the thin partition. An hour later the new roomers moved in.

CHAPTER 17

"For a few days I peddled kitchen utensils, graters, knives, vegetable peelers; small objects for which no suspicious-looking suitcase is needed. Twice I came home earlier than usual and found Helen gone. I waited, growing more and more worried; but the concierge assured me that no one had come for her, that she had gone out a few hours before, that she often went out.

"It was late when she came in. Her face was hostile. She did not look at me. I didn't know what to do, but not to ask would have been stranger than asking. 'Helen, where have you been?' I asked finally.

" 'Out for a walk.'

" 'In this weather?'

" 'Yes, in this weather. Don't try to keep tabs on me.'

" 'I'm not trying to keep tabs on you,' I said. 'I was only worried that the police had picked you up.'

"She laughed harshly. 'The police will never get me.'

217

" 'I wish I could believe that.'

"She glared at me. 'If you keep on asking questions, I'll go out again. I can't stand being watched all the time, can't you see that? The houses outside don't watch me. I'm of no interest to them. And I'm of no interest to the people on the street. They don't ask me questions and they don't watch me.'

"I saw what she meant. Outside, no one knew of her sickness. Outside, she was not a patient, but a woman. And she wanted to go on being a woman. She wanted to live; to be a patient meant a slow death.

"At night she cried in her sleep. In the morning everything was forgotten. It was the darkness she could not bear. It settled like a poisoned spiderweb on her terrified heart. I saw that she needed more and more sedatives. I spoke to Lewisohn, formerly a doctor, now a peddler of horoscopes. He told me it was too late for anything else. Just what Dubois had told me.

"She often came home late after that. She was afraid I would question her. I didn't. Once a bunch of roses was delivered when I was alone. I went out, and when I came back the roses were gone. She began to drink. Friends found it necessary to tell me that they had seen her in bars—not alone. I clung to my last hope—the American consulate. By now I had permission to wait in the lobby; but the days passed and nothing happened.

"Then I was caught. I was twenty paces from the consulate when suddenly the police set up a cordon. I tried to get through and that made them suspicious. Once inside, you were safe. I saw Lachmann disappear in the doorway and broke loose in an attempt to follow him, but a gendarme thrust out his leg and tripped me. 'Keep a good hold on that one,' said a smiling young man in civilian clothes. 'He's in too much of a hurry.' Our papers were checked. Six of us were held. The police withdrew, leaving us in the hands of a group of civilians. We were loaded into a closed truck and taken to a house

218

in the suburbs. It was isolated, with a big garden around it. It sounds like a Class B film," said Schwarz. "But have the last years been anything but a stupid bloodthirsty movie?"

"Was it the Gestapo?" I asked.

Schwarz nodded. "Today it seems a miracle that they hadn't laid hands on me before. I knew that Georg wouldn't stop looking for us. The smiling young man mentioned Georg the moment he saw my papers. Unfortunately, I had Helen's passport on me, too; I had thought I might need it at the consulate. 'At last we've got our little fish,' said the young man. 'The female won't be long in coming.' He smiled and punched me in the face. He seemed to have rings on all his fingers. 'Do you agree with me, Schwarz?'

"I wiped the blood off my lips. There were two other men in the room, also in plain clothes. 'Or mightn't it be wiser,' the young man said, 'to tell us the address?'

" 'I haven't got it,' I answered. 'I've been looking for my wife myself. We quarreled a week ago and she ran away.'

" 'Quarreled? How nasty!' Again the young man hit me in the face. 'There, that's for quarreling with your wife.'

" 'Should we swing him, chief?' asked one of the gorillas.

"The young man with the girlish face smiled. 'Tell him what swinging is, Möller.'

"Möller explained that a telephone wire would be tied around my genitals, and then they'd swing me. 'Know what it's like?' asked the young man. 'After all, you've been in a camp.'

" 'I didn't know. 'My invention,' he said. 'But we can start with something simpler. We bind off your jewels so tight that not a drop of blood can get through. In an hour or so you'll be making a fine hullabaloo. To quiet you down, we stuff your little mouth with sawdust.'

"His eyes were light blue and strangely glassy. 'We're full of interesting little ideas,' he went on. 'Have you ever stopped to think what can be done with a little fire?'

"The gorillas laughed.

" 'With a fine red-hot wire,' said the smiling young man. 'Remarkable results are obtained by introducing it slowly into the ears or up through the nostrils, Mr. Schwarz. We're very fortunate in having you here to help us with our experiments.'

"He stepped hard on my feet. I could smell his perfume. I did not move. I knew it was useless to resist and even more to make a display of courage. My tormentors would have been only too delighted to break down my resistance. At the next blow, administered with a cane, I collapsed with a moan. They all guffawed. 'Revive him, Möller,' said the young man tenderly.

"Möller drew at his cigarette and pressed it to my eyelid. It was as if fire had been poured into my eye. The three roared with laughter. 'Get up, son,' said the Smile.

"I staggered to my feet. I was hardly up when he struck me again. 'This is only warming-up exercises,' he explained. 'We have time, a whole lifetime—yours. The next time you take it into your head to malinger, we have a marvelous surprise in store for you. You'll hit the ceiling.'

" 'I wasn't malingering,' I said. 'I've got a bad heart. It's perfectly possible that I won't get up next time, whatever you do.'

"The Smile turned to the gorillas. 'Our boy says his heart is bad. Should we believe him?'

"He hit me again, but I could see I had made an impression. He couldn't hand me over to Georg dead. 'Have you remembered that address?' he asked. 'It would be easier to tell us now while you still have some teeth.'

" 'I don't know it. I wish I did.'

" 'Our boy's a hero. How touching! Too bad that nobody but us will ever know.'

"He kicked me until he was tired. I lay on the floor, trying to protect my face and genitals. 'Seems like enough for now,' he said finally. 'Lock him up in the cellar. After dinner we'll really get started. Night sessions are so stimulating!'

"I was familiar with this sort of thing. It was as much a part of German culture as Goethe and Schiller, and I had been through it in the camp. But I had my poison on me. They had searched me, but not very carefully; they hadn't found it. I also had a razor blade inserted in a strip of cork—sewn loosely into the cuff of my trousers; they hadn't found that either.

"I lay in the darkness. Of course I was in despair. But strange to say, what really got me down wasn't so much the dark prospects as the thought of my stupidity in getting caught.

"Lachmann had seen them arrest me. He didn't know it was the Gestapo, because the French police seemed to be involved. But if I were not back in twenty-four hours at the most, Helen would try to reach me through the police and probably find out who had arrested me. But would the Smile wait for that to happen? I assumed that Georg would be notified immediately. If Georg was in Marseille, he would 'interview' me that night.

"He was in Marseille, all right. Helen's eyes had not deceived her. He came and gave me his personal attention. I won't bore you with the details. When I passed out, they poured water on me and dragged me back to the cellar. It was only the poison I had that enabled me to hold out. Luckily Georg had no patience with the refined tortures that the Smile had promised me; but in his own way he was no slouch.

"He came back later that night. He brought in a stool and there he sat in all his barrel-chested self-righteousness, a symbol of the absolute power we thought we had left behind us in the nineteenth century and which nevertheless—or perhaps for that very reason—became the hallmark of the twentieth. That day I saw two embodiments of evil—the Smile and

Georg, absolute evil and unadulterated brutality. If distinctions are in order, the Smile was the worse of the two—he tortured for the pleasure of it, Georg to impose his will. Meanwhile I had thought up a plan. I had to get out of that house. When Georg came back, I acted as if I were completely broken. I'd tell him everything, I said, if he would spare me. He had the well-fed, contemptuous grin of a man who has never been in such a situation and consequently believes that if he were he would behave like a hero in a schoolbook. The fact is that his type goes to pieces completely."

"I know," I said. "I once heard a Gestapo officer screaming because he had squashed his thumb in an iron chain he was beating somebody to death with. The man who was being beaten didn't let out a peep."

"Georg kicked me," said Schwarz. " 'Oho,' he said. 'So now we're trying to bargain?'

" 'I'm not trying to bargain,' I replied. 'But if you take Helen to Germany, she'll run away or kill herself.'

" 'Nonsense!' Georg snarled.

" 'Life doesn't mean very much to Helen,' I said. 'She knows she has cancer and that it's incurable.'

"He stared at me. 'That's a lie, you swine. She hasn't got cancer. It's one of those women's ailments.'

" 'She has cancer. It was discovered the first time she was operated on in Zurich. Even then it was too late. The doctor told her so.'

" 'What doctor?'

" 'The surgeon who operated on her. She wanted to know.'

" 'The inhuman swine!' Georg roared. 'But I'll get him too! Switzerland will be German in another year.'

" 'I wanted Helen to go back,' I said. 'She refused. But I think she'd go if I were to break with her.'

" 'That's ridiculous.'

" 'I could be so beastly that she'd hate me for the rest of her life,' I said.

222

"I saw that Georg's mind was working. I had propped up my head in my hands and was watching him. I had a pain between the eyes from trying to force my will upon him.

" 'How?' he answered finally.

" 'She thinks I'd find her repulsive if I knew of her sickness. That's her greatest fear. If I said that, she'd be through with me for good.'

"Georg pondered. I could follow his thoughts. He saw that my suggestion offered him his best chance. Even if he tortured Helen's address out of me, she would go on hating him; but if I behaved like a scoundrel, she would hate me and he could step forward as her savior and say: 'I told you so.'

" 'Where does she live?' he asked.

"I gave a false address. 'But there are half a dozen ways out,' I said, 'through cellars and other streets. If the police try to arrest her, she can easily escape. She won't run away if I go alone.'

" 'Or I,' said Georg.

" 'She'd think you had killed me. She has poison.'

" 'Nonsense!'

"I waited. 'And what do you ask in return?' Georg asked.

" 'That you let me go.'

"He smiled for a moment, showing his teeth like a beast of prey. I knew that he'd never let me go. 'All right,' he said. 'Come along with me. That way you won't try any tricks. You'll tell her in my presence.'

"I nodded. 'Let's go,' he said. He stood up. 'Clean yourself up at the faucet over there.'

" 'I'm taking him with me,' he said to one of the gorillas, who was lounging in a room decorated with antlers. The gorilla saluted and escorted us to Georg's car. 'Get in here beside me,' said Georg. 'Do you know the way?'

" 'Not from here. From the Canebière.'

"We drove off into the cold windy night. I had hoped to drop out of the car when it slowed or stopped; but Georg had locked my door. It wouldn't have done any good to scream; no one would think of responding to cries from a German car, and before my scream was half out, Georg would have knocked me unconscious. 'You'd better be telling me the truth,' Georg snarled, 'or I'll have you skinned and rolled in pepper.'

"I huddled in my seat. When Georg jammed on the brakes to avoid an unlighted cart, I let myself fall forward. 'Coward,' Georg snapped at me. 'This is no time to play sick.'

" 'I feel faint,' I said, slowly picking myself up.

" 'Weakling!'

"I had ripped open the threads in my cuff. The second time he had to brake I located the razor blade; the third time, I bumped my head against the windshield. When I settled back in the seat, I had the blade in my hand."

Schwarz looked up. His forehead was bathed in sweat. "He would never have let me go," he said. "Do you believe me?"

"Of course I believe you."

"As we were rounding a curve, I shouted as loud as I could: 'Watch out on the left!'

"The unexpected cry took Georg unawares. His head turned automatically to the left; he braked and gripped the wheel. I lashed out at him. It wasn't a big blade, but it caught him in the side of the neck. I pulled it forward hard across his windpipe. He let go the wheel and clutched his throat. Then he sagged against the door. His arm hit the handle. The car hurtled into a clump of bushes. The door flew open, and Georg fell out. He was wheezing and bleeding heavily.

"I climbed out and listened. All I could hear was the roaring of the motor. I turned it off. The wind seemed to howl in the silence, but it was the blood in my ears. I watched Georg and looked for the blade with the strip of cork. It glinted on the running board. I picked it up and waited. I thought Georg might jump up at any moment. Then a quiver ran through his legs and he was still. I threw the blade away, but picked it up again and stuck it in the ground. I turned off the lights and listened. Not a sound. I hadn't thought about what to do next; now I had to act quickly. Every minute's head start counted.

"I removed Georg's clothes and tied them up in a bundle. Then I dragged the body into the bushes. He wouldn't be found for some time, and then it would take a while to identify him. If I were in luck, they would list him as unknown. I checked the car. It was undamaged. I drove it back on the road. I vomited. In the car I found a flashlight. There was blood on the seat and on the door. Both were leather and easy to clean. There was water in the ditch, and I used Georg's shirt as a rag. I also wiped the running board. I inspected the whole car with the flashlight and kept wiping until it was clean. Then I washed myself and got in. It nauseated me to be sitting in Georg's place; I had the feeling that he would leap at me out of the darkness. I drove off.

"I left the car in a side street a little way from the house. It had begun to rain. I crossed the street, breathing deeply. Gradually I began to feel the aches in my body. I stopped outside a fish store; there was a mirror at the side of the window. I couldn't see much in the dark silver, but as far as I could make out, my face was swollen. I took a deep breath of the damp air. I could hardly believe that I had been there that same afternoon.

"I managed to slip by the concierge unseen. She was already asleep and just mumbled something. It was not unusual for me to come in late. Quickly I mounted the stairs.

"Helen was not there. I stared at the bed and the clothes cupboard. Awakened by the light, the canary began to sing. The cat came to the window with its phosphorescent eyes and peered in like a damned soul. I waited for a time. Then I crept over to Lachmann's door and knocked softly.

"He awoke at once. Fugitives are light sleepers. 'Are

225

you—' he began. Then he took a look at me and fell silent. 'Have you seen my wife?' I asked.

"He shook his head. 'She's been away. She wasn't back an hour ago.'

" 'Thank God.'

"He looked at me as if I had gone mad. 'Thank God,' I repeated. 'Then she probably hasn't been arrested. She's just gone out.'

" 'Just gone out,' Lachmann repeated. 'What's happened to you?' he asked then.

" 'They questioned me. I got away.'

" 'The police?'

" 'The Gestapo. It's all over. Go back to sleep.'

" 'Does the Gestapo know where you are?'

" 'If they did, I wouldn't be here. I'll be gone before morning.'

" 'Wait a second.' Lachmann rummaged about and came back with some rosaries and holy pictures. 'Here, take these with you. Sometimes they do wonders. They got Hirsch across the border. The people in the Pyrenees are very religious. These things have been blessed by the Pope himself.'

" 'Really?'

"His smile was beautiful. 'If they save us,' he said, 'they've been blessed by God himself. Good-by, Schwarz.'

"I went back to the room and packed our things. I felt utterly empty, but tense, like a drum with nothing inside. In Helen's drawer I discovered a packet of letters addressed to her in care of General Delivery, Marseille. I thought nothing and put them in her bag. I also put in her evening dress from Paris. Then I sat down at the washbasin and turned on the water. My burnt nails ached and it hurt me to breathe. I looked out at the wet roofs and thought nothing.

"At last I heard Helen's steps. She stood in the doorway like a beautiful ravaged ghost. 'What are you doing?' She knew nothing. 'What's wrong?'

" 'We've got to get out of Marseille,' I said. 'Right away.'

" 'Georg?'

"I nodded. I had decided to tell her as little as possible. 'What have they done to you?' she asked in a fright, and came closer.

" 'They arrested me. I escaped. They'll be looking for me.'

" 'Where can we go?'

" 'Spain.'

" 'How?'

" 'As far as possible in a car. Can you make it quick?'

" 'Yes.'

"She winced. 'Are you in pain?' I asked.

"She nodded. Who is that in the doorway? I thought. Who is it? She was a stranger to me. 'Are there any ampoules left?' I asked.

" 'Not very many.'

" 'We'll get some more.'

" 'Leave me for a moment,' she said.

"I stood in the hallway. Doors opened a crack. Faces appeared with the eyes of lemurs. One-eyed faces with crooked mouths. Lachmann in long gray underdrawers darted up the stairs like a grasshopper and pressed a half-full bottle of cognac into my hand. 'It will come in handy,' he whispered. 'V.S.O.P.'

"I took a good swig on the spot.

" 'Could you sell me another bottle?' I asked. 'Here. I have plenty of money.'

"My first impulse had been to throw Georg's briefcase away, but I had quickly changed my mind. In it I had found a considerable sum of money—and, better still, his passport, along with Helen's and my own.

"I had weighted down Georg's clothes with a stone and tossed them in the harbor. Then after carefully examining Georg's passport under the flashlight, I went to Gregorius's room and woke him up. Would he fix up Georg's passport for me with my photo? At first he was horrified and flatly refused.

227

His business was 'rectifying' the passports of refugees and in the performance of it he felt more righteous than God, whom he held responsible for the whole mess—but he had never before laid eyes on the passport of a high Gestapo official. I told him that he wouldn't have to sign his work like a painting, that the responsibility was all mine, and that no one would know he had anything to do with it.

" 'What if they torture you?'

"I showed him my hand and face. 'I'll be gone in an hour,' I said. 'As a refugee, I wouldn't get ten miles with my face in this state. And I've got to get out of France. This is my only chance. Here's my passport. Photograph the picture and put the copy on the Gestapo passport. What's the charge? I have money.' Gregorius finally consented.

"Lachmann brought the second bottle of cognac. I paid him and went back to my room. Helen was standing by the bedside table. The drawer where the letters had been was open. She banged it shut and came over to me. 'Did Georg do that?' she asked.

" 'It was a committee,' I said.

" 'Damn his soul!' She went to the window. The cat fled. She opened the shutters. 'Damn his soul!' she repeated with the deep passionate conviction of a medicine man cursing the enemies of his tribe. 'Damn his soul in this world and the next. . . .'

"I took hold of her clenched fists and drew her away from the window. 'We've got to be going.'

"We went down the stairs. Eyes followed us from every door. A gray arm motioned. 'Schwarz! Don't take a knapsack. The police are on the lookout for knapsacks. I have an artificial leather suitcase. Cheap and very chic . . .'

" 'Thank you,' I said. 'I don't need a suitcase. I need luck.'

" 'We'll keep our fingers crossed.'

"Helen had gone ahead. I could hear a dripping street-walker who had taken refuge in the doorway advising her to stay home, you couldn't do any business in this rain. Good, I thought; as far as I was concerned, the streets couldn't be too deserted. 'Where did that come from?' asked Helen when she saw the car. 'Stolen,' I said. 'It ought to take us part of the way. Get in.'

"It was still dark. The rain streamed down the windshield. If there was still any blood on the running board, it would be washed away now. I stopped a little way from the house where Gregorius lived. 'Stand under there,' I said to Helen, pointing to the glass overhang protecting the entrance of a store dealing in fishing equipment.

" 'Can't I stay in the car?'

" 'No. If someone turns up, act as if you were waiting for customers. I'll be right back.'

"Gregorius had finished. His fear had given way to artist's pride. 'The only difficulty was the uniform,' he explained. 'Your picture has civilian clothes. So I cut off his head.'

"He had detached Georg's picture, cut out the head and neck, laid the uniform over my photo, and photographed the montage. 'Obersturmbannführer Schwarz,' he said proudly. He had already dried and attached the copy. 'The stamp came out pretty well. If they look at it carefully, I have to admit, you're done for—you would be even if it were authentic. Here's your old passport—unharmed.'

"He gave me both passports and what was left of Georg's photo. I tore up the photograph into small pieces on my way down the stairs and threw the fragments into the water that was racing down the gutter.

"Helen was waiting. I had checked the gas; the tank was full. With luck that would take us across the border. In the glove compartment I found a *carnet,* the document required for taking a car across borders—it had been used twice. I decided not to cross where the car had already been seen. I also found a Michelin map, a pair of gloves, and a motorist's atlas of Europe.

"We drove through the rain. We still had a few hours before daylight, and we headed for Perpignan. I decided to stay on the main road until it was light. 'Would you like me to drive?' Helen asked after a time. 'Your hands.'

" 'Can you? You haven't slept.'

" 'Neither have you.'

"I looked at her. She seemed fresh and calm, though I don't see how she managed it. 'Like some cognac?'

" 'No. I'll drive until we can get some coffee.'

" 'Lachmann gave me another bottle of cognac.'

"I took it out of my coat pocket. Helen shook her head. She had her injection.

" 'Later,' she said to me very gently. 'Try to sleep. We'll take turns driving.'

"Helen was a better driver than I. After a while she began to sing; monotonous, childish songs. I had been all keyed up; now the humming of the car and her soft singsong began to lull me. I knew that I ought to sleep, but I kept waking up. The gray countryside flew by, and we used the bright lights, ignoring the blackout regulations.

" 'Did you kill him?' Helen asked suddenly.

" 'Yes.'

" 'Did you have to?'

" 'Yes.'

"We drove on. I stared at the road; all sorts of things drifted through my mind, and then I passed out like a stone. When I awoke, the rain had stopped. It was morning, the car was humming, Helen was at the wheel, and I had the feeling that I had dreamt it all. 'What I told you isn't true,' I said.

" 'I know,' she said.

" 'It was somebody else,' I said.

" 'I know.'

"She did not look at me.

CHAPTER 18

"I decided to get a Spanish visa for Helen at the last town before the border. The crowd outside the consulate was terrifying. I knew the police might already be on the lookout for the car, but I had to take the chance. There was no other way. Georg's passport already had a visa.

"I drove up slowly. The people began to move only when they saw the German license plates. They made a lane for us. Some of the refugees fled. Through an avenue of hatred we moved toward the entrance. A gendarme saluted. That hadn't happened to me in a long time. Negligently I returned the salute and went in. The gendarme stepped aside for me. You've got to be a murderer, I thought bitterly, to be treated with respect.

"I was given Helen's visa the moment I showed my passport. The vice-consul looked at my face. He could not see my hands. I had put on the gloves I had found in the car. 'A souvenir of the war,' I said. 'Close combat.' He nodded sympathetically. 'We, too, have had our years of struggle. *Heil* Hitler! A great man, like our Caudillo.'

"I came out. A void had formed around the car. In the back seat sat a frightened boy of eleven or twelve. He sat huddled in the corner with his hands over his mouth, and all I could see of his face was the eyes. 'We've got to take him with us,' said Helen.

" 'Why?'

" 'He has papers that expire in two days. If they catch him, he'll be sent back to Germany.'

"I felt the sweat on my back under my shirt. Helen looked at me. She was very calm. 'We have taken a life,' she said to me in English. 'It's our duty to save one.'

" 'Let's see your papers,' I said to the boy.

"Without a word he held out a residence permit. I took it and went back into the consulate. It was very hard for me to go back; the car seemed to be shouting its secret from a hundred loud-speakers. Nonchalantly I told the secretary that I had forgotten about needing another visa—in line of duty, for an identification on the other side of the border. He hesitated when he saw the paper; then he smiled with an air of complicity and gave me the visa.

"I got in. The crowd was even more hostile than before. They probably thought I was carrying the boy off to a camp.

"I left the city, hoping that my luck would hold. The wheel felt sizzling hot in my hands. I thought we might have to abandon the car any minute but I had no idea what to do then. Helen could not cross the mountains over mule paths in such weather; she was too weak, and loss of the car would be the end of this weird protection by our enemies. Neither of us had a permit to leave France. And that was more important on foot than in an expensive car.

"We drove on. It was a strange day. Reality seemed to have sunk into an abyss. We drove along a high narrow ridge beneath low-lying clouds, as in the cabin of a funicular. The closest likeness I could think of was one of those old Chinese ink drawings, showing travelers moving along monotonously amid mountain peaks, clouds, and waterfalls. The boy huddled in the back seat and barely moved. All he had learned in the course of his short life was to distrust everybody and everything. He remembered nothing else. When the guardians of National Socialist culture bashed in his grandfather's skull, he had been three years old; he had been seven when his father was hanged, and nine when his mother was gassed—a true child of the twentieth century. He had somehow escaped from the concentration camp and had crossed the borders by his own resources. If he had been caught, he would have been sent back to the concentration camp and hanged. Now he was trying to get to Lisbon, where he had an uncle, a watchmaker, as his mother had told him the night before she was gassed, when she had given him her blessing and a few last bits of advice.

"Everything went well. No one on the French border asked for an exit visa. I briefly presented my passport and filled out the blanks for the car. The gendarmes saluted, the gate went up, and we left France. A few minutes later the Spanish customs guards were admiring the car and asking how many miles it did on a gallon. I told them something or other, and they began to rave about their Hispano-Suiza. I told them I had had one and described the emblem on the radiator—a crane in flight. They were delighted. I asked where I could fill up on gas. They had a special supply for friends of Spain. I had no pesetas. They exchanged my francs. We bade each other good-by with effusive formality.

"I leaned back. The mountain ridge and the clouds vanished. A strange country lay before us, a country that no longer looked like Europe. We were not yet safe, but it meant a good deal to be out of France. I saw the streets, the donkeys, the people, the costumes, the stony countryside—we were in Africa. This country beyond the Pyrenees, I felt, was the real Occident. Then I saw that Helen was crying.

" 'Now you're where you wanted to be,' she said.

"I didn't know what she meant. I was still too bowled over by the ease with which we had made it. I thought of the politeness, the greetings, the smiles—this hadn't happened to me in years, and I had had to kill in order to be treated like a human being. 'Why are you crying?' I asked. 'We aren't safe yet. Spain is full of Gestapo agents. We've got to get through as quickly as possible.'

"We slept in a small village. I would have liked to abandon the car somewhere and go on by train. But I decided against it. Spain was unsafe; the quickest mode of travel was the best. In some inexplicable way the car became a kind of dark mascot; its technical perfection even dispelled my horror of it. My need of the car made me forget about Georg. He had been a threat hanging over my life too long; now he was gone and I felt little more than relief; I thought of the Smile; he was still alive and perhaps he was trying to locate us by telephone. All countries extradite for murder. It had been self-defense— but I would have had to prove that in the city where the crime was committed.

"We reached the Portuguese border late the following night. I had obtained visas without difficulty on the way. At the border I left Helen in the car with the engine running. If anything went wrong, she would start up and drive straight at me, I would jump in, and we would break through to the Portuguese side. Nothing much could have happened to us; it was a small station, and before the guards had time to aim and fire in the darkness, we would be gone. What would happen in Portugal was another question.

"Nothing happened. The uniformed guards stood in the gusty darkness like figures in a Goya painting. They saluted, and we drove to the Portuguese station, where we were ad-

mitted just as easily. As we were starting off, one of the guards
came running after us, shouting at us to stop. After a moment's hesitation I complied; if I had gone on, the car could
easily have been stopped at the next town. I stopped. We
barely breathed.

"The guard came up. 'Your *carnet*,' he said. 'You left it on
the desk. You'll need it to come back with.'

" 'Thank you very much.'

"Behind me the little boy heaved an enormous sigh of relief. I myself had a sense of weightlessness for a moment.
'Now you're in Portugal,' I said to the boy. He slowly took
his hands away from his mouth and leaned back for the first
time. He had been crouched forward during the whole trip.

"Villages flew by. Dogs barked. The fire of a blacksmith's
shop glowed in the early morning; the blacksmith was shoe-
ing a white horse. It had stopped raining. I waited for the
feeling of release that I had been looking forward to for so
long; but it did not come. Helen sat silent beside me. I wanted
to be happy, but I felt empty.

"In Lisbon I phoned the American consulate in Marseille.
I told them what had happened up to the moment when
Georg had appeared. The man on the wire said, well, then I
was safe. All I could get out of him was a promise that if a
visa were granted, he would forward it to the consulate in
Lisbon.

"The car that had protected us for so long had to be got
rid of. 'Sell it,' said Helen.

" 'Shouldn't I let it roll into the sea someplace?'

" 'That won't change anything,' she said. 'You need the
money. Sell it.'

"She was right. It was very easy to sell. The purchaser told
me he would pay the duty and have the car painted black.
He was a dealer. I sold him the car in Georg's name. A week

later I saw it with Portuguese plates. There were several like it in Lisbon; I recognized it only by a slight dent in the left fender. I burned Georg's passport."

Schwarz looked at his watch. "There isn't much more to tell. Once each week I went to the consulate. For a time we stayed at a hotel on the money from the sale of the car. I wanted Helen to enjoy as much comfort as possible. We found a doctor who helped her to get sedatives. I even took her to the casino. I rented a tuxedo for it. Helen still had her evening dress from Paris, and I bought her a pair of golden slippers. I had forgotten her others in Marseille. Do you know the casino?"

"Yes, unfortunately. I was there last night. It was a mistake."

"I wanted her to play," said Schwarz. "She won. She had an incredible streak of luck. She threw out chips at random and the numbers came.

"The last days had little connection with reality. It was as though our life at the castle had begun again. We both put on a bit of an act; but for the first time I had the feeling that she belonged entirely to me, although she was slipping away from me by the hour, into the arms of the most ruthless of lovers. She had not yet surrendered to him; but she had stopped fighting. There were nights and nights of torment, when she wept; but then came almost unearthly moments, when sweetness, sadness, wisdom, and a love without bodily limits attained such an intensity that I scarcely dared to move. 'My darling,' she said to me one night, and it was the only time she ever spoke of it. 'We won't see your Promised Land together.'

"I had taken her to the doctor's that afternoon. Now suddenly I was overwhelmed by the sense of impotent rebellion that comes to a man who is unable to hold what he loves. 'Helen,' I said in a suffocating voice, 'what has become of us?'

236

"She said nothing. Then she shook her head and laughed. 'We did our best,' she said. 'And that's enough.'

"Then came the day when they told me at the consulate that the unbelievable had happened. The two visas had come. The drunken whim of a chance acquaintance had brought about what no amount of desperate pleas could accomplish. I laughed. It was hysteria. If you're capable of laughing, there's plenty to laugh at in the world today. Don't you agree?"

"We've got to stop laughing sometime," I said.

"The strange part of it is that we laughed a good deal in the last days," Schwarz went on. "We seemed to be in a port, sheltered from every wind. The bitterness had run out, there were no tears left, and our grief had become so transparent that it was often indistinguishable from an ironic, melancholy gaiety. We moved into a small apartment. With incredible blindness I went on with my plan of escape to America. For a long time there were no boats, and then finally a sailing was announced. I sold my last Degas drawing and bought the tickets. I was happy. I thought we were saved. In spite of everything! In spite of the doctor!

"The sailing was postponed for a few days. Then the day before yesterday I went back to the office of the shipping line. The date had been set for today. I told Helen and went out to buy something or other. When I came back, she was dead. All the mirrors in the room were smashed. Her evening dress lay torn on the floor. She was lying beside it; she was not lying on the bed.

"My first thought was that she had been murdered by a burglar. Then that she had been killed by a Gestapo agent; but he would have been after me, not her. It was only when I saw that nothing was damaged apart from the mirrors and the dress that I understood. I remembered the poison I had given her, which she claimed to have lost. I stood and stared

237

and then I looked for a letter. There was none. There was nothing. She had gone without a word. Can you understand that?"

"Yes," I said.

"You understand?"

"Yes," I replied. "What could she have written?"

"Something. Why. Or . . ."

He fell silent. He was probably thinking of last words, of a last token of love, of something that he might have taken with him into his loneliness. He had shorn off a good many conventional ideas, but apparently not this one. "If she had once begun," I said, "she could never have stopped writing. By not writing she told you more than she could ever have said in words."

He thought it over. "Did you see the sign in the travel bureau?" he whispered then. "Postponed for twenty-four hours. She would have lived a day longer if she had known."

"No."

"She didn't want to go. That's why she did it."

I shook my head. "She couldn't stand the pain any longer," I said.

"I can't believe that," he replied. "Why should she have done it just when everything was settled for the trip? Or did she think she wouldn't be admitted to America with her sickness?"

"Shouldn't we leave it to a dying woman to decide when she's at the end of her rope?" I said. "It seems to me that's the least we can do."

He stared at me. "She held out as long as she possibly could," I said. "For your sake, can't you see that? For your sake alone. Once she knew you were saved, she gave up."

"And what if I hadn't been so blind? What if I hadn't insisted on going to America?"

"Mr. Schwarz," I said, "that would not have cured her."

He moved his head strangely. "She's gone," he whispered,

238

"and suddenly it's as if she had never been. I looked at her, and there was no answer. What have I done? Did I kill her or did I make her happy? Did she love me, or was I only a crutch that she leaned on when it suited her? I can't find an answer."

"Must you have one?"

"No," he said. "Forgive me. Probably not."

"There is no answer. There never is—except for the one you give yourself."

"I've told you the story," he said after a while, "because I have to know. What has my life been? Has it been an empty, meaningless life, the life of a useless cuckold, a murderer. . . ?"

"I don't know," I said. "But if you prefer, it was also the life of a man who loved, or, if that appeals to you, of a kind of saint. But what good are names? It was your life. Isn't that enough?"

"It was! But now?"

"It will live as long as you."

"It's only we who are keeping it," Schwarz whispered. "You and I; there's no one else." He stared at me. "Don't forget that. Someone has to hold it. It mustn't die. There are only two of us. It's not safe with me. But it mustn't die. It's got to go on living. With you it's safe."

For all my skepticism a strange feeling came over me. What did this man want? Did he want to bequeath me his past along with his passport? Was he planning to take his life?

"Why should it die in you?" I asked. "You will go on living, Mr. Schwarz."

"I am not going to kill myself," Schwarz replied calmly. "Not when I know that the Smile is still alive. But my mind will try to destroy the memory, chew it to bits, reduce it, falsify it, domesticate it, make it into something I can go on living with. Even a few weeks from now, I'd be unable to tell you what I've told you today. That's why I wanted you to listen to me. You won't falsify it because for you it holds no danger. And somewhere it's got to endure." Suddenly he was utterly forlorn. "Somebody has to preserve it intact, at least for a while." He drew two passports from his pocket and set them down in front of me. "Here is Helen's passport, too. The tickets you have already. Now you've got American visas. For two." A shadowy smile passed over his face and he fell silent.

I gaped at the passports. With an enormous effort I managed to ask: "And you really don't need them any more?"

"You can give me yours in exchange," he said. "I'll need it only for a day or two. Just for the border."

I looked at him.

"In the Foreign Legion they don't ask for passports. I don't have to tell you that they accept refugees. And as long as there are barbarians alive like the Smile, it would be a crime to kill myself, to waste a life that could be spent fighting them."

I took my passport from my pocket and gave it to him.

"Thank you," I said. "Thank you with all my heart, Mr. Schwarz."

"There's some money, too. I won't need much." Schwarz looked at his watch. "Would you do one more thing for me? They'll be coming for her in half an hour. Would you come with me?"

"Yes."

Schwarz paid the check. We went out into the screaming morning.

Outside lay the ship, white and restless on the Tagus.

I stood in the room beside Schwarz. The mirror frames were still hanging there—empty. The broken glass had been cleared away. "Ought I to have spent the last night with her?" Schwarz asked.

"You were with her."

The woman lay in the coffin as dead people do; her face

seemed infinitely aloof. Nothing concerned her, neither Schwarz nor I nor herself. It was no longer possible to imagine how she had looked. What lay there was a statue, and Schwarz alone had an image of how she was while she breathed. But Schwarz was now convinced that I shared it. "Some letters . . ." he said. "Only yesterday . . ."

He took some letters from a drawer. "I haven't read them," he said. "Take them."

I took the letters and was going to put them into the coffin. Then I thought better of it—now, at last, the dead woman belonged to Schwarz alone, or so he believed. Other people's letters had become irrelevant—he didn't want her to take them with her, but on the other hand he didn't wish to destroy them, because after all they had been hers. "I'll take them," I said and put them in my pocket. "They have lost their meaning. They mean less than a small banknote that you spend for a dish of soup."

"Crutches," he replied. "I know. She once called them crutches that she needed to go on being true to me. Do you understand that? It's absurd. . . ."

"No," I said, and then very cautiously, with all the compassion I had: "Why can't you at last leave her in peace? She loved you and she stayed with you as long as she could."

He nodded. Suddenly he looked very frail. "That's what I wanted to know," he murmured.

It was very hot in the room—the dead woman, the pungent smell, the flies, the spent candles, and the sun outside. Schwarz saw my glance.

"A woman helped me," he said. "It's hard in a strange country. The doctor. The police. They took her away. Then last night they brought her back. Autopsy. The cause of death." He gave me a helpless look. "They . . . some of her is gone . . . they told me not to uncover her. . . ."

The pallbearers came. The coffin was closed. Schwarz seemed to be about to faint. "I'll go with you," I said.

It was not very far. The morning was bright and the wind

241

raced like a sheep dog pursuing a flock of fleecy clouds. At the cemetery Schwarz stood small and forsaken beneath the vast sky.

"Do you want to go back to your apartment?" I asked him.

"No."

He had taken a suitcase with him. "Do you know someone who can fix the passports?" I asked.

"Gregorius. He got here last week."

We went to see Gregorius. He quickly arranged my passport for Schwarz; there was no need to be too meticulous. Schwarz had on him a card from a recruiting station for the Foreign Legion. He would only have to cross the border. Once at the Legion post, he could throw my passport away. The Legion wasn't interested in the past.

"What became of the little boy you brought to Lisbon?" I asked.

"His uncle hates him; but the boy is happy. He thinks it's better to be hated by a member of his family than by strangers."

I looked at the man who now bore my name. "I wish you the best of luck," I said, taking care not to call him Schwarz. I could think of nothing else to say.

"I won't be seeing you again," he said. "It's just as well. I've told you too much to want to see you again."

I wasn't so sure of that. It seemed possible that he would want to see me later on for that very reason. I alone, he believed, possessed an unfalsified image of his life. But that could make him hate me; perhaps he would feel that I had taken his wife from him, this time irrevocably—if he really believed that his own memory deceived him and only mine remained clear.

I saw him going down the street, suitcase in hand, a pitiful figure, the eternal cuckold and heroic lover. But had he not possessed the woman he loved more profoundly than all those stupid conquerors? And what do we really possess? Why do we make so much fuss about things which at best are

242

merely lent us for a little while; and why all this talk about degrees of possession, when the illusory word "possess" means merely to embrace the air?

I had a passport photo of my wife on me; in those days you were always needing photographs for identification papers. Gregorius went right to work. I stayed with him. I was afraid to let the two passports out of my sight.

By noon they were done. I rushed to the hole we were living in. Ruth was sitting by the window, watching the fishermen's children in the yard. "Did you lose?" she asked when I appeared in the doorway.

I held up the passports. "We're leaving tomorrow. We'll have other names, each a different one, and we'll have to get married again in America."

I hardly gave a thought to the fact that I was now bearing the passport of a man who might be wanted for murder. We sailed the following afternoon and reached America without difficulty. But the lovers' passports did not bring us luck: Ruth divorced me six months later. To make it legal we had first to get married again. Later, Ruth married the rich American who had given Schwarz his affidavit. The whole thing struck him as too funny for words; he was best man at our second wedding. A week later we were divorced in Mexico.

I spent the rest of the war in America. Strangely enough, I began to take an interest in painting, which previously had meant next to nothing to me—an inheritance, it seemed to me, from the dead and remote original Schwarz. I often thought of the other Schwarz, who was perhaps still alive, and the two of them merged into a hazy ghost, whose presence I sometimes felt. It even seems to influence me, though I know that such notions are pure nonsense. I finally found employment in an art store, and in my room hung several prints of Degas drawings, of which I had grown very fond.

I often thought of Helen, whom I had only seen dead, and

for a time, when I was living alone, I even dreamed of her. The first night at sea, I had thrown the letters Schwarz had given me overboard without reading them. In one of the envelopes I felt a small hard object. I had removed it in the darkness. Later, under the light, I saw that it was a flat piece of amber, in which thousands of years ago a tiny gnat had been captured and petrified. I had kept it—the death struggle of a gnat, preserved in a cage of golden tears, while its fellows had frozen or been eaten, and vanished from the face of the earth.

After the war I went back to Europe. I had some difficulty in establishing my identity, because at that time there were thousands of members of the master race in Germany trying to lose theirs. I gave the Schwarz passport to a Russian who had fled across the border—a new wave of refugees had begun. Heaven only knows what has become of it since. As for Schwarz, I never heard anything more of him. I even went to Osnabrück once and asked about him, though I had forgotten his real name. But the city was in ruins, no one had heard of him, and no one was interested. On the way back to the station I thought I recognized him. I ran after him. But it was a postal clerk, who told me that his name was Jansen and that he had three children.